MURDER AT ST MARGARET

An Oxford Key Mystery

LYNN MORRISON

The Marketing Chair Press

Cover design by Emilie Yane Lopes

Published by

The Marketing Chair Press

Oxford, England

LynnMorrisonWriter.com

Paperback ISBN: 978-1-8380391-0-3

To Alex, Adele, Giorgia, Leo and Stella

(And yes, I know those last two are cats.)

CONTENTS

Chapter One

The stall door next to mine crashes open. Peeking underneath, I watch as a pair of practical black rubber clogs stomps their way to the basins. I freeze in place at the sound of an angry muttering.

The words, mumbled in a growly voice, are hard to understand. "Interrupting me... how dare she... right in the middle of dinner prep... won't be on my shoulders if the roast chicken is burnt... ringing my phone and demanding I come straight over... I'll show her straight over..."

My legs start to tingle, a sure sign I need to get out of this position before they go numb. I'm working up the courage to stand up when I hear her stomping resume, followed by another door slamming. I slide the latch and open a slight crack, peeking out to make sure the woman is gone. After crossing to the sinks, I take my time. The last thing I want is to run into whoever that was.

Stopping for a last glance in the bathroom mirror, I fluff my blonde curls with my damp hands. The full day of moving combined with the humid air of the packed train compartment did me no favours. The stylist took my request for a serious cut to heart; I can barely get it up into a ponytail. I straighten my collar, smiling at the pair of cherries embroidered on my jumper. A touch of vintage felt proper for my welcome to one of the UK's oldest institutions.

Having successfully exited the bathroom undetected, I make my way towards the lit doorway further along the hall. The sign next to it says 'College Principal'. I tap a gentle knock before stepping into the cosy reception room. The older woman sitting behind the desk smiles a welcome. "Have a seat over there. Dr Radcliffe is finishing up a quick chat and will be right with you."

Her white hair is cut in a cute pageboy style, her jewel-tone dress accessorised by a vibrant floral scarf and an oversized golden broach. Her desk is in perfect order, not even a stray post-it note out of alignment. The tidy desk has one laptop, one phone, and a framed photo of an older man. Despite the regimental order of her workspace, the woman exudes an air of friendliness. Her blue eyes sparkle with merriment as she leans over the desk as though inviting me into her home for a chat.

I cross the room to perch on the upholstered chair the woman indicates, setting my flowery bag by my cherry red flats. Everything is as I imagined it would be. The mahogany walls offer a rich backdrop for gilt-framed Cotswold landscapes painted by a master. A shelf-lined wall showcases leather-bound books, priceless antiques and commemorative photos of rowing regattas.

The woman opens a desk drawer and lifts out a small cut-glass bowl. She places it on the corner of her desk and nudges it in my direction. "Go on, take one. I find a little sugar helps settle the nerves. Is this your first time in Oxford?"

I shake my head as I unwrap a bright red sweet. "Other than a quick trip for the interview, I visited once before as a child on a school tour of the museum. All I can remember is a long room with lots of sculptures of naked men."

She chuckles in response to my honest, if somewhat ribald, response. "That'd be the Ashmolean. It's the tip of the iceberg, plenty more places to explore. I guess you'll have opportunities enough to do so in your new role. Lillian rang me up as soon as you accepted the job, asking if we could put you up in our faculty housing until you find your feet. Given our Autumn Gala is the first event on your To Do list, I could hardly say no."

"I really appreciate your help, Mrs... um, sorry, I didn't catch your name."

"It's my fault for not introducing myself. There's no need to be so formal, you can call me Harry. Short for Harriet. I'm the Principal's executive assistant."

"I imagine I'll be spending a lot of time with you. As you've likely guessed, I'm Natalie Payne. Please call me Nat, most people do once they get to know me."

Harry's warm welcome has put me at ease, but based on the seniority of her role and the glint in her eye, I'm guessing she has a core of steel inside her.

A flurry of raised voices coming from behind the closed inner door interrupts any further conversation. When we hear the crash of glass breaking, Harry winces and offers me a weak smile. I cling to my smile but shift on the edge of the cushioned seat. My eyebrows arch into question marks as I nod towards the exit, a silent query to see if I should make excuses and come back later.

Harry shakes her head and motions me to stay where I am. "Don't you worry, love. Dr Radcliffe is a gem. It's that other woman in there. She's stirring up all the trouble."

The heavy inner office door slams open, a broad-shouldered and thick-waisted woman in a stained chef's coat comes barrelling out of it straight into the reception. I spy a familiar pair of black clogs on her feet. So much for my efforts to avoid her.

She doesn't spare a glance at me, glaring at Harry before turning back around and continuing with her angry rant. "How dare you tell me what I have to do! The kitchen and dining hall are my domain and I must have complete and total freedom."

A voice calls out from the inner office, "Of course, you are in control, but surely you can see how your decisions can affect others?"

The chef is undeterred, her face glowing red with fury. "What happened to them is no fault of mine! If you want me to remain here as Head Chef, I'll thank you to remember that. Now if you've no other false complaints to hold against me, I have to finish preparing dinner."

When the chef stomps out of the room, slamming the reception door behind herself, both Harry and I breathe a sigh of relief.

"The glass paperweight?" asks Harry as a middle-aged woman in pressed trousers and a silk blouse appears in the doorway.

"Got it in one. I'm lucky she smashed it onto my desk instead of my head." The woman spots me smiling in my chair. "You must be Ms Payne. Do come in. I'm so sorry about the delay... and that you had to witness that."

I murmur polite reassurances as I gather my bag. Harry winks at me, offering reassurance with her expression that I'm not walking into the proverbial lion's den.

Fixing my smile back in place, I straighten my shoulders and follow. I soak in more of the detail as I trail behind her into the next room. My last job locked me in the unforgiving modern glass and clean lines of London's exhibition halls. The college Principal's office is the exact opposite, located in the east wing of a sprawling mansion. The Edwardian architecture echoes in the decor, the space filled by an antique hardwood desk, claw-footed chairs and velvet sofas that scream to be stroked. Floor-to-ceiling bookshelves line the walls, embossed leather covers mixing in with well-worn paperbacks and a few popular self-help novels. The room strikes a balance between well-respected and welcoming.

A life-size portrait of a man in an old-fashioned white wig dominates the space above the walnut fireplace mantle. His dour expression is so piercing that it almost feels as if he's glaring at me. I choose the chair that faces in the opposite direction. Better to have Mr MacCreepy at my back than staring me in the face throughout my first meeting.

"I'm Scarlett Radcliffe, the Principal here at St. Margaret College at the University of Oxford. I'm really pleased to welcome you to our team."

"This is an incredible opportunity, particularly for someone my age. I'm thrilled to be here." My eyes are bright with genuine enthusiasm.

Dr Radcliffe settles into her padded leather chair. "When your predecessor, Lillian, announced her retirement, we didn't know how we'd ever find someone who could work her magic in planning our ceremonies and events. Before she left, Lillian assured us you are more than competent for the job." Pausing, she leans in my direction, "Did you know that Lillian was only 30 when she took on the role? I imagine you reminded her of herself."

Dr Radcliffe digs around on her desk before coming up with a familiar looking document. "I'm ashamed to say I've had little time to review your CV, despite Harry continually moving it to the top of my pile. Would you mind talking me through it? It will help me learn more about you, which will be useful later when Harry quizzes me on our catch-up."

I clear my throat and drive into my career highlights. "Although my CV covers my professional experience, my passion for events started much earlier. I've been planning my birthday parties since I was out of nappies. My mother let me help with her charity events in my teens, and by the time I headed off to uni, I knew what I wanted to be when I grew up."

I pause for a breath before continuing. "I stayed near home, attending City, University of London where I studied Business and Marketing. From there, they offered me an internship at Disneyland Paris. It was a dream come true to work behind the scenes at the park. No one in the world is better at event planning. I learned so much from seeing first hand the tricks they used to make it look like things happen by magic."

Dr Radcliffe leans over her desk, her head resting on her hand, engrossed in my story. "I've experienced the magic of Disney myself. I can imagine a lot of work goes into planning their events. When did you come back to the UK?"

"I stayed at Disney for a year and a half. I had the chance of taking a full-time role in Orlando, but I wasn't up for moving that far away. Paris was adventure enough. I found a job with a corporate events agency in London and spent the last few years there."

"And now Oxford." Dr Radcliffe eyes me before nodding. "You'll fit right in, plenty of former London diehards here in the area. Everyone moves up here to raise their families, trying to escape the London house prices. Not much of a discount anymore, I'm afraid. But nothing for you to worry about now, you're welcome to stay here in the college for the next six months. Is anyone joining you?"

"No family for me, just myself. I'm dedicated to my job."

Dr Radcliffe smiles, "Much like our grad students and junior professors. So many of them are single that I've stopped offering a plus one on my dinner invitations."

I straighten up in my seat, trying to brush off the feeling that the old portrait is huffing his disapproval onto the back of my neck. I am a confident, grown woman, and I don't need a man to feel complete. Jumping ahead, I shift the conversation. "It's incredibly generous of the college to put me up for so long. I am sure the house will be perfect, if what I've seen so far is any sign."

The college fills an entire city block with a mix of hundred-year-old Edwardian buildings and modern halls tucked away behind a tall, wrought-iron fence. Each building is named for an earlier benefactor or notable college fellow, the halls hung with ageing portraits and commemorative plaques. I felt like I was stepping back a century when I walked in the front door. Only the sheer history of Oxford keeps the elements of modern technology from reminding me I'm still in the 21st century.

Dr Radcliffe rises from her chair, inviting me to follow. "I appreciate you stopping by to introduce yourself. I'm sure you want to unpack, so I won't keep you long. Harry will get you a set of keys and show you to the flat. Shall we meet back here tomorrow morning, say 7am? I know it's early, but I have an all-day meeting I can't postpone."

I pick up my bag and follow. "That's fine. I'm an early riser. I'd love a proper tour, and then to meet the key staff."

"Perfect. Do you have any other questions before you head off?"

I mull over whether it is appropriate to ask about the angry staff member or not. Better to know if she's someone important so I can start strategising on how to win her over.

"The key staff members, do they include the woman who stomped her way out of here?"

Dr Radcliffe chuckles and nods her head. "Unfortunately, yes. Mrs Smythe will be someone you can't avoid. As you must have overheard, she's the head chef here. In fact, she's one of the top chefs in the country, as she often reminds us. We have to fall in line with her demands, regardless of whether they are rational or even palatable. The other colleges here in Oxford keep trying to lure her away."

I smile at her candour and reassure her, "There's one in every bunch, even at Disney. I'm sure I can find a common interest to connect with her."

"We'll be very impressed if you do. Good night, Ms Payne."

Chapter Two

I follow Harry as she winds her way through a maze of
flowerbeds. Despite the crisp outdoor air, the flowers bloom
with a riot of colours. Squirrels dart across our path, chattering as
they climb into hideaways in the trees. Although I can see other
people walking around, the perfumed air carries a spirit of
tranquillity throughout the garden.

Glancing over at Harry, I confess, "I'm still trying to wrap my
head around Oxford's structure. I know it's made up of different
colleges, but until today I hadn't grasped how independent they
are of one another. Can you explain how it all works?"

Harry nods her head in understanding. "Our international
visitors expect to find a few buildings in the corner of a sprawling
campus," she says. "But each college is its own kingdom, and the
university departments and administration buildings are sprinkled
along the streets in between them. Some roles, like mine for
example, are at the college level. Other positions, like yours or the
library or the museums, are centralised."

She winks at me. "It will make your job challenging, but also
that much more interesting. Lillian imagined herself as a

travelling minstrel, visiting courts to offer an entertaining escape from everyday life."

My eyes light up at the thought. "Oh, I love that!"

"It isn't all sugar plums and roses, luv," Harry cautions. "You're beholden to the king in each castle, or should I say the principal in each college. When one would annoy or anger Lillian, I'd remind her she could soon move on to another college and start again."

I mull over her words, wondering if I know what I'm getting myself into with this job.

As we exit the landscaped gardens, Harry slows her steps. She points towards a slender iron pole, saying, "You'll soon learn your way around, but until then, keep an eye out for the signposts. Our administrative offices are in the main building."

We veer off onto a narrow concrete pathway lining a field of lush green grass. Shade trees dapple the lawn, surrounding themselves with an autumn blanket of red, gold and orange. Here and there are wrought iron benches, each meticulously labelled with donor names and other honourees. Every single blossom, bush and tree has been hand-selected to cultivate a sense of harmony. Together they urge you to grab a picnic blanket and basket and wile away an afternoon in their company.

Harry nods towards a series of ivy-covered, red brick buildings. "The Michaelmas term started this week; the students are getting resettled back into their rooms. They'll be outdoors sunning themselves this weekend, weather permitting. For now, they're trying to make friends with their new roommates and prepare for their first tutorials."

Further along, Harry points out a shadowed hall looming at the far end of the pathway. "The sizeable building in the distance is our newest, designed as a conference and events centre as well as providing more office space. Prince William himself came over to open it for us."

Wow. I'm stunned. *The* Prince William? I make a mental note to put him on every guest list.

I match my steps to Harry's, settling in beside her. "Did you know Lillian well?" I'm curious about my predecessor, particularly since she isn't here to help me settle into the role.

Harry's countenance brightens. "Oh Lillian, I miss her. She and I were dear friends. I trusted her to organise spectacular events, and she always depended on me to help her navigate the executive assistants' network amongst the Oxford dons. Although the colleges and departments are spread out, we assistants are closely connected. It's the only way anything gets done here."

I laugh in understanding. My mom taught me at a young age that the assistants hold the keys to the castle. If I want to be successful, I need to stay on their good side.

"I hope it's not presumptuous for me to say I'd like us to have a similar relationship."

Harry beams over her shoulder. "I'd love that, Nat. I really would. It's good you'll be staying here; it will give us plenty of opportunities to get to know one another better."

Harry points towards the back entrance of what appears to be an Edwardian home. "Number 84 Woodstock Road. A lovely old home, I hope you'll be comfortable living here. This entrance takes you straight into the ground-floor flat. The front door opens onto the common front hall and the stairwell, and you'd need to use your badge to get through the gate over there. If you're inside the college, this is the easiest way into the flat."

She leads me up the narrow set of concrete steps to a dark blue painted door. Black paint flakes off the metal handrail, silvery glimpses breaking through here and there. Rather than make the space rundown, they lend an air of authenticity. Harry pulls a bulky keyring from her pocket, sorting through a mix of skeleton keys until she finds the one modern key hidden away in the bunch. She deftly opens the door and steps inside, reaching for hidden light switches to brighten up the shadowed space.

She steps inside of the kitchen and beckons me to follow. "Come in, come in. Let's get you settled." She crosses the room, dusting off countertops and straightening the salt shaker. "I had everything scrubbed clean before you arrived. This was one of the original college buildings. It was used for both lodging and lessons."

As I look around, I'm already envisioning Edwardian flat decor on a budget. The crown moulding is begging for some period artwork to fill the bare walls. "This building has great bones," I gush and mean it.

Harry continues through the house, keeping up the informal tour. "This was a large family home, before the college bought it. Down here was the living room, study and kitchen of the original house. The upper floor flat suffers from lower ceilings and smaller rooms since it was designed as bedrooms. This particular unit is the jewel."

As we walk into the living room, I spot my suitcase and boxes waiting inside the front door. The open curtains in the bay windows allow light to flood the room. The house is set back from the road with a gravelled drive for several cars to park in the front. Looming evergreen trees block out the sounds of passing traffic. The velvet-lined window seat cries out for long afternoons with a book and mugs of tea.

The rest of the furniture is comfortable and inviting with an eclectic mix of college cast-offs recovered to look new. A deep sofa, an armchair with a footstool and a dinged-up coffee table round out the furnishings. There is a TV tucked away inside the remains of the old fireplace.

Harry looks around the room. "I can see the porter has been here and dropped off your things. Always helpful to know that someone nearby has a spare key." She plumps up the sofa cushions before pointing back in the direction of the garden.

"The bedroom and bath are off the kitchen. There are clean linens on the bed and in the cupboard, and a washer/dryer in the kitchen. We can't have our professors airing their unmentionables in the college garden." We both snicker at the thought.

She opens a kitchen drawer and pulls out a set of keys. "I'll let you make yourself at home. You're unlikely to see your neighbour unless you run into one another at the front entrance. There are offices down in the basement, but they have a separate entry from the garden-side."

"Is there a student living upstairs?" I'm already worrying about the potential for late night noise.

"No, Edward Thomas lives up there, one of our professors. He's been living up there alone since he arrived a few years ago, the poor dear. I keep hoping he'll fall for a young lady, move out and start a family, but he seems to have wed his work instead."

My shoulders drop in relief. "Married to work I can understand. I'm sure we won't bother one another at all."

She passes the keys over, each one tagged in identification. "I stocked a few foodstuffs in the kitchen to tide you over until you can make it to the shops. You've got free meals in the dining hall, but I guessed you'd want to unpack and settle in tonight."

I open the fridge to find it packed with milk, bread, butter, jam, eggs, fresh fruit and vegetables and even a small box of chocolate-covered eclairs. I could get on board with this version of staples.

"Thank you so much, Harry, that's really thoughtful. I hadn't even thought about food or shopping. You've saved me a ton of hassle. I hope you'll let me invite you to dinner one night to say thanks properly."

"I'd love that, but no rush. You'll soon have enough on your plate. We can get to know each another over lunches in the dining hall." Harry pats me on the hand before letting herself out the door. "My number is on the pad by the telephone if you need anything, tonight or any other time. You can follow the same pathway tomorrow morning; I'll have the coffee machine on before you arrive."

❖

As the door shuts behind Harry, I exhale a breath I didn't realise I'd been holding. I've been preparing my entire life for this opportunity, heading the events team at a major cultural centre. Short of working for the royal family, it doesn't get more significant than Oxford. Part of me wants to crawl into the window seat and wrap myself in daydreams. The other part of me realises that if I do, I won't get anything else done.

Practicality wins the day.

I cross back into the living room and open my suitcase. Inside are several framed photos, each encased in layers of tissue paper. I unwrap them and carry them over to the empty mantle, placing them in a neat row. My parents and best friends smile at me, but my attention lingers on the photo of my grandfather.

When I was little, my grandfather told me stories about a magical version of Oxford. He'd been a librarian here before he retired. My dad would tell him to stop filling my head with nonsense, but my grandfather was undeterred. I loved snuggling up next to him on the sofa. He'd sneak a bowl of crisps out of the kitchen, sharing them for as long as I would sit quietly and listen. He passed away while I was in primary school, but he'd be proud to see me continue the family legacy here at Oxford.

I pull myself from my reverie and get back to work unpacking, tearing open a box to find my collection of throw pillows. I left most of my belongings back at my parents' house in London, but a girl needs a few personal touches to make a place feel like home. The next two hours fly by as I spend them putting away clothes and setting out framed prints and knickknacks around the rooms. By the time I put my Wonder Woman tea mug in the kitchen cupboard, it doesn't look like the same house anymore. I pick up my journal from the kitchen table and tick 'unpack' off my lengthy To Do list. It isn't an exaggeration to say that my entire existence lies within its leather cover. Every idea, activity and plan is noted with detail. I glow in satisfaction when I can tick them off my lists.

Famished, I turn back towards the refrigerator and its intriguing contents.

"Oh my god, aged Lincolnshire poacher cheddar. My favourite."

I unearth a cutting board and frying pan in a cluttered kitchen cabinet and assemble a posh toastie. Chef Smythe wouldn't approve, but it will hit the spot.

Right as I set my plate down on the scuffed coffee table, ready to relax to whatever the BBC offers, I hear a soft knock at the back door.

I claw my way back up from the sunken cushions, heading for the kitchen. "Might be Harry, maybe she forgot to give me some kind of instructions."

I grab the keys from the counter and cross to the door, twisting the locks.

No one is there.

"Hello? Hello? Hmm, I swear I heard a knock," I mutter. "Guess it must have been my imagination."

After closing and locking the door, I turn once again towards the smell of warm cheese emanating from the living room.

I take one step and tumble over a furry barrier.

"Mrrriaowwww!" the friendly cat rubs its furry little head against my arm.

Sprawled across the wooden kitchen floor, I watch in shock as it nudges my palm, begging for a deep scratch between the ears.

"Lucky for you, I like cats, you little devil. Otherwise, I'd be more upset about the giant bruise forming on my leg." I stroke its back before picking myself up again. Dusting my jumper off, I eyeball my guest. I always wanted a pet, but my mother was allergic and then my busy work schedule made it out of the question. A communal college cat could be the perfect pet for a busy gal.

"Do you live here at the college?"

"Mrrrriaowwww."

"I'm Nat. What's your name, college cat?"

Staring down, I wait for a response. The cat blinks at me in return.

"Oh god, I'm talking to a cat and I'm expecting it to answer."

The cat, solid black except for two tufts of white fur around the neckline, winds in and out of my feet, alternating miaows with purrs in a cacophony only a cat can make. I wonder how I'll walk with a cat underfoot. Maybe it will wander around the flat and ignore me now that it's inside.

"Rightie-o, I guess Harry forgot to mention that I have a roommate. Now where did I leave that cheese toastie?"

I am no sooner seated on the sofa before the cat leaps up and curls around beside me.

"Miaow?"

"Did the word cheese perk you up? Are you hungry?" An answering paw attempts to swipe the sandwich from my hand. "I've let you in the house, but I draw the line at sharing a plate. Come on, I'll find you something."

Four more slices of Lincolnshire poacher later, laid out on a plate for my guest, I bite into my now-soggy sandwich. After all my unpacking, I'm too tired to care. I follow the sandwich with a packet of jammy dodgers and a small glass from the bottle of wine Harry left on the counter. As the rain drizzles down my sash windows, I realise I can hardly toss the cat back outside in these conditions.

"Cat," I prod it gently to gain its attention. "This is how it's going to work."

The cat slits open one eyelid and gives a short trill of a response.

"Excellent, you're awake. Here are the rules. I'm going to sleep now. I sleep in the bedroom. You sleep here. Me, there. You, here. Got it?"

The cat squints one eye open, gives a giant yawn and then goes right back to sleep.

"I'll take that as cat-language for a yes. Good night, college cat. Don't poop in my suitcase." I close the suitcase, just to be safe. You never know with cats.

In retrospect, I should have reiterated the point about not sleeping in my bed instead.

Chapter Three

When I agreed to meet Dr Radcliffe at seven in the morning, I had forgotten one key detail. It's still dark. The pale morning light hints at a sunrise but fails to help me find my way back to the main building.

"Oh, thank goodness," I murmur as I use my phone to spotlight a signpost. After a few more steps, I find the familiar pathway between the landscaped flowerbeds. I retrace my steps until I spy the yellowing light hanging at the main building's back door.

Harry is waiting for me in the hallway, perfectly coiffed despite the early hour. Handing me a cup, she shoos me into reception.

"Bless you, Harry, you're a star!" I take the St Margaret's mug from her and gulp my first sip of hot coffee. All I could find this morning were a teakettle and a bag of unground coffee beans. I'm an early riser, but much of my morning enthusiasm is fuelled by coffee.

As the caffeine hits my bloodstream, I launch into my first concern of the day. "Harry, I think I have a cat."

Harry settles into her desk chair and begins sorting through a stack of files. "That's lovely, dear. Is it a friendly cat?"

"What? Yes, no, um I guess so? It's just that I didn't know I had a cat. Yesterday morning I did not have a cat. Does the college have a community cat?"

She pauses, lifting her head in surprise. "Black with strange white markings?"

"That's the one," I confirm.

Her eyebrows rush towards her hairline, "How odd! That cat followed Lillian around everywhere. I assumed it was hers."

I shrug my shoulders, as much at a loss as she is. "Maybe goes with the job instead of with the person? It showed up at my house last night, was curled in my bed this morning, and then followed me out the door. I lost it in the garden on my way over here."

Harry tilts her head to the side in consideration before going back to her sorting. "On the bright side, Nat, everyone's used to the Ceremonies team having a cat."

I can't believe her nonchalance. I thought I was borrowing a communal cat, not inheriting one. Clearing my throat to catch her eye, I try again. "You're definitely confirming that I have a cat? Regardless of whether I want it?"

Harry nods, snickering behind her own steaming mug. "The cat's name is H if that helps."

"Aitch?" I repeat, sure I've misunderstood.

"No, H, like the letter," she clarifies.

I don't even try to wrap my brain around that one. Any further questions go on hold when Dr Radcliffe comes striding into the office, unbuttoning her jacket as she walks.

She bustles past me and says, "I'm pleased to see you here already, Natalie. Punctuality is an under-appreciated virtue. Let me put my briefcase on my desk and then I'll take you around. We'll pop by your office first so you can do the same."

I blow into my cup before chugging the rest while I wait for

Dr Radcliffe to dart into her office. I swallow the last sip in time for her to step back into the reception.

She motions me to follow her and we head for the doorway. "Right-o, we're off then. Harry, I'll aim to be back in time for my first meeting. Dial my mobile if I lose track of time and don't show up." Harry nods and waves us on our way.

Dr Radcliffe turns to the left, leading me into another doorway-lined hallway. She passes several before stopping, pushing open a large wooden door labelled 'Ceremonies'. "This is your office. You've got two assistants. They sit in a larger shared office with the other junior staff. I'll ask Harry to introduce you to them later this morning."

The office isn't as grand as Dr Radcliffe's, but that was to be expected. Nonetheless, I want to throw myself into the large leather desk chair and spin around in front of the antique oak desk. It has a roll top, closed tight, no doubt hiding away a myriad of wonders. My mind squeals in excitement.

There's a small wooden table with two upholstered chairs, ideal for intimate meetings, and large, sunny windows which open onto the college gardens. A deep floral rug provides a finishing touch.

Stepping into the room, my eye lands on the last piece of furniture. A cat bed. Oh lord, I'm definitely stuck with a cat.

Dr Radcliffe waits in the doorway as I wander in. "You can set your things down; they'll be perfectly safe here within the college. The security team patrols around regularly."

I cross the room to the desk and give the roll top a gentle tug, but it doesn't move.

Now I really want in. I glance at Dr Radcliffe, eyebrow raised. "It seems to be locked. Do you know if there's a key somewhere?"

"Oh yes, the key, what did Harry tell me?" she raises one hand to her mouth, casting her eyes towards the ceiling as she searches through her memory for the answer. "Now I remember. Lillian left strict instructions that we were to put it into the top right-hand drawer, and no one was to touch it until you arrived."

I open the drawer to find it empty except for a single mid-sized skeleton key. The weak, early morning light glints off the copper finish.

I reluctantly push the drawer closed, leaving the key in place. If I pick it up, I won't be able to stop myself from diving straight into any files and instruction packs which might hide inside. I pull a fountain pen and bright blue notebook from my handbag and stash the bag under the desk.

As we turn to leave, a muffled miaow and small thud catch our attention. A ball of black fur and two yellow eyes peer in through the window.

Dr Radcliffe stares open-mouthed. "My word, is that Lillian's cat?"

I glare at the window, annoyance painted across my face. "Now it's my cat. As best as Harry can guess, it came along with the job offer."

To my shock, Dr Radcliffe crosses the room and gives the window an expert tug, as though inviting an animal into the office is a normal activity. "We can hardly leave it outside, now can we?"

"Mriaoowwwww."

The cat leaps in, landing on one of the visitor chairs. He arches his back, begging for a gentle stroke. Dr Radcliffe gives him a welcoming pat. "And good morning to you, Ceremonies cat. Come along, you probably know this place as well as I do."

With another miaow, he drops beside her heels and follows her out of the doorway.

I stare in wonder as Dr Radcliffe chats away with the cat. Is everyone here slightly crazy? Maybe something's in the water. I make a mental note to get a filter.

The cat darts in and out of doorways, stopping to sniff a corner or bat a tuft of dust. Dr Radcliffe chatters away as we walk around the main building, providing an overview of the full University, St Margaret college and its environs.

"The University is made up of thirty-eight different colleges, St Margaret being one of them. Each college recruits their own students, but they all graduate with a degree from the University. Here at St Margaret, we have 800 students in total. The main Oxford shopping district is about a mile from here."

I wrack my brain for a reference point, failing to find anything other than the total number of university students. "Is that a lot for an Oxford college? Sorry if I should know that already."

Dr Radcliffe waves off my apology. "It's your first day, I'll give you a bit of leeway. To answer your question, yes. We're one of the largest of the Oxford colleges. St Margaret started as a women's school, but we now accept both sexes."

We stop in the college library, examining a collection of objets d'art on display in the atrium. I sigh wistfully. "What I've seen so far is gorgeous. I wish I'd had such a tranquil environment when I was a student."

Dr Radcliffe opens a set of French doors and steps out onto a small balcony. I can see the top of the iron fence bordering the grounds. She leans over the railing, explaining, "The grounds are enclosed by the fence, and tall hedges line most of the garden areas to keep out prying eyes."

The grounds reek of privilege, leaving me feeling like an interloper. "I've heard about the town and gown concept, but I didn't realise it was still accurate."

Dr Radcliffe smiles gently. "We don't mean to be so exclusive, but we owe it to our students, both past and present, to give a protected enclave where they can study and learn enough to rise to the top of their chosen fields."

She guides us back out into the main hallway. We slow to a stop in front of one of the enormous portraits lining the hall.

"This one is a particular favourite of mine. Catherine Morgan, one of our early benefactors. She was passionately involved in the fight for the women's vote and became interested in the university when she heard about the challenges women faced in trying to get an education. She defied expectations for how a wealthy woman should live her life."

"Sounds like my kind of woman," I agree, staring into the blue eyes of the older woman in the painting. The old-fashioned pin curls soften any harsh lines in her face, and her cunning smile makes me think of the Mona Lisa.

"Indeed. She never married. They say it's because she feared giving a man control of the fortune she would inherit. In reality, I suspect her head was turned in a different direction. When she passed away, she left most of her money to her lifelong female companion and bequeathed a substantial amount to the college."

A loud miaow triggers my startle reflex. I'd forgotten it was following us.

"And it would appear that Cat is also a fan. Look at the time! We'd better get a move on. Chef Smythe will be fit to be tied if we interrupt her in the kitchen once breakfast starts."

Our unlikely trio continues along the long hallway, arriving at a set of swinging double-doors marking the entrance to the dining hall. Dr Radcliffe pushes one open to reveal a broad L-shaped room. Our steps echo as we come inside and let the door swing shut behind us.

Metal rails and shuttered windows line the narrow end where we've entered. I can imagine a line of hungry students waiting to gather trays and collect their food. Tall windows line the righthand wall, providing glimpses of the manicured gardens. In between the windows are stands for cutlery and a small refrigerator with bottled drinks.

Further ahead, I spot the start of several rows of polished wooden tables. Intricately carved wooden seats are tucked underneath, so close together I can't help wondering how often diners elbow one another. Overall, I'd rate the room as 96% typical college dining hall and 4% Harry Potter.

Dr Radcliffe casts a surprised glance at the shutters. "I'm surprised the food windows are still closed. Chef Smythe always has at least one open so she can shout at the late-arriving staff."

"Lovely," I mutter before reminding myself that I can achieve anything I set my mind to, including making this horrid woman like me. At least a little.

"Trust me, wait until you taste her scones and homemade strawberry jam. She's famous for them, they practically melt in your mouth."

She raps on a shutter to announce our arrival. "Chef Smythe, are you here? I'd like you to meet our newest staff member."

The echo of her knock is the only response. "Strange, she might be back in the refrigerator. Let's go into the kitchen."

We cross the room, my mouth watering at the thought of a bacon roll or a few slices of buttered toast. The cat sticks by our side, sniffing the air, searching for the smell of fresh-cooked meat.

We pass the last shuttered window, striding around a small cashier station.

"With any luck, perhaps we can talk Chef Smythe into warming a scone or two. I know it's early, but they are honestly magnificent," Dr Radcliffe explains as we round a tower of metal tray racks, turning into the open doorway. We halt, staring in horror at the scene in front of us.

Chef Smythe is waiting in the kitchen. I recognise the soles of her black rubber shoes as they dangle off the edge of the metal kitchen island. Her body lies face down, a pool of deep red staining the floor.

I gasp as my eyes land on a large wooden handle. The fluorescent kitchen lights glint off the shiny steel of the meat cleaver sticking straight up from her back.

My vision goes grey as I mutter the only words that come into my mind. "I don't think I'm getting one of her scones soon."

❖

Dr Radcliffe leads me over to a table, the chair scraping the floor as she pulls it out and nudges me into it before rushing back into the kitchen. I take deep breaths until she returns, fumbling in her jacket pockets, searching for her mobile. She takes two tries to get past the fingerprint reader, cursing under her breath.

"Harry, thank goodness. I need you to call the police and then our security team. Send them to the dining hall... It's Chef Smythe. She's dead... Yes, I'm sure... Please hurry. Thanks."

Harry's sharp intake of breath is so loud, even I can hear it.

I watch as she slides her phone back into a pocket before covering her face with her hand. Dr Radcliffe takes three deep breaths, in and out. That's all she allows before pulling herself back together. By the time she lowers her hand, she is once again in control. She looks me straight in the eyes, "Ms Payne, I need to secure the doors until the security team arrives. Do not move from this space. Keep breathing deep, I'll be right back with you."

I take a few more calming breaths, focusing on the sounds of her heels echoing around the room. My stomach is in a knot. I concentrate on the swish of the door and murmured voices that signal the security team to keep from being sick. I try not to think about the scene I've witnessed, but it is burnt into my brain. The images flicker in and out of focus in time with my breathing. The rubber shoes, their flour-dusted, non-slip soles on display for all to see. A stain of darkest crimson, dripping from the table to pool on the tile floor. Last, but not least, the knife with its unforgiving steel blade.

Shuddering, I fight to hold in the tears scratching the backs of my eyelids. A furry face brushes against my legs, reminding me I'm not alone. I force my head back up, blood rushing through my body as circulation is restored.

"Come here, cat." He jumps into my lap and bumps his head under my chin. I bury my face in his furry warmth. He doesn't complain at the wetness. His deep purr sinks into my chest, comforting me until I find the strength to pull myself back together.

Dr Radcliffe is once again back in front of me. At a glance, she is calm and collected, but her crossed arms cannot hide the slight tremor in her hands. "The police are securing the scene and a Detective Constable will be here shortly. I'd send you home, but they told me we must stay put until the Detective can speak with us."

I nod my understanding. "Don't worry, I'll stay here with you as long as needed. The shock must be worse for you since you knew Chef Smythe well. Would you like a cup of tea? Would that help?"

Her mask slips for a moment, so quick I almost miss it. "That's a great idea, Natalie. I'll ask Harry to bring us each one. A proper builder's cup to give us both strength." She doesn't wait for an answer, ringing Harry with an additional set of instructions.

The hours pass by in a haze, snatches of conversation interspersed with images of yellow police tape, uniformed officers and flashes of crime scene photographers.

"Tell me what you saw."

"Did you touch anything?"

"Did Dr Radcliffe seem surprised?"

I answer question after question until Dr Radcliffe puts her foot down, insisting we've both shared everything we know. Harry steps forward, pulling me to my feet and tucking me under her arm as she guides me out of the dining hall and back to my office.

"Let's get your handbag, Nat, then I'll walk you back to the flat." She releases me long enough to allow me to gather my things. I half listen as Harry chats with the cat while I struggle to remember whether I had anything other than my handbag with me. "Come along, H. Be a good boy and keep our young lady company today."

The walk to the flat passes in a flash with Harry chattering the entire way. "I wish I could hide away here with you, but Dr

Radcliffe needs my help to contact staff members and to sort out student meals for the rest of the day. It'll be good to stay busy, keep my mind off it."

I rush to reassure her I'm okay now that I'm free from my captivity. "I'll find something on the television to watch, and the cat will stay by my side."

She squeezes my arm, as much for me as for herself. "Don't worry about dinner, I'll drop something from the caterer by later. Your body needs comfort food. It will help you remember that you are okay."

I stare at the TV after she leaves, watching a Bake-off marathon until Harry returns, a pair of foil-covered plates in hand. She settles next to me on the sofa, picking at her food as we watch the Bake-off contestants try to make a meringue pie. When the episode ends, she presses a small pill into my hand. "The Detective suggested you and Dr Radcliffe might have trouble sleeping this evening. He asked the doctor to give you something to help. I promised I'd get you both to take one of these pills, so no arguing with me."

I follow her into the kitchen, thanking her for everything and once again voicing my hope that she is okay. Standing on the doorstep, she waits until I turn the lock and wave permission for her to go.

I barely have time to wash my face and slip into my nightclothes before oblivion slips over me, the rumbles of the cat's purr lulling me to sleep.

Chapter Four

I wake to a bright sunlight streaming in my windows. In my
haste to get into bed last night, I forgot to close my curtains
and set my alarm. Memories of yesterday's events flood my mind.
A murder at an Oxford college. I heard one of the security guards
comment that it had never happened before. Just my luck to
stumble across the scene.

It's tempting to pull the covers over my head, staying tucked
away in the quiet of my bedroom, but I imagine Harry would
bang the back door down if I failed to turn up. Rolling over, I let
the warm rays clear away the last of the cobwebs in my brain.
Yesterday was a nightmare brought to life, but today doesn't have
to be. I've made a new friend in Harry. Today I'll get to meet my
team for the first time. There are plenty of good reasons to get
out of the bed. With that thought, I push down the covers,
encouraged that this new day will be better than the one before.

I'm barely upright before the cat leaps onto the bed next to
me, howling his disapproval of my lie-in. "All right, I'm coming. I
guess you want some food. Maybe a can of tuna?"

He scoffs his food before leaping onto the tabletop and
plonking a paw in the middle of my bowl of Crunchy Nut. Waving

my spoon at him, I grumble, "I wasn't done with that, cat." He counters by sticking his head in my bowl and lapping up the milk. Well played.

His bright yellow cat eyes shrink into slits, paw ready to swipe should I detour from my morning preparations. I shower in record time but stall in front of my cupboard. I turn to the cat for advice, "Should I opt for sophisticated or personable?" I lay two different options on the bed, a simple white sweater set versus a navy dress spotted with tiny ladybirds.

The cat comes to the rescue, leaping on the bed, and curling up on the sweater set. By the time I get him off it, the damage has been done. I roll my eyes as I look at the outcome, muttering, "Next time, can you give advice without shedding half your fur on my clothing?" However, I'm secretly pleased with his choice, much preferring to be myself on my second attempt at a first day at work.

I toss a few hair bands onto the floor to distract him while I struggle with my hair. When it's clear it isn't going to look any better, I snap my fingers, letting the cat know I'm done. He herds me into the kitchen and out the door. After locking up, I turn to find him staring up at me from the back steps, eyes bright with intelligence. "H, you are the strangest cat I have ever met in my life."

I've no risk of getting lost this morning with H taking the lead through the college grounds. His tail swishes left and right, his steps light and eager. Everyone we pass calls hello.

Hello to the cat, that is.

When we enter the flower garden, it hits me just how weird my life has become. "Yesterday, I stumbled across a crime scene. Today, I'm following a cat. Am I ever going to have a regular old, average, run-of-the-mill day here at St Margaret?" I could almost swear I hear the cat snicker. That's impossible.

"Let's go to my office, set my bag down and then see if we can find some coffee. I'm sure Harry can show us where to go." The

cat must agree as he marches straight to the door marked
"Ceremonies", his tail furiously swishing as I hunt for the door
key in the depths of my handbag. The lock tumbles over, the door
opening with a satisfying click. The cat shoves his nose into the
gap, pushing his way into the room.

"Miaow," sauntering over to the desk, he reaches up with his
front paws to perch onto the handle of the top right drawer.

"Coffee first, H." My announcement is greeted by a hiss.
"Okay... drawer first, then coffee?" He settles back onto his
haunches. I take that as a yes.

I cross the room, spinning my desk chair until it faces the
closed rolltop. I slide into it and drop my handbag at my feet. The
cat doesn't twitch.

Wrapping my fingers around the brass handle, I give a gentle
tug. The drawer slides smoothly open, the copper skeleton key
once again taking on a slight glow in the now streaming sunlight.
I pick it up and carefully insert it into the old fashioned lock on
the front of the rolltop. It turns over with a slight click and an
electric zing I feel all the way up to my elbow.

Something grasps onto my leg.

A raspy male voice shatters the silence. "Oi, about time you
used the key, missie. I've been stuck miaowin' at everyone since
the old bag Lillian 'ightailed it off to the 'ighlands."

I was sure I'd been alone in the small office. I inch around,
working up the courage to look down at my left leg. Yellow cat
eyes blink up at me, but the familiarity ends there. Wisps of
smoke trail out of wide nostrils, the long black snout pulling back
in a terrifying semblance of a smile. Behind a pair of wings, its
spiky tail taps a rhythm against the desk.

My mouth drops open while the rest of my body freezes into
place, air whooshing out of my chest. There is, undeniably, a baby
dragon in my office, its head reaching up to my knees.

I sway in my seat, something I didn't know could even happen
before now. I rub my eyes and look again.

Still there, one small black dragon with leathery grey wings. I hide my face in my hands.

"I'm still asleep in my bed. All this is a sleeping pill-induced dream. There isn't really a dragon attached to my leg."

Warm breath huffs across my legs as the raspy voice harrumphs. "I ain't a dragon, mate. I'm a wyvern. See the wings? Wings equal wyvern. Plus, I ain't got t-rex arms neither. Got a right bicep goin' in this wing, iffen I do say so myself."

Slowly breathing in and out, I cast my eyes upward, making a silent prayer that yesterday's shock hasn't driven me around the bend. The sensation retreats from my leg. It was probably a blood clot.

The sound of a sneeze calls my attention back to the ground, where I find the baby dragon stomping out a small fire in my carpet. The shriek I've been holding in turns out to be more powerful than I am.

"Lor luv a duck, lady." The beast tilts his head sideways as he digs a black talon into his ear. "You're blowin' out my eardrums down 'ere. Guess you're gonna need something more than me jabberin' away for you to believe me. Now where did Lillian put that note?" He squints at me, rubbing his chin.

The banging sound of the wooden rolltop flying up snaps me out of my reverie. The little creature, dragon, wyvern, whatever it was, is shuffling around, sending papers cascading towards the ground.

"Ere it is. I knew she left you a letter." He waves a sheet of paper around in front of me. I can't believe I'm saying this, but I take the paper from the wyvern. His little hand brushes mine as I do so.

Still not real.

I read,

"Dear Natalie,

Welcome to the University of Oxford Department of Ceremonies. By now you've probably met our wyvern Humphrey and are wondering whether you've lost the plot entirely or perhaps fallen into an alternate universe. I assure you; you have done neither.

You are the Carimoniae Praefectus, one of a handful of individuals throughout history who holds responsibility for keeping alive the magic of Oxford. Yes, magic is real. For hundreds of years, Oxford has thrived because of its connection with the earth's magical field, allowing ghostly scholars and curious creatures to continue walking the halls long after their demise.

As the ceremonial prefect, you must curate events which uphold and extend the traditions of the colleges, provide relief from studies, and foster lasting memories which feed into the magical system.

Why you? The ability to see the magic lies in your veins, handed down through the generations. Not everyone heeds the call, but those who do find a career beyond their wildest dreams.

Humphrey, or H as he prefers, will ensure you soon meet the other two prefects, working in the library and museum, respectively. They will give you more information and answer all your questions. I am sorry that I am not there to welcome and guide you in person. Last year I began showing signs of early dementia. Whilst the doctors reassure me that my slide will be gradual, it was clear I could no longer uphold the responsibilities of my role.

I wish you the absolute best of luck. The magic assures me you're up to the task.

Kind regards,

Lillian

P.S. H prefers Lincolnshire Poacher to any other cheddar. And don't let him convince you to pour him a stout. It won't end well for either of you. Trust me."

"Magic???" I blurt out.

Humphrey nods, sending wisps of steam curling into the air. "'Ow else do you think a gooseberry puddin' like you ends up with such a noble title? It's the magic."

"Magic!" I repeat, dumbfounded. "I can do magic? Is that what the letter said?" I skim the page again, my eyes leaping from one paragraph to another. The words haven't changed in the last few seconds; it's right there in black and white.

Magic is in my veins.

❖

I look at Humphrey, something niggling in the back of my mind. "You're the cat, right?" His nod confirms my suspicions. "I knew it! I knew something was weird about you."

The little guy in question is having none of it, rolling his eyes and shaking his snout. "You're full of porky pies iffen you believe that. You had no idea, natterin' away to an old cat." He lets a little chuckle slip before straightening himself back up.

I pick Lillian's letter up again to read it more closely. Poor woman, it must have devastated her to leave her job after so many years, not to mention dealing with a dementia diagnosis.

Unfortunately, though, that leaves me holding the bag with no one here but a wyvern to explain what it is exactly I'm supposed to do. How did I end up here?

I cough a few times to interrupt H's battle with the ash floating in the air. "Lillian's note says I inherited my magical abilities... but how did she know?"

H takes a last swipe at the ash before answering. "Your grandda asked me a similar question."

A lightning bolt strikes through my brain. "My grandfather?"

"Well, I did say it runs in families. Your grandda was the first 'uman I met after I became a cat."

All those stories my grandfather told me about magical Oxford. That's why the little beast's name is so familiar. Humphrey the mischievous wyvern was a favourite of mine. How could I have forgotten?

My grandfather died years ago, his stories fading into the depths of my memory. I fish a scene out at random, my grandfather mid-story, my dad interrupting to call us to dinner. My dad... "What about my dad? Does he know magic is real?"

H shakes his head, "Nah, the wee lad 'ad 'is sights set on London. 'E was getting outta 'ere at all costs, the magic would 'ave been a prison sentence for a chap like 'im. Your grandda never told 'im."

"I still don't understand, H. If he had the right bloodline, why couldn't he see the magic? How could his father keep it a secret?"

H crosses the room and roots around on the desk until he finds the old skeleton key. "I spent the first few 'undred years of my life as a gargoyle. I dunno who the original discoverers were or 'ow they married up the 'uman field with the magical field. What I know from spendin' time with your grandda is this: One, you gotta 'ave the right bloodline. Iffen you do, you can put one of the three skeleton keys into the lock to make the connection between yourself and the magic."

"So that's why I couldn't see you until I used the key." I look at it, sitting there in H's hand. Other than a slight glow, the object in question seems mundane.

I cross my legs, still deep in thought. "I've got so many questions; I don't know where to start. The magic? This prefectus thing? Do I get a wand?" I spin to my desk, searching through the disarray. "Where's my journal gone? I need to make some notes."

Papers fly again as Humphrey leaps onto the desk, wings whipping my hair into disarray. "No notes." He meets my eyes, his stern gaze holding me hostage. "Look, mate, you can't tell any muggins about our secret. Iffen you want to stay 'ere and work with magic...." I nod in confirmation, encouraging him to continue, "...iffen you want to be the prefect, you gotta keep quiet."

I think about that for a moment. It feels wrong to keep a secret of this magnitude from my father. All those times he thought grandfather was inventing fairy tales, he should know the truth. "What happens if I tell someone... or if I say cheers, but no thanks?"

"We kill you." The wyvern doesn't blink as he says this.

"Kill me?" the words squeak out. "Seriously?"

When the colour drains out of my face, Humphrey breaks out full-on belly laughs. The falling to the floor type.

"Mate, your face! You shoulda seen it. Kill ya? Ha hahahahaha. Iffen you told somebody, what would they do? They'd tell you to get right into the sea, that's what. No one would believe ya. And walkin' away? Who would walk away? It's magic."

Still struggling to accept this is more than a figment of my imagination, I arch my finger, silently beckoning him to step closer. Hesitantly, I lean over, asking permission to stroke his wyvern forehead. Are wyverns slimy? I run a finger between his ears and am overjoyed to feel a dry, leathery skin.

"Are you purring?" He's definitely purring.

Humphrey quickly straightens up and coughs. "No, of course not. That would be weird, bruv. What's wrong with you?"

I let him hold on to some semblance of dignity. "Can we get back to my questions? I don't understand any of this. How does the Head of Ceremonies, of all people here in Oxford, end up as a magical prefect? Why isn't it one of the professors or college principals?"

Humphrey hops back up on top of my desk, sits down and crosses his legs. "Listen up, missie. I been watching the lads in this place for four 'undred years. Students and professors, assignments and long 'ours studyin'. You can find that at any university. That ain't what makes Oxford special."

I wave aside his explanation. "I get that, but you've got all this history and the buildings themselves. I grew up on stories about Oxford. There are plenty of things that make it stand apart from every other city in the world."

He glares me back into silence. "Yeah, we got all that, but think about it. What do people talk about years after they graduate? It sure ain't the buildins'. It's the ceremonies. The events. The parties. Them fancy 'igh table dinners where they're rubbin' elbows with the silk britches types."

The wheels in my head are spinning as I connect the dots. "You're telling me that there's magic, and my events help it exist?" Leaning forward, I ask, "Wait a minute, do the people at Disneyland have magic? That would explain a lot."

Humphrey frowns. "The only magic Disney 'as is that tunnel system runnin' under the ground. This is real old magic, only found in two places in the world – here and Cambridge."

"Really?" I always wondered how they stayed on top of the rankings. Five hundred years is a long time to remain in the lead. But magic? My mind races as I consider how far the magic might extend. "What, specifically I mean, is magical here?"

"What ain't magical at Oxford? There're gargoyles like me, ghosts, the portraits..."

The angry old white man in Dr Radcliffe's office springs to mind. I flash back to the meeting, remembering the feeling of a heated glare on the back of my neck. I knew that creepy portrait was staring at me!

"...books in the library...hello? Nat? Are you listening to me? You gotta take this seriously."

"Seriously? It's magic! You're a talking wyvern-cat-gargoyle who gave me a letter saying I'm a magical prefect. I don't know whether to jump for joy or worry that there's been a gas leak. How does a wyvern come to be at Oxford in the first place? And Humphrey? Where'd that name come from?"

"Please, call me H. Not 'Umphrey. That's a name not even my mum could love. As to being at Oxford, I got way more 'istory in this town than anything within St Margaret's walls. I started my days as a gargoyle, one of the original carvings at the Bodleian."

I stare up at the ceiling as my mind races through the stories my grandfather used to tell.

"That's the main library, right?"

"Flmphhh, 'the main library' she says." His head shakes in disgust. His barbed tail thumps until he is sure I'm paying close attention.

"The Bodleian ain't your county library. It's over four 'undred years old, for starters, second oldest in Europe."

"So, you were a gargoyle at the library, but now you're a cat. And a wyvern?" My confusion is written across my face.

"I ain't 'ad to explain this to someone new in ages." H marches a couple of laps on the carpet while he gets his thoughts in order. "Well, mate, it's like this. After several 'undred years of wind and rain, my carvin' started to wear away."

I follow his talons as he traces the path, "First the top of my wing, then my legs... when I was barely a 'ead left, I started to worry. I'd been watching people and animals walk by for centuries. I never saw no one worried 'bout what was 'appenin' to me." He lets loose a blast of black steam, his anger clear.

"Then one day, right when I was 'bout to give up, I nodded off and woke up on the ground. I was one of them. And a cat! Bloody lucky call, that one. My neighbour Sid ended up bein' a squirrel. No Lincolnshire poacher cheddar for 'im; 'e's gotta 'unt around for chestnuts."

Sid? I make a mental note to come back to that name later. "Right, then you, um, reincarnated?"

Snout nodding in approval, H confirms, "Guess you can call it that. A black cat with white markings for my wings, missie." He waves the wings in question, fluttering up a few feet into the air.

The picture is coming together in my head, but I've still got a question. "Ok, gargoyle into cat. How do you get back to being a wyvern?"

"That's tied to the magic. Unless you're born to the right family, I'm a cat. Bloody ridiculous with all the miaowing and whatnot. Thankfully, I can usually con somebody into sharing their curry with me."

"Can I only see you as a wyvern inside the college? What happens if we leave St Margaret?"

"We can go most anywhere in Oxford, and you'll see a wyvern. Everybody else sees a cat. Now what you say about meetin' some of the other lads in my magical gang?"

Chapter Five

I'm gathering up my handbag to leave when the reality of what I'm doing sets in, freezing me in place. "Um, H? I've got a few more questions before I'm ready to leave this office."

H glances back, mid-flight towards the closed office door. "But my mates! Everyone is wantin' to meet ya."

I grab his tail to halt his progress. "Trust me, I am really excited to meet everyone, but it's nine in the morning. What if someone catches me talking to you? Or to a portrait? Or thin air?"

His glare softens when he sees the concern written across my face. "Don't you worry none, missie. The magic makes it so people accept whatever they see. Cat wanderin' the 'allways, no problem. Lady chattin' with a painting, that's just fine." H flies up until his eyes are level with mine, reaching out with a hand to pat my cheek. "Don't worry iffen someone sees you."

"What about when you breathe fire? Won't people notice the burn in my... where did it go?" I spin around, searching for the spot that H set on fire when he sneezed earlier. Aside from basic wear and tear, the carpet is perfect.

"The magic fixes everything back again. 'Cept the ash... that sticks around." H swoops across the room, dislodging the last bits of ash from the carpet in question.

Once again, I grab H by the tail before he can get to the door. "Lor luvin, Nat. It's a tail, not a bell pull. What now?"

I struggle to speak past the lump in my throat. "I'm nervous. I mean, magic? Ghosts? Am I really ready for all of this?"

His eyes travel from the polka dot ballet flats on my feet, up the length of my ladybird dress until he finally meets my eyes. "Look at you self, Nat. You 're a strong missie, confident. Your grandda prolly told you all about us. You're not meetin' strangers, you're finally gettin' to know your wider family."

That's the inspiration I needed to get moving. My answering smile reassures H that it's safe to turn his back on me. I'm ready to go, no further plans to pull on his tail before we go.

After opening my office door, I nudge H aside and stick my head out to peek down the hallway. No humans wandering about. Everyone must be off playing catch-up on all the work they didn't get done yesterday. Seemed like every person in the college found an excuse to stop by the dining hall and spy on the bobbies investigating the scene.

I wave H out and lock the door behind us. As we turn, I rub my eyes, checking to make sure they are working properly.

How on earth was I oblivious to all this activity yesterday and this morning? The hallway is buzzing with ghostly figures dressed in clothes covering every decade in the last century.

Pausing, I watch them bustle from room to room, carrying paper-filled folders or large textbooks. "Ghostly college admins? Is that really how they're spending their afterlife?" I shudder, horrified at the thought of passing eternity shuffling papers from one room to another.

I spy a well-dressed man hurrying in our direction. He looks to be in his mid-thirties, and I'm guessing he's from the earlier days of the college as he has a pocket watch tucked into his waistcoat. I attempt to flag him down, but my hand passes right through him as he rushes past.

Fortunately, H is there to snag him with a claw. "'Old up Bartie, I want you to meet Nat. She's our new prefect. Old Alfred was her grandda." Facing to me, H completes the introductions. "Nat, this is Bartholomew."

Bartholomew's eyes light up in satisfaction. "Welcome, Ms Nat. Sorry for not stopping, but I wasn't sure you could see us yet. We're all chuffed you're here. Many of us knew your grandda well."

I nod hello, mindful of the stacks of papers in his arms. "I'm pleased to meet you, Bartholomew. I still can't believe those fairy tales my grandfather told me all those years ago were real."

"Please call me Bartie, like your grandda did. I'm not surprised to hear he told you about us. He desperately hoped your dad would follow in his footsteps, but it wasn't meant to be. Sounds like he made a head start on planting the seed in your mind."

Laughing, I agree, "That he did, although he was canny about it. I never had a clue what he was doing, but here I am. H has promised to take me on a tour of the magic. I hate to ask because you look like you're in the middle of something, but would you have a minute to tell me what you do here?"

"I do!" Bartie flags down one of the ghostly women, passing the papers over to her with a quick set of instructions to deliver them to one professor. "I'm the Head of Eternal Affairs here at St Margaret. Besides H, I will be your primary contact at the college."

"What does the Head of Eternal Affairs do?"

Bartie chuckles, "What don't I do might be the easier question. As you've seen, I've got a small team of ghosts to help with the administration. We monitor all the research our living professors and students are undertaking, matching them up with right magical support." Seeing the next question on my lips, he continues on, "We have over a hundred years of history within these walls, plus the wider resources of the university. Mankind has a tendency to forget history. We don't. That's why we refer to ourselves as Eternal. When the living need help, I call in an Eternal expert to give them a nudge or locate a book with the missing piece of information."

My eyes widen as I grasp the size of his task. "Keeping up with that much information, knowing how to find it, and for so many students and professors. That seems impossible!"

Still hovering beside me, H elbows me. "Not impossible, Nat. It's magic."

Bartie clears his throat, capturing our attention. "All of us Eternals are terribly sorry about your experience yesterday. A murder at St Margaret! I never thought I'd see anything like that."

Since he's brought up the murder, perhaps he has some ghostly file indicating whodunnit. From what I overheard yesterday, it didn't sound as though the police had identified any immediate suspects. With a bit of magical luck, maybe I can point them in the right direction. "Speaking of the murder, Bartie, you don't know who the culprit might be?"

"I'm afraid not, Ms Nat. Much like live human beings, we can only see what happens directly in front of us. There are no ghosts in the kitchen and the portraits of the old principals which hang in the dining hall face each other. They can't see beyond the high table... of course, I could say that about all the professors," Bartie chuckles. "Whatever happened was limited to the kitchen itself. We didn't see or hear anyone out of the ordinary enter or exit the dining hall between Chef Smythe's arrival early yesterday and that of yourself and Dr Radcliffe."

Not the answer I hoped to get, but I hadn't really given any thought into how I'd explain my knowledge to the local police. H said they see and hear what they expect, but I don't think anyone expects you to say that a ghost told you.

"Thanks anyway, Bartie." Stepping to the side, I wave Bartie off. "It's been a pleasure to meet you. I don't want to keep you from your work any longer, so I'll trust that we'll see each other again soon."

Bartie gives me a polite nod and a friendly smile before continuing on his way.

❖

I follow H as he passes the security guard standing in the porter's lodge doorway but stall on the pavement before we exit the front gate. "I thought you said there are portraits and books and, well, other magical things at St Margaret. How come we're leaving?"

H reaches out a hand and tugs me along. "I'm taking you to the Bodleian. It's the best place to start iffen you really want to understand your job. You can meet one of the other prefects." Happy that I'm following along, he flaps his wings, flying above the pavement.

Speeding up my pace, I catch up to walk alongside him. "Will you at least tell me what we're passing on the way? I came straight into the college yesterday and didn't exactly get a tour."

"Sure thing, missie. There ain't a secret in this town I don't know... well exceptin' who killed Chef Smythe."

The memory of yesterday hangs over us as we wait for the crosswalk light to change. Finally, the traffic slows, letting us head deeper into a neighbourhood. Lining the shaded streets are well-appointed homes tucked away behind elaborate iron gates, luxury cars parked in every drive. All signs point to these homes being well beyond anything I could afford. I sigh, picking up my pace to once again catch H.

After two blocks we hit a large circular drive with a tiny, gated park in the middle. One of those like you see in the movies, where only the people in the neighbourhood have a key to get in. Wonder if my magical key works there? I make a mental note to check one weekend.

A block of stately cream-coloured buildings line the crescent, reminding me somewhat of the famous street in Bath. "These houses are gorgeous. And big. Are they owned by university faculty?"

"Nah, nowadays, these Victorian behemoths cost a fair penny more than a professor makes. But they are part of the 'istory of St Margaret."

Looking around, I spot no obvious clues. "How's that, H?"

"When the professors moved into these 'omes, they brought their wives and their wee ones. And iffen there's one thing a professor cares about, its education. Back then, women couldn't get a degree at Oxford, but they could study iffen a college would let'em in. Remember Dr Radcliffe explaining that St Margaret started as a women's college? Well, there you go. Don't seem so long ago to me, sure did make life 'ere more interestin'."

As we continue, passing by another couple of colleges and more private homes, I mull over how H must view the world. Four hundred years of history he's seen, first from above and then from the ground. He's right to point out that not that long ago I would have been an interloper in a man's world. We women are still fighting the battle, I mused.

We slip down a brick-lined alley, past a narrow gate, and emerge into a wooded wonderland.

"Welcome to the University Park, Nat," H announces. "Seventy acres of peace and quiet, with none of them pesky bicycles tryin' to run a mate down."

By unspoken agreement, H and I slow our pace, taking in the calming ambiance of the shade trees and grassy pitches. The only sounds are children laughing and ducks quacking. I stop to read one of the information signs, bursting into laughter when I spot a goose chasing H around a small pond.

With a fiery breath, H sends the goose scurrying back to the safety of the water.

Stifling back my laughter, I check in with him, "Everything all right?"

"That's my mate, Laurie. He's still spittin' about transformin' from a tragic Greek mask into a goose. Cain't say I blame him." After dusting himself off, H steers me back onto one of the pathways. "Enough wasting time. Shake a leg, missie, still more streets to cover."

H regales me with stories about my grandfather as we stroll past the cricket fields. Many of them are ones I heard years before, but this time told from the wyvern's point of view. It's been years since my grandfather passed away; hearing his stories reminds me of all of those afternoons I spent curled up next to him on the sofa.

I had been inconsolable in those weeks after his death, but gradually time acted as a bandage over the wounds. Discovering that H and the magic of Oxford are real makes me remember all the warmth and love my grandfather gave me, triggering none of the pain of the loss. By the time H and I reach the croquet lawn, it feels like we're old friends.

We exit the park in front of Keble College with its distinctive red bricks and neo-gothic architecture, following the signs which point left towards the town centre.

My head swivels as we pass landmark after landmark. H points out the university museums, sending my imagination into overdrive with tales of dinosaur skeletons come to life. I barely overcome the urge to duck inside the museum and check out the scene for myself. The road carries on, the distance on the town centre signs shrinking as we glide by Rhodes House and alongside the Trinity College walls.

Finally, a giant roundabout comes into view, marking our arrival in the heart of Oxford. With the clean lines of the newly built Weston Library at our backs, we pause, waiting for an opening in the traffic.

I look left and right, sizing up the mix of cars, double-decker

buses, cyclists and pedestrians before stepping into the roadway. I
hear H calling my name as I reach the pavement on the other side
of the road. Turning back, I'm just in time to catch him darting
underneath a bright red double-decker and nearly knocking a
cyclist over in his rush to catch up.

He steps onto the sidewalk, breathless from his exertions.
"Nat! Didn't you 'ear me? You gotta be careful 'ere!"

Leaning over, I help him wipe the bicycle tyre tracks off his
tail. "Um H, I know you're supposed to be my guide, but I'm from
London. I lived in Paris. An Oxford roundabout has nothing on
Piccadilly Circus. Based on the look on that cyclist's face, I think
you'd better stay close to me next time."

Feeling confident, I take the lead up the concrete stairs,
guiding us under the arched entry of the Clarendon Building,
following signs towards the central library quad. The library
building looms over the pavement, crenelated towers and carved
gargoyles lining the top. I eye them carefully but can't guess
which one used to be H's home. Carrying on through another
arched passageway, I see wooden boards reminding us that silence
is required as the buildings are used for research and studies.

We emerge into the library quadrangle, my eyes wide as I
stand in the middle of the open-air square and try to take in the
buildings surrounding me. One end is marked by a five-story
tower, each level decorated with different styles of architecture.
The walls of the surrounding buildings are divided into long,
narrow rectangles, evoking visions of unbroken rows of book
spines waiting to be picked off the shelves.

H interrupts my efforts to translate the Latin text above one
of the four arched doorways. "I remember when Ole Pembrokey
used to pass through 'ere."

"Who? Pembrokey?" I replay the last few minutes, wondering
whether I missed a verbal cue.

His little wings batting, H floats over to the large statue
erected in front of the main library entrance. He huffs a fiery

breath onto the nameplate, using a leathery hand to buff it into a shine. "Pembrokey, can't you read? 'E was a bigwig in the early years. Always 'ad 'is loaf in a book, but the ladies liked 'im well enough. Even made it into one of Old Shakey's plays."

Shakey? He can't mean... "Um, H, do you mean Shakespeare?"

Dumbstruck, I follow H, curious to see how he will handle the crowd of tourists blocking the library entrance. Between the gaggle of teenagers engrossed in their efforts to take the perfect selfies and the older tourists with their noses buried in guidebooks, it won't be easy.

To my surprise, H skirts the group, choosing one of the smaller doors off the side of the main entrance. The label above the stone archway says Schola Musicae, but a laminated plastic sign below reads "Staff Entrance", conveying its current purpose. Safely inside, we move towards the front desk when I spot a young woman beckoning me from across the room. Her long blonde hair is pulled up in a messy bun, held in place by a few wayward pencils. Dressed in a snarky t-shirt and jeans, she nearly blends into a group of students. The name badge hanging from around her neck is the only sign of her status.

Beaming with delight, she leans over, exchanging high fives with H before rising up to say hello. "Welcome, you must be Natalie, I'm pleased to see you've joined us here at the University. I'm Mathilde, the bibliothecae praefectus."

I breathe a sigh of relief, thrilled to see another human being acknowledge the existence of magic. "Hi Mathilde, I am really, really pleased to meet you. Please call me Nat."

Mathilde laughs and pats me on the shoulder. "Worried you were losing your mind?" I nod a yes. "Happens to all of us. Our prefect team is small but critical. We've been busy preparing for your arrival."

She spins around, leading us over to a framed scroll work displayed on one wall. "Nat, before I can take you any further into the library, I need you to recite the library oath. It's been a requirement for entry since the 1400s."

I squint, struggling to make out the faded writing on the yellowed paper. Mathilde gives the gilt-edged frame a sharp rap, and magically the words come into focus. I clear my throat, "*I hereby undertake not to remove from the Library, nor to mark, deface, or injure in any way, any volume, document or other object belonging to it or in its custody; not to bring into the Library, or kindle therein, any fire or flame, and not to smoke in the Library; and I promise to obey all rules of the Library.*"

Mathilde smiles in approval. "I know it seems old-fashioned, but it is ceremonial habits like these which help reinforce the connection with the magical plane. Now, why don't we go to my office, make ourselves comfortable and get to know one another."

We wind our way through the stacks and up an old stairwell. Once we're seated in a tiny office, I ask, "Now can someone explain what it is a prefect does? Is there a guidebook?"

"Ha! I wish." Mathilde shakes her head. "Kate, she's the third prefect, you'll meet her soon. She moved to Oxford four months ago, and I've only been here for about three weeks myself. Our predecessors were nearing the mandatory retirement age and had been looking for someone to inherit their positions. Lillian was meant to stay on for a while and be our mentor, expecting to be here for another decade. Her diagnosis was sudden; I can't say I blame her for choosing to leave so quickly." She shakes her head before giving me a small smile. "We were lucky to have the handover period we did. I'll tell you what I know, and then we can all work together to fill in the gaps."

Smiling, I nod my head in encouragement. "I already feel better knowing that I'm not alone. My grandfather told me stories about a magical Oxford, but learning that those stories were real is a lot to take in."

Mathilde sits up in her chair. "Magical stories? Your grandfather? There hasn't been a prefect in my family for several generations, same for Kate as far as I know. It seems there are enough families with magic in their blood that it skips around. I'd love to hear what he told you, if you're up for sharing."

"Absolutely," I reassure her. "We'll consider it as comparing notes. You must be patient with me. He died nearly 20 years ago. I need to sit down one evening and fish them out of my childhood memories. I'll write everything I can remember and then share."

H thumps his tail, reminding us he's here to help. "I'll fix what the missie gets wrong. I spent the first three 'undred years as a carvin' on the side of this very buildin', so I don't know them in much detail. But for the last sixty, I'm your expert."

Mathilde inclines her head in a gracious nod and says, "Thanks for that, H. Unfortunately, I don't know that much about the beginning, either. Lillian said legend has it that a few hundred years ago, a group of researchers had an experiment go awry on them and somehow they accidentally uncovered the existence of the earth's magical plane."

Blinking, I struggle to make sense of her statement. "The earth? Like the whole planet? But I thought H said that the only places with magic are Oxford and Cambridge?"

Mathilde stands up, slipping into lecturer mode. "The magical plane wraps around the entire planet, but... and this is the important part... you can only access it under the right conditions. This is what the researchers discovered - the conditions you need in place to bring it into alignment with the earth's magnetic field. They did several experiments, eventually building up an infrastructure here in Oxford and over in Cambridge. By bringing the magical field into alignment, they turned the two university towns into safe havens."

I consider her words before asking for a clarification. "What do you mean by safe haven?"

Pacing around, Mathilde explains, "In the early years, scholars were subject to the whims of the rich, dependent on them for funding. The magical field increased the attraction to the universities. More scholars came to study, the wealthy felt compelled to leave behind donations. New colleges sprang up around the towns. From the outside, Oxford and Cambridge's success looks like the result of a self-fulfilling prophecy. But to those few of us on the inside, we know the truth."

"Magic?" I ask.

Mathilde winks back her confirmation. "Magic."

I lean back in my seat, taking it all in. "Ok, I can believe most of that. But how did they keep it a secret for all these years? I thought researchers like to shout when they make a discovery? Something like this would be monumental, to say the least."

Mathilde frowns, turning to H to see if he can offer any insights. "I was a wee carvin' on the wall back then. Awake, but couldn't see much from my perch."

Shrugging, Mathilde makes a guess. "Maybe something happened that made them fear telling others? England wasn't exactly the stablest country before the 17th century. If there are any notes left, they're probably hidden away in the archives of one of the oldest colleges."

Thinking of 1600s England reminds me of a song I learned in grammar school. I sing the opening bars, drawing a laugh from Mathilde, "Divorced, beheaded, died. Divorced, beheaded, survived..." I grab a breath before commenting, "If it was around the time of Henry VIII, I can see how they wanted to avoid offering him any excuses to rid himself of more wives. Any guesses on when they introduced the prefect's role? And why us, I mean, our families?"

Dropping back into her chair, Mathilde replies, "Lillian thought we might be descendants of the original researchers. Something they did during their experiments shaped our DNA. It is frustrating for a librarian such as myself to not know the full history. I'm looking forward to digging into the library archives, to see if I can construct my family tree and understand at least that part of the mystery."

I shift in my seat, "That would explain how we can see the magic, but not why they limited the number of prefects to three."

Mathilde grabs a pen and paper, scratching down three lines of text on the page. "The Latin versions of our titles make it clearer: *bibliothecae, musei and caerimoniae.* The bibliothecae praefectus was left in charge of all written materials." She waves at herself, "That's me. They put another person as the musei praefectus in charge of looking after magical artefacts, that's Kate. Last, but not least," she smiles, "they left the caerimoniae praefectus overseeing all the people. I should warn you that the term 'People' has a broader meaning, here. It includes the ghosts and all the portraits, and not to forget the little beasts like H over there."

I wink at H, "Sounds like I'm your new boss." He singes the hem of my dress in reply.

Laughing, Mathilde clarifies, "You'll soon see that the human beings are your main concern. The Eternals are there to assist you in planning your ceremonies and events. We all have our part to play with the magic, my books, Kate's statues and buildings and your ceremonies. As a prefect, we're responsible for keeping our areas in perfect working order. The magic calls to members of our families. It guides people like me and you and Kate, shaping our choices so we end up as experts in the needed fields."

I blink, trying to make sense of Mathilde's words. "So, you're saying that magic made me be an event planner?"

"In short, yes. Let me give you an example. Before you got this job, were you actively looking for one?"

I cast my mind back. "Huh. No, actually, I wasn't. Even if I was, I wouldn't have been looking for roles outside of London. I don't really remember applying. Lillian phoned one day and invited me for an interview, and that was that."

"No missie, that was magic," H interjects.

My body stills completely, stunned by this revelation. "Magic made me into an event planner and then brought me to Oxford, so I could oversee all the university's ceremonies? And the ceremonies are critical to keeping the magic... alive?"

"Not alive, but accessible," Mathilde explains. "The magic needs to be in alignment so that Oxford can continue to enjoy the benefits it provides. Lillian explained to me that three of us, you, me and Kate, help to triangulate the field. I keep all of our books secure and help bring new knowledge in. Kate inspires through art and architecture. And you entertain and enrapture through ceremony. Does that make sense?"

I nod, finally starting to understand how I fit in, and how much responsibility sits on our shoulders.

Satisfied, Mathilde reclines in her seat. "Speaking of ceremonies, I understand you've got St Margaret autumn gala to plan straightaway. How are you finding it there?"

Just like that, all the excitement I'd been feeling evaporates. My stomach churns as visions of yesterday flash through my mind. "It's been a rollercoaster since I arrived. Between finding out about the magic and discovering Chef Smythe..." My voice trails off as I run out of words.

Seeing me upset, Mathilde rises from behind her desk to take the chair next to mine. "Did you have a run-in with her already? Her scones are famous, but I've heard she's a beast."

A frown creases my face. "Oh no, Mathilde, you haven't heard? She's... she's dead. Dr Radcliffe and I discovered her body in the college kitchen."

Mathilde's eyes fly open. "What? WHAT?!?! Oh my god, Nat, that's awful. What happened?"

I suck in air, hunting for strength. "I met Dr Radcliffe early in the morning. She was showing me around the college, giving me some history. We ended up in the dining hall. It was silent when we walked in. Probably should have been our first clue that something was awry. But we were chatting, and she was waxing on about Chef Smythe's scones."

Mathilde grips my hand between her own. "Where did you find her?" she asks.

Squeezing her hand in thanks, searching my mind for the best words to describe the scene, I opt for the bare minimum. No point in giving anyone else nightmares. "She was in the kitchen, draped face down on the metal island. Meat cleaver sticking from her back." I shiver as the vision flames to life in my mind.

Releasing my hand, Mathilde pulls me into a gentle hug. "Thank goodness you were with Dr Radcliffe. Lillian introduced me to her, she seemed lovely."

"She is lovely. We were stuck there in the dining hall for hours, being questioned by various detectives. Harry, her assistant, stayed with us as much as she could. We all propped one another up, I guess. Not the best circumstances to start a friendship, but here we are."

Reassured that I'm okay, Mathilde leans back in her chair. "Wow, a murder. At a college. I've never heard of such a thing."

"Ahem." The sound of H clearing his throat captures both of our attention. "I was 'opin' to give you missies a chance to settle in, but it looks like that choice is outta my hands. I'm gonna 'ave to tell ya."

Mathilde is the first to react. "What are you talking about, H? What choice?"

"There's a reason you three gooseberry puddins are all new. The magic ain't workin' like it should. You said it, Tildy. Oxford's supposed to be a haven. Ever since Kate got here, things 'ave been wonky. We thought it was the ole bag. You know, Lillian."

I arch an eyebrow and ask, "Are you saying that the magic started failing because of Lillian's dementia? What made you think she was the cause?"

"Books went missing, antiques were misplaced, we all thought she was movin' things round and forgettin' where she put 'em. That's why she left so quickly. But a murder?" H shakes his head. "For the first time in my four 'undred years in this town, somethin' is wrong with the magic. It ain't in perfect alignment no more."

I look to Mathilde, but she seems as unconvinced as I am. "Granted murder is a terrible crime, but surely one death doesn't mean that you weren't on the right track with Lillian. How do you know for sure that the missing items weren't her fault? Maybe the murder is a freak accident?"

H sneezes, accidentally lighting a stack of papers on fire. He rushes to stomp it out before replying, "I had my suspicions when I saw Chef Smythe, but I knew for sure this morning. It was when you couldn't touch Bartie. If the fields were aligned, 'e'd have been as solid to you as I am."

Nearly in unison, Mathilde and I lean backwards, flabbergasted by this revelation.

H's expression is deathly serious. "You three missies are responsible for keepin' the magical alignment in place. We'll all 'elp, but we can't do it without you. You need to make a plan."

I glance over at Mathilde, but she is still shellshocked. I should be falling apart, but the stress of the last twenty-four hours seems to have helped me find my steel nerves. This is our magical inheritance, and the future of the town is in our hands. Now what can we do about it?

I look over towards Mathilde, waiting for her to speak up. When the silence stretches to uncomfortable lengths, H gives Mathilde a gentle prod.

Mathilde's face drains of colour, worry forming a knot between her eyebrows. "Me? A plan? Ummm, I guess, well.." Her voice trails off as she shifts uncomfortably in her seat. "I could do some research, maybe? Look in some older books?"

H flaps his wings in agitation, rising to hover a few feet in the air, small jets of flame shooting out of his nostrils. "We ain't got time for you missies to stick your 'eads in a book. We already lost four months blaming the ole bag. Now somebody's dead."

Mathilde wilts under H's heated gaze. When she offers no further suggestions, his head turns in my direction.

"Me? But I just got here... Yesterday." I can feel drops of sweat forming at my hairline. "What about Kate?"

Shaking her head, Mathilde discards my suggestion. "Kate's been here the longest, but from what I've seen, she's a bigger picture type. She's comes up with all kinds of amazing ideas, but she leaves the details to her projects team."

H snorts a cloud of smoke, forming a perfectly shaped arrow pointing at my head. "You got To Do lists all over your flat. I bet you got a pen and paper in your bag. You 're a natural planner."

I stop shaking my head when his smoke turns into flames. Unless I'm ready to singe off a few curls, it looks like I'm in charge here, whether I like it or not. What would my grandfather do if he were here? He wouldn't shy away from a challenge, that's certain. He'd push up his sleeves and get to work.

Picturing my grandfather, it hits me that this is more than a problem with the magic. It's my family's legacy. Mine, Kate's, and Mathilde's. Generations before us have spent their lives keeping the magic in alignment exactly so that something like this won't happen. Although we're all too new to be to blame for whatever caused the problem in the first place, we will be at fault if we don't fix it.

Almost as one, Mathilde and H lean forward in anticipation of my guidance. I straighten my shoulders and clear all doubts from my head. I can do this. After pulling my pen and notebook from my bag, I dive in. "If the magical issue is resulting in deaths, we need to act fast. Why don't we start with a list of causes we should check out?"

Both H and Mathilde nod their heads, encouraging me to continue. "H, you said you think the magic isn't aligned properly.

Is it some kind of web? Does it use statues or monuments or something set-up around Oxford?"

Mathilde answers, "I have no idea how it works, but your guess seems like a reasonable place to start. There are sculptures and monuments everywhere. Kate would be the best person to look into the idea; both fall under her area of expertise."

I make note of the assignment, adding, "Let's get her to check whether any have been damaged recently. Or stolen."

Mathilde pipes back up with another suggestion, "I'll look into our records to determine if any books are missing. While I'm there, I'll check the library archives to see if there is anything in the university history that might give us a clue. Maybe one of the original city limits maps will have information. We've got books in all the colleges, who knows, there could be old notes tucked away in one of them."

"That's the spirit!" I quickly jot down the plans. Looking over my notes, I realise that the only person left without an assignment is me. "Ok, so ceremonies. We know they're important, but they can't go missing."

H flaps again to get my attention. "Ceremonies can't go missin', but they can get cancelled. Iffen we ain't careful, the gala might not take place. It's 'ard to feel like partyin' with a murderer on the loose."

Gripping my pen, I write mine and H's names and our assignment, reading it aloud when the ink is dry. "Nat and H - Find the murderer."

Chapter Six

Although I felt positive when we left the library, the long walk home gives me plenty of time to think about how much responsibility I'm taking on. As my feet pound on the cobblestones, I focus my brain on organising all my tasks into some kind of list.

The autumn gala has to take the top spot. It has to be a success. But H is right. If the police don't quickly identify the culprit, Dr Radcliffe could be forced to delay the event, or even cancel it. I need to nose around and find out what I can.

"One step at a time," I remind myself, waving at the security guard as H and I enter the college gates.

I open the door to the main building to find Harry wearing a path in the front vestibule. The stress lines fade from her face, her eyes lighting up when she sees me come inside.

"Nat, where have you been? I was worried when you didn't show up this morning, and then when Robert in security told me you'd left on a walk, I didn't know what to think. How are you doing today?"

I give her arm a quick squeeze to thank her for her concern.

"Thanks for worrying about me, Harry. I came in this morning but felt like I needed some fresh air."

"Oh hon, you should have called me if you wanted to go for a walk. You didn't need to go on your own."

I wave towards H who has sauntered ahead in the hallway. "I had a little friend along with me. I'm okay now, other than feeling terrible for everyone here. It must be difficult for all of you who knew Chef Smythe for so long."

Harry matches her steps to mine as we walk down the hallways towards my office. There are enough students and professors milling around the halls to make conversation challenging, so she waits until we're inside my office to respond. H heads straight for the cat bed, circling around several times before flopping onto his side. He plays his cat role to perfection, making me wish I could see him as a fluffy black puffball again. I'm envious of Harry, Dr Radcliffe and everyone else here who can't see him for the wyvern he really is.

After Harry and I settle into the chairs around my small meeting table, I lean forward, laying my open arms on the top in an invitation for her to continue.

"I'm not sure Chef Smythe's demeanour was conducive to building deep friendships. She wasn't exactly loved, but murder? I can't believe it! It is so awful." Fishing a tissue out of her pocket, Harry adds, "She was the absolute best chef in all the college circuit, second to none. How will we ever replace her? And the autumn gala!" She blots away a few wayward tears, the stress lines reappearing on her forehead, "It's less than a month away. Who is going to cater it? Where will we find someone on such short notice?"

A caterer? I've been so caught up in all the magic I hadn't even given a thought to the practical implications of a dead head chef. "Surely the sous-chef must be capable..." I suggest.

"She would be, except she handed in her notice as soon as she heard the news. Said she was finally getting out of here. I guess she didn't want to stay working where her former mentor had died."

I lean back in my chair. "She might have a point there. However, I will not let a staff shortage stand in the way of my first event being a roaring success." Casting my eyes upwards, I search for another idea. "Could we borrow a chef from another college?"

That idea gets an immediate no from Harry. "Too much poaching between colleges. The other college principals would never allow it, particularly since we'll be looking for a full-time replacement."

Shifting in my seat, my eyes wander around the room, hoping to find inspiration. H gives a little huff of hot air on my ankles, motioning towards a framed picture hanging on the wall. Rising from my chair, I quirk up an eyebrow, trying to interpret H's message. The painting isn't particularly special, a watercolour showing Oxford's high street, lined with shops. I stare for a few seconds until, finally, it hits me. "Harry, I wonder, is there anyone I could approach outside the university? Maybe a chef in town?"

"That's a brilliant idea, Nat!" A hint of a smile wipes some worry from her face. "You could start with the chef at La Maison Oxford. He is the second-best..." her voice trailing off as she blots another tear. "Well now, I guess he's the best chef in Oxford."

Snagging a stack of post-it notes and a pen, I jot down the restaurant name. "I'll track him down immediately. Surely he'll jump at the chance to showcase his talents and claim the dominant spot."

"That's a nice thought, dear, but he's a wild card. He and Chef Smythe had what can only be described as an unhealthy competitive relationship. He's undoubtedly dreaming up a special dessert to celebrate her passing and his move up the rankings. He might say yes, but there's an equal chance that he may not be interested in stepping into her old shoes, even for a night."

Popping the cap back on the pen, I stick the post-it inside my notebook. "I've got nothing to lose. Might as well give it a try, right?"

"That's our girl. Right back into the swing of things." Glancing at her watch, Harry passes me my handbag. "If you leave now, you can catch him before his restaurant opens for lunch. You'd better leave the cat with me while you go. Chef Rousseau will chase you out the door if you bring an animal into his sanctuary. Come here, little puss puss."

Rising from his cat bed, H meanders his way over to Harry, arching his back for a rub. He even has the gall to wink at me before launching into something that sounds remarkably like a purr.

Leaning over, Harry trails a hand down H's back. "This little beast and I are old friends, aren't we? I spent many an evening with him and Lillian. Never could understand why she called him H though. Surely he must have a proper name and not a letter."

His glare promises retribution if I rat him out. "He doesn't seem to have a proper home or permanent owner, so why should his name be any different, I guess."

Harry gives him a fond pat, encouraging H to arch his head up so she can scratch his chin. "Lillian often asked me to babysit him. What kind of trouble can a cat get into, I'd ask. She'd shake her head and say that he'd magic up some kind of nonsense in no time if left to his own devices. Her exact words were that 'it'd be beyond all my expectations'."

That's for sure.

With a final stroke down H's back, Harry rights herself before rising from her chair. "C'mon little fellow, maybe I can find some nice cheese for you in the college kitchen."

❖

Thankfully La Maison Oxford is only a mile from the college. Robert, the security guard working in the porter's lodge, helps me unlock one of the college bicycles after providing a quick set of directions. "Straight down the road until you get to the shops. You can't miss them. La Maison will be on your right, past the Marks & Spencer."

I drop my handbag into the bicycle basket, testing the gears before pedalling into the street. The glorious sensation of the wind in my hair re-energises me. All too quickly, I spot the restaurant exactly where Robert said it would be.

As I lock the bicycle up, I peer into the front windows. Despite being in the middle of a line of English shops, the restaurant screams Parisian bistro with its eclectic mix of tables and chairs, Pernod bottles on display and the obligatory skinny French woman manning the host desk. My foot is barely in the door before she's shooing me back out again.

"I'm sorry, madame, but the restaurant doesn't open for another hour."

I hold my hands out to reassure the French hostess that I'm not looking for a table. "My name is Natalie Payne. I'm Head of Ceremonies at the University. Is Chef Rousseau available for a short chat?"

"Chef Rousseau is very busy with the food preparation." Her accent turns every word into a dagger.

After my year in France, I know there's only one way I'll get past someone like her. Sheer persistence. I wedge my foot in the doorway, forcing her to continue our conversation. "I'll only take a moment..." Gritting my teeth, I lean into the door, watching her face for the exact moment she realises I outweigh her by more than a stone. When her eyes flash wide, I grab hold of the door, preventing it from flying into her as she steps back from the pressure.

Now inside, I brush some imaginary dust off my skirt, allowing the hostess a moment to accept that I'm here and she will have to deal with me. "Perhaps you didn't hear me clearly the first time. Natalie Payne. Head of Ceremonies. *The University*. Could you let Chef Rousseau know I'd like a word?"

She stares me down, but we both know she's fighting a losing battle. At last, she sniffs, flips her hair and turns towards the back of the restaurant. "Peut-être, maybe he will make a few minutes available for you. Wait here a moment."

When the wait stretches closer to five minutes, I grab a menu and seat myself at the nearest table. Might as well find out what kind of food is his specialty while I wait. The paper is still warm from the printer, indicating that he either changes it daily or has added something new.

"Zuppe du jour, Poisson du jour, Pasto du jour... nothing that would require a reprint," I note. Then I catch the extra line right at the bottom.

"Scones al Rousseau with homemade jam and locally sourced clotted cream - second to none in Oxford"

Hmm, definitely didn't wait for the body to get cold before he came up with that one.

The sour-faced hostess returns with a tiny French man behind her. The hostess is a waif, but somehow Chef Rousseau is even smaller. He reminds me of a bobble-head doll, his entire body existing in a state of constant motion. He must burn away every calorie that goes in - a rather convenient ability for a French chef. He stalls in front of me, but doesn't stop moving, shuffling his feet, hands smoothing up and down his white apron, his head swivelling between me and the kitchen in the back. I can't help feeling that he's left a pot of food on the stovetop. Unlucky for him. Whatever guilt I had felt over interrupting him evaporated when I spotted that menu addition.

The hostess moves to stand behind me, the weakest attempt at bodyguarding I've ever seen. A decent breeze and these two will both blow out the back door. Chef Rousseau sneers a welcome, his strong French accent punctuating every word.

"Meeez Payne, I can only spare a moment, I am very busy in the kitchen."

I flick the menu in my hands. "Yes, I imagine you must be very busy working on your new dessert special."

At least he has the decency to look somewhat ashamed. "Hehehe, I cannot say I am sorry. I heard you and Dr Radcliffe found Madame Horrible yesterday. Word travels around très vite in Oxford, particularly in our small circle of culinary experts."

Harry was right about this guy. Not an ounce of sympathy in him. I skip straight to business. "Then you can guess why I am here."

"The autumn gala?" He glances back at the hostess, his sneer back in place. "I cannot help you, even if I so desired..." Catching my eye, he puts the final nail in the coffin, "... and I do not."

Undaunted, I settle back into my chair. "Chef Rousseau, you seem awfully firm in your position. You haven't even heard my offer. Our gala could be your crowning achievement, confirming your status as the pre-eminent chef in Oxfordshire."

His bobble head shakes from side to side. "Non. The sous-chef phoned me this morning; I am agreeing with her. There can be no cooking happening until the bad air is cleaned out of the room. And this can only happen when we know who has done the deed. If it is one of her jealous underlings, I am safer here in my kitchen with my own people."

This is not good. Where did that rumour start? If I can't convince Chef Rousseau, Oxford local, to at least consider, I'll be facing an uphill battle with anyone else. "The gala isn't in the dining hall. You could use your own kitchen. Your own staff and suppliers." The hostess echoes Chef Rousseau's movements, their heads shaking in concert before I can get all my words out.

The hostess steps around the Chef, circling behind me to tug on my chair, indicating my time is up. She straightens the flatware out, glaring at me, "He cannot do it. Chef Rousseau is not available, he is already booked to prepare dinner at the Palace."

My eyebrows shoot skyward. "Buckingham?"

"Blenheim Palace, Madame Payne," clarifies Rousseau. "It is outside Oxford, magnifique and worthy of my time and effort. I was there two nights ago. The family had me stay over and prepare breakfast. Now, I am running late and cannot spare another moment of my time. Au revoir et à bientôt."

On the cycle back to the college, I hope his cooking is warmer than his heart. I'm not sure he even has one. I'm relieved that he isn't available. He'd probably come up with another new delicacy themed around the death of our chef - not exactly the type of food that inspires alumni to make donations.

If he hadn't told me about being away at Blenheim the night of the murder, I'd have nudged the police to look in his direction. Apparently, the only thing he's guilty of is incredibly poor taste, which is unfortunate for a chef.

Even more unfortunately, all this talk of cooking and food has made my stomach wake up. I burned through my bowl of Crunchy Nut blocks ago. I wonder if Uber Eats exists in Oxford.

Forty-five minutes later, H and I are together again in my office, surrounded by greasy pizza boxes.

I shift in my seat, trying to ease the indigestion caused by inhaling six slices of pizza, while digging out my notepad. "We need to come up with a plan."

Rolling his eyes, H frowns at my suggestion. "Have you lost your loaf? We already did that with Tildy. This morning? At the library." He throws his clawed hands in the air, breaking up the tendril of smoke snaking from his nostrils. "You pulled a ruler out of your handbag and drew lines in your notebook. We gotta go through all that again? Already?"

I nudge the last slice of pizza in H's direction. Maybe a full belly will make him more amenable to my afternoon plans. "We're nowhere near done planning, H. All we covered this morning was the magic issue. We've still got a new chef to find, a murder to solve and something else... what was it again? Oh yeah, A WHOLE EVENT TO PLAN."

I shake my head in disbelief. "Honestly, H, you spent the last 35 years shadowing an event planner. How can you already be sick of writing and sorting out tasks?"

H lets out a small burp and accidentally lights one of the empty pizza boxes on fire. I quickly smother it out with some napkins, arching my eyebrow to let him know he still owes me a response. "The ole bag, she was more of a wing an' a prayer type. Not a planner like you are. All us Eternals would step in and sort things out."

I stare, sure I must have misheard him. "Well, we won't be doing any of that, mister. Oh, no. But at least you've reminded me that the Ceremonies team is bigger than it seems on paper. How many Eternals are there here at St Margaret?" I ask.

H rubs his chin, tallying up the numbers. "Around 15 more between wispies and portraits, including myself. No other animals 'ere."

Fifteen sets of eyes, ears and hands. Plus, my two assistants whom I still need to meet. I abandon my search for my notebook, grabbing a flip chart and writing 'ACTION PLAN' in bubble letters across the top. "I'm feeling better already, H."

"Knock, knock," Harry calls out as she pushes open the door to my office. "I thought I'd better check on you before I head home for the even... what on earth?"

Whatever else Harry was aiming to say is lost in her reaction to the chaos of my office. Every flat surface in my office is covered with wadded up paper balls, markers, old pizza boxes and empty flip charts. I've been outlining tasks and putting them into handwritten charts as fast as H could fly around and stick them to the wall. We covered up the windows hours ago and I have no idea whether it is 5pm or 5am.

"Hi Harry. I'd offer you a place to sit but..." I trail off, shrugging as I take in the room.

Harry is frozen in the doorway, still shellshocked by the scene before her. "I know we expected you to jump straight into things, but I didn't think you'd go *A Beautiful Mind* on us until at least the second week."

I step back, surveying my work. "Trust me, Harry, there is plenty of method in my madness."

Using a foot to clear a pathway, Harry picks her way into the office, shutting the door behind her. "At least I can see you found something to distract yourself since I saw you this morning."

Rising to stand, my back cracks in four different places. How long was I sitting in that corner of the floor? "Was it only this morning? Feels like I've been locked away in here for days. Speaking of, I really need to pop to the loo. Clear yourself off a chair while I'm out." I make a mad dash down the hallway as every ounce of soda I drank has me dying for a wee.

I return to find Harry ensconced in a chair, head tilted as she tries to read one of the charts lying on my meeting table. "Do you always illustrate your roles and responsibilities lists?"

Some people would be embarrassed to be called out on their doodling. Not me. "It's all part of my system. I'm a very visual learner, the drawings help me remember the information better and buy me time to think through any roadblocks or brain freezes. I discovered this approach when I was a child and I've been doing it ever since. Now it's the latest trend with a fancy name: *Bullet Journaling*. Anyway, enough about me. What brings you here?"

Harry arches an eyebrow my way. "I came to find out how you're doing before I leave. You've had quite a first couple of days."

Mumbles drift over from the corner where the cat bed sits. "You don't know the 'alf of it, missie. Gah! Watch it!"

I didn't nudge him that hard; I promise. Thankfully, Harry heard miaows instead of words.

"I won't lie to you, Harry. I was feeling somewhat overwhelmed this morning. I've been shut in here for the last," I look down at my watch and gasp in shock, "... six hours! Wow. Ok, where was I? Oh yes, I knew if I organised my thoughts a bit I'd surely find a way to get it all done. You know, plan a gala, find a new chef, the basics. I've got it all under control."

Harry appears unconvinced, but she's too polite to put that into words. "If you say so, Nat." She surveys the space, jumping in her seat when one of my flip chart pages peels off the wall and falls to the floor. "This is a new approach to event planning for us; we seem to have gone from no notes to all the notes in the world. But if it works for you, who am I to judge?"

I switch my smile up a notch or two, reassuring her I am okay. As I grab a handful of papers off the table, a greasy napkin clings to the back of them. Harry peels it off the back, dropping it into the bin beside my desk. "I thought I'd ask if you need anything, Nat, but I see that what you need is for someone to make you go home for the night. Shall I help you tidy this place back up before you go?"

A sigh of relief slips from between my lips. "I can't remember whether I've said this today or not, but Harry... you're a gem."

As Harry gathers up the various pieces of rubbish from around the room, I sort through the papers on the table. The sight of the roles and responsibilities chart reminds me I need to check an assignment with Harry. I was planning to ask her in the morning, but since she's standing right here, I might as well see if she's up for it.

"Harry, I've been thinking about the murder. I don't suppose you received any updates from the police force?"

"None so far. They had the dining hall closed all day yesterday, gathering evidence, what little there was. No signs of a struggle and the knife was one from our own kitchen. The back door was unlocked, but Chef Smythe parked outside and usually came in that way. Nothing unusual about that. The police are stumped."

"From what you've told me and what I saw yesterday, it seems like plenty of people had a motive."

Harry drops a stack of pizza boxes into the bin before turning in my direction. "Edward always says to look at the immediate family, but Chef Smythe was a widow. Her husband died young in an accident."

"Edward?" I ask. "Who's Edward?"

"Edward Thomas, your upstairs neighbour. He's a world-renowned criminologist researcher, and he's acting as the college liaison with the police force. Whatever he doesn't know about motives isn't worth knowing," Harry explains. "I'll introduce you the next time I see you two together."

"That'd be nice given how close we live to one another. In the meantime, I thought that maybe I should talk to some kitchen staff? Maybe I can convince some of them to stay on and help with the gala."

Harry ties up the rubbish bag and flashes me a hopeful smile. "I think that's a great idea, Nat. Maybe you can convince the sous-chef to reconsider. The sooner we can put all this behind us, the better."

"Perfect, it's a plan!" I announce before heading over to a window. I grasp a fat black marker and make a very satisfying check next to the first item on my To Do list.

Chapter Seven

T he following morning passes by in a whirlwind of activity,
mostly spent getting to know my two assistants.

"Will? And you're Jill?" I eyeball the two, sure that they must
be having one on. They sit side by side, batting their lashes in
unison, the very picture of innocence. Despite their similar
sounding names and shared mannerisms, I don't have any worries
I'll get them confused. Jill's dark copper skin and colourful head
wrap stand in sharp contrast to Will's pallid pink complexion and
mousy brown hair.

"Please call me Nat. I'm sorry it's taken me so long to
introduce myself. I'd planned to come by on my first day, but..."
My voice trails off as I stop myself from going any further down
that pathway. I clear my throat before starting again. "Ahem,
where was I? Introducing myself, that's it. I'm assuming you've
both seen my CV?" I pause, waiting for both heads to nod before
continuing.

"Then I'll skip the boring bits. I love the challenge of creating
something new and unexpected. I'm a hard worker, but I make
sure we all have a bit of fun while we get the job done." I smile,

making sure both Jill and Will are still with me. "Enough about me, how long have you two been working here?"

"Two years," starts Will.

"And seven months," continues Jill.

"We both started on the same day," Will finishes. As if on cue, both pick up their St Margaret mugs and sip their tea. When they set them back down, I realise that their desks are organised exactly the same, with the phone on the left, laptop in the middle, and pen pot and notepads sitting on the right.

I glance down at H, my questioning gaze asking whether my assistants are part of the Eternal team. His answering chuckle sears the backs of my ankles. I guess that's a no.

"So, how do you two like to work? Together?"

"Oh no, we prefer to divide and conquer," says Will.

"We've got different work styles," explains Jill.

I give H a gentle shove with my toes when my ankles heat again. If I have to keep a straight face, so does he, "Right. I'd hoped to spend some time getting to know you each better, but unfortunately, the clock is against us right now. We need to jump straight into gala planning. Perhaps we could start with an overview of last year's event?"

Three hours pass before we make it back to my office. By then, both H and I are dragging our heels. I glance at my watch, amazed to see it is one in the afternoon. No wonder my stomach is growling. "H, how would you like to go on a little trip to the dining hall?"

H falls to the floor, rolling around while holding his stomach. "Finally! Lor luv, mate. I'm starvin'. I was fading away listening to the lad wax on about last year's gala menu. All I ate for breakfast was a few crumbs."

"Crumbs?" I shake my head at his poor recollection. "You had four cheese scones for breakfast! I'd hardly call that suffering. But fine, come on. Maybe we can find a bowl of milk to wash those crumbs of yours down."

H flies up to hover in front of me, wings spread-wide and an angry spurt of flame slipping from his nostrils. "Cream. Not milk. Clotted, ideally. Iffen they're out of 'em, a few slices of Cornish cruncher, or Wensleydale. Wookey Hole is pretty good, Lancashire'll do in a pinch or even that Red Leicester. Iffen none of them are in the larder, then I'll take some Boursin or whipping cream… And don't get me started on the double cream…"

"Basically, all cheese and milk products?" I interrupt H's monologue.

"Ain't nothin' else worth eating." His glare leaves me wondering whether his cat-side is more dominant than he wants to admit.

"Never mind, let's go. At least you've given me an excuse to talk to the kitchen staff. My visit to Chef Rousseau yesterday was not 'magnifique', I'm sad to say. In fact, he was pretty darn horrible. Hopefully, today goes better."

The closer we get to those swinging dining hall doors, the more I have to steel myself to enter the room. Thankfully, it's a few minutes shy of lunch closing. If I have a breakdown, at least the whole student body won't be on hand to witness it.

My pace slows as my nerves overtake the hunger pains. Do we really need to eat today? My mind flashes back to my first morning. Shuttered serving windows, the blood-stained cleaver, yellow police tape, dark blue uniforms swarming about the space. My brain says to move, but my legs are no longer listening.

Realising he's lost me, H turns back, flapping his wings until he hovers in front of my face where he can spot the anxiety in my eyes. "Listen up, missie. You gotta go back in the dinin' 'all sometime. The longer you wait, it ain't gettin' any easier. Close your eyes, clear your mind and think about steamin' 'ot Yorkshire puddins. Nod your loaf when you 're with me."

I let the vision of a golden-brown Yorkshire swimming in rich, dark gravy wipe every other thought from my mind. Gradually my stomach unclenched, hunger once again surging to the forefront.

I blink a few times, straighten my back and take the last few steps, sheer determination powering my stride as I push through the double doors. The room inside looks... normal. The clatter of dishes and hum of voices fill the space, t-shirt clad students crowding the benches at the trestle tables. The serving woman smiles at me, nodding towards the stack of trays that mark the start of the serving line. I walk ahead, wanting to replace every picture in my head with a new one before I attempt to eat.

I spot Dr Radcliffe eating at the high table. It's the first time I've seen her since our horrid discovery. With her back to the room she hasn't seen me come in, not that she'd notice anyway given the tall man blustering down onto her. What is it with this place? Why is someone angry every time I step into a room?

The man looks like a young Colin Firth with his stately, aristocratic features, sharp eyes and slim build all wrapped up in a buttoned cardigan - complete with elbow patches. He is years younger than the ancient professor sitting beside him, but faint lines around his bright blue eyes confirm his status as professor and not student.

His wavy hair is nearly standing on end. When he pulls his fingers through it, I can see why his hair gel is losing the battle. Thanks to his posh accent, I can hear every syllable coming out of his mouth. "... And Disneyland, of all places? Will she have us dressing up in mouse costumes? We have enough challenges right now without adding an incompetent newcomer into the mix."

I can't solve the problems with the magic or figure out what happened to Chef Smythe, but incredibly rude men who underestimate me... now *that* I can handle. He wants an incompetent youth, he'll get one. I straighten up my fox print dress and march right up to the end of the table as though I haven't heard a word.

"Hiya Dr Radcliffe, I'm super glad I've run into you. I'm back from the costume shop, they were short a few mouse ears, but not to worry, they could place a special order on my behalf." I back my ridiculous statement up with a 1000-watt smile that shows every shiny white tooth in my mouth.

Professor Rude sticks his nose in the air, harrumphs, and stomps off. Thankfully Dr Radcliffe's chuckles assure me she understood exactly what I was doing.

"Well done, Ms Payne, that ought to put him in his place for a bit. I was worried you might catch the first bus out of town after our terrible morning, but I can see you're made of sterner material."

Moving around the table, I lean against the chair opposite Dr Radcliffe. "Bad things can happen anywhere. Even at Disneyland, I saw more than one pickpocket while working events inside the park. Both then and now, the best thing we can do is hope for a quick end to the police investigation and some luck with hiring a new chef."

"A rapid end would be my preference. Everyone will be on pins and needles until they solve the crime. As you've just seen, even some of our most supportive professors are running short on patience. But enough of that; Harry mentioned you would try to track down Chef Rousseau. Any luck so far?" asks Dr Radcliffe.

I can't hold back a frown as I respond to her question. "I got a few minutes of his time yesterday, but I wouldn't class it as a lucky event. Is it a requirement that all top chefs have personality disorders?"

Dr Radcliffe answers with a grim smile, "I suspect a certain amount of cut-throat mentality is required to climb your way to the top spot."

I mull over her statement as she finishes the last few bites on her plate. "The kitchen couldn't have been a great place to work, regardless of how nice the rest of the college staff seem to be."

Tucking her napkin under her plate, Dr Radcliffe replies, "I won't lie to you, I had several complaints about Chef Smythe, but I always knew that was the price we paid to have the best chef in town. It's a challenge I face in more departments than this one.

Our professors and some of our students can be as trying as Chef Smythe was. But the people here at St Margaret do genuinely care about one another."

Glancing up, my eyes scan the room before landing on the grumpy professor. If it weren't for the elbow patches, I'd think it was a different man standing there. He's barely recognisable with his features smoothed out as he clasps the shoulder of a distraught kitchen server, murmuring reassuring words.

Straightening, I share my next steps. "I'll check around with some kitchen staff, maybe I'll convince the sous-chef to stay on or find someone who has connections with other chefs. I have little time to sort out catering arrangements for the gala."

"The gala is an important fundraising event. I hope you find a chef, Ms Payne. Please check in later with Harry so we can hear how you get on."

Fundraising? If only Dr Radcliffe knew how important this gala is.

Leaving Dr Radcliffe in peace to finish her meal, I skirt the edges of the trestle tables, glancing underneath for H, but he's nowhere to be found. I don't know why I'm surprised when I finally locate him purring in the lap of the dining hall's young blonde cashier.

"H! There you are. I'm so sorry, I hope he isn't bothering you."

The young woman waves away my concern. "No need to worry, I've known H for ages. I'm chuffed to see he's still around and didn't leave with Lillian."

I glare at H until he leaps down and sits quietly at my feet. The queue of hungry students has disappeared, and the staff are already clearing up the empty food pans from the counter.

"You must be Ms Payne. We heard you were due to start. I'm Beatrice. I guess you want lunch?"

I look back down the line to see nothing left but pans of steaming water. "Maybe just a sandwich?"

"Don't be silly. There's plenty left, I'm sure. Most of the

people coming in today have been more interested in trying to see into the kitchen than getting a plate of food. I'll pop into the back and fix us both a plate. Meat or veg?"

"Veg please." H sinks a claw into my ankle. "And some clotted cream, if you've got any to spare."

Beatrice giggles and heads off, motioning me towards the long trestle tables.

I gather up cutlery, fill water glasses and set us up across from one another at the table. I expected to have to work harder to get an introduction to the kitchen team. With some luck and gentle probing, Beatrice might give me some useful insights which I can use to talk the sous-chef into sticking around.

"I hope you like puff pastry," Beatrice says as she lays a perfectly plated meal before me. I spear a roasted potato and jump into the discussion.

"You must feel terrible about what happened with Chef Smythe."

Rather than answer, Beatrice's eyes fill up, huge salty drops leaking out to drip right onto her gravy-covered plate. Oh god, what if they're related? I didn't think to ask Harry about extended family.

"I didn't mean to do it. It was an accident!"

H and I both stare at her in shock. Magic or not, apparently we unmasked the murderer by lunchtime.

Fortunately, Beatrice is oblivious to our momentary loss of words. "I had flubbed a big exam that afternoon, and I forgot that the left bread loaf was the gluten-free one and," she breaks off into sobs again.

"And then you confronted her?" I ask, ready to push back my chair and dart away from the table.

"What? No, of course not. I didn't do anything to Chef Smythe. It was her who did something to me. I made a simple mistake, and she shouted at me for nearly an hour. Nonstop!"

"Over bread?" My mind whirs as I try to make sense of her comment.

"Exactly! I have so much stress with my studies, but does she see any of that? All she ever saw was her precious kitchen. I made a tiny error at High Table and she threatened to have me fired."

I can't help but repeat myself. "Over bread?"

Beatrice's eyes well up again, her hand trembling, a cadence of tiny clinks sounding as her fork hits the plate. "I work so hard, you know. I study every night, attend all my lectures and tutorials. And I'm never late to work in the morning... I wanted to run away and never look back again. I wouldn't be here now if it weren't for Claudia."

I look at H for a clue, but he shrugs and goes back to licking out his bowl of cream. "How did Claudia help you?"

Beatrice sniffles up a bit before giving up and blowing her nose in her napkin. "Claudia had to work under Chef Smythe day in and day out. She found me crying in the storeroom after everyone left. She should have been head chef somewhere, but Chef Smythe refused to give her a recommendation. Pure jealousy because she knew how talented she is! She needed Claudia to stay put because Claudia helped make her look even better."

Ahh, now I know.

"The sous-chef!"

Beatrice nods in confirmation. "Claudia is so nice and generous. She sat down right there beside me in the storeroom. She didn't care that the floor was a little dusty or that it was well past closing time. She told me all the things she wished she could say to Chef Smythe, and I did the same. The last thing she said to me was that she hoped someday someone would take care of our Mrs Smythe problem. I guess someone finally did."

"I hate to ask this, and please don't cry again, but where were you the other day? Dr Radcliffe and I were here for hours, I never saw you arrive."

Beatrice sips her water, taking a moment to get her emotions back under control. "Even after my chat with Claudia, I still felt like rubbish. Then Chef Smythe yelled at me again at breakfast the next day. I was so stressed I kept getting everyone's change wrong. I couldn't deal with the thought of going back in there again. I called in sick at dinner."

My next question slips out before I have time to think it through. "Did you stay in your room the whole night?"

Nodding, Beatrice replies, "All I wanted was my mum, you know? I called her, and she completely understood my troubles. She told me to come back home for the evening and she made my favourite meal. I stayed there until I came back yesterday morning."

Eyes wide, I realise how narrowly Beatrice escaped being involved. "If you hadn't been away, you might have witnessed the crime."

Beatrice's eyes fill again. "I might have saved her... or I might have been another victim. I keep second-guessing myself for having skipped out. I never behave that way."

Passing her a tissue, I give her a gentle smile. "Don't blame yourself. How were you to know? I can't speak for everyone, but H and I are both glad you're sitting here. Otherwise we'd be eating cold sandwiches back in my office. This is miles better. Hopefully, now things will calm down and you'll be able to study and work without being berated on a regular basis."

Beatrice smiles weakly at my reassurance. "I hope so, that's the one thing I'm counting on."

Before I can take another bite, H leaps onto the table and blurts out an urgent request.

"Oi Nat, I finished the cream. Can you ask iffen she's got any poacher back there?"

❖

After Beatrice rushes off to make it to her afternoon class, H and I are left behind to mull over her words.

"You gonna finish up that bread roll?" H asks, one hand holding a slice of cheese while the other one taps on the item in question.

I pass him the roll and shudder as he slides the cheese inside before shoving the whole thing into his snout. "That was quite a tale Beatrice told, H. I have got a nagging suspicion about this Claudia person. From what Beatrice said, she's overworked and overlooked, and was permanently trapped in the shadow of Chef Smythe. I bet she asked again for a reference the other morning and when the chef said no, she lost it and stabbed Chef Smythe with the closest knife to hand."

H's mouth hangs open, little pieces of half-eaten breadcrumbs clinging to the drool falling down his snout. "You know, that ain't 'alf crazy. You need to go tell 'Arry and Dr Radcliffe. Err, and maybe the Bobbies who were investigatin' the scene?"

Moving toward the edge of the table, H flaps a wing, preparing to take off. I grab his leg and scoot him back across the wooden tabletop. "Eeerp, watch the tendons, I ain't made of stone no more."

I pass him my half-eaten slice of cake as a peace offering. "I can't go to them with my suspicions unless we have some proof. Beatrice isn't going to point the finger at her best friend. I need you to sneak in there and see what you can find out. Maybe try to whisper a conversation starter or two? Lay out a few knives and see if she reacts? You're old and magical, you'll figure something out."

H pauses mid-lick, "Alright, mate, I'll do it. But only because I want some more of this cake."

"Cool, I'll drop my tray off and say goodbye so they know that I've gone. You can hide under the table until no one's looking and then find a way into the kitchen. I'll wait outside, I saw a small seating nook out in the hallway." I high five H and try not to wince as his claw catches me between two fingers.

I gather my items onto my tray and cross the room to the towering metal racks. It doesn't take too much effort to make a ruckus given the number of half-empty, wobbly glasses ready to take a small tumble. I stick my head into the kitchen doorway, mentally patting myself on the back for my ability to get anywhere near this space, and call a loud goodbye and thank you to Beatrice. She's deep in conversation with a skinny brunette in a chef's hat.

"Come on, H, let's get back to work!" I call out as I exit the dining hall. H looks confused, but then shakes his head and follows me.

"What are you doing?" I hiss.

"You called me and said to get back to work." He hisses right back again, looking even more confused than before.

"That was PRETEND, so they'd think you were gone as well. You were meant to stay behind without them knowing. If we're going to be a team, you'll have to learn to catch my meaning," I hiss in return.

H definitely has more to say on the topic, but he mutters it too quietly for me to hear as he does a 360, heading back in the kitchen's direction. I cross my fingers and toes before pushing my way through the swinging doors.

Outside in the hall I attempt to make myself comfortable on an old-fashioned fainting sofa while I wait for H to report back. Are you supposed to lounge across it? Perch? I contort my body into several positions, each one more uncomfortable than the one before, before giving up and sitting far enough back that I can lean against the wall behind me and dangle my legs off the edge.

I eyeball my dress and wonder for the second time today whether the fox print was really a good choice. Foxes, hunting dogs, closets, Narnia... it seemed appropriately Oxonian when I saw it in the store. Hopefully my understated jewellery, sensible shoes and black patent leather belt are pulling the look together.

I lose track of time, caught up in people-watching all the students as they walk up and down the hallway. A loud clattering sound coming from the dining hall catches my attention, making me look up in time to see the doors swing open seemingly on their own. Shoving them closed again, H leans his wings against them, breathing harder than any self-respecting, magical wyvern should ever do.

I stand up and straighten my dress. "Did you get a confession?"

"A confession? I nearly got my loaf chopped off! I'm four 'undred years old and I ain't never seen a woman so quick to draw a knife. She found me 'idin' in the pots and pans and flipped. I barely made it out of there with my loaf on my shoulders."

I shiver at the thought. "That sounds awful, but also somehow promising. I think I should talk to her, see if I can get her to say something incriminating we can take to the police. Come on, let's catch her while she's still here."

"Catch 'er? I'm more worried bout Claudia catchin' me," H whines.

"Hmm, you might have a point there. Better not bring you back into the kitchen area so soon. She'll know we're up to something." I mull over my options, but none of them look appealing. So far, my Oxford chef interactions haven't exactly gone swimmingly.

"I can't go alone in case she is the murderer. You're going to have to hide under one of the tables. Sorry to make you do that, but..." I barely get the words out before H loops around towards the dining hall.

"'Ave you seen 'ow many crumbs are down there?"

"Hopefully you'll be able to hear any calls for help over your chewing."

❖

I quietly push the swinging doors open wide enough for myself and H to slip back through. We don't need to attract any attention yet.

Inside, the kitchen serving windows are locked up tight, but I can hear enough dishes rattling to be reassured I haven't missed her. I glance at H, hoping he will have some guidance. "What do you think, H? Any tips for starting a conversation with Claudia?"

An imperial tone rings out a response. "If you're talking about our sous-chef, I wouldn't advise going in with any approach other than flattery."

Unless H has suddenly developed a woman's voice, we're not as alone as I thought. I can't see anyone, but wait - is that an arm sticking out of the portrait up by the high tables?

By the time I get up there, the older woman in the portrait is lounging comfortably on a wooden chair, a stack of books on one side and her loyal German shepherd on the other. She flicks her wrist, a cup of tea magically appearing before she motions me to have a seat in front of her painting.

"Hullo dahling Natalie, I'm Dr Rosemary Thicke, one of the previous principals here at St Margaret. I couldn't help overhearing your question to your boon companion there."

"Hello Dr. Thicke, nice to meet you. I'd love to stay for a chat, but I'm in a rush to catch our sous-chef before she leaves. I don't suppose you have any experience with her, do you?"

"Ah yes, Claudia. I've dealt with my fair share of difficult individuals, and she fits into that category. She seems nice to those she likes, but for everyone else, her eyes shoot daggers."

If Claudia is volatile enough to commit a murder, I need to tread lightly. I don't want to set her off, merely get a few pieces of information I can use to convince the police to take me seriously. I turn my eyes up to the portrait and ask for help. "You must have plenty of opportunities to observe Claudia, Dr Thicke. What approach would you advise?"

"Hmmm, let me think for a moment." Dr Thicke sips her tea as she mulls over options. "Yes, yes, that might work. As you can see, I've watched over many a high table dinner from my esteemed position here in the hall. Whilst our Chef Smythe was the genius behind most of the menu, there was one area she always delegated off to her sous chef - the appetiser course. That was Claudia's space alone to showcase her talents. Compliment her on her beetroot foam from last week and she'll wax on for much longer than you'll want. Hopefully, you can flatter her right into whatever you need."

"Beetroot foam? I heard something about that. Perfect, I'll start there and then segue straight to begging her to stay on to cater the gala. Got it. Thanks so much for your help, Dr Thicke. I'd better run if I hope to catch Claudia."

"Anytime, dahling. Next time bring a cuppa along and I'll tell you about some of my own adventures."

"I'd love that." I wave goodbye before turning towards the kitchen.

Before going into the kitchen, I glance over my shoulder to confirm H is in position. I spot his wings between the chair legs, sitting comfortably under a table, shoving a handful of crumbs in his mouth. He gives me a salute, waving me on my way. Deep breath and in I go.

"Hello? Is anyone still here?" Bingo. Assuming she was the woman in the chef's hat, Claudia seems to be the last person left in the kitchen. I've caught her as she gives the cooking area a final wipe down. Her white chef hat lies abandoned on a corner desk, her chef's coat unbuttoned and stained. Unfortunately, she seems much less pleased to see me than I am to find her.

Her voice crackles with a harsh growl. "I don't know who you are, but I've had about enough of the lookie-loos coming into my kitchen today. I've only got a few hours before I have to be back here for dinner, and I don't intend to use them playing tour guide to a crime scene."

I shiver at the reminder. "Thanks, but I had enough of a look the other morning with Dr Radcliffe. If you're Claudia, it's actually you I'm hoping to track down."

"Natalie Payne?"

"The one and only." I hold out a hand as I introduce myself. Her grip is strong, palm callused. And damp. That's what I get for interrupting a sponge down. She gives me an apologetic smile as she wipes her hands on her coat and smoothes her dark hair back into her ponytail.

Peppy smile in place, I turn on the charm. "I've heard so many absolutely amazing things about your cooking, I didn't want to miss the chance to meet you before you go."

Claudia raises one eyebrow. "Somehow I doubt that. The only chef who got any praise here was Chef Smythe. She made sure of that."

I paint on a confused look. Two can play the eyebrow game. "Oh, are you not the genius behind last week's English beetroot foam with a parmesan crisp? My assistants have been raving about it since they heard about your departure."

Claudia's face lights up, the switch from scowl to smile happening in an instant. I'm in.

"Yes, that was mine. I didn't think anyone noticed. It took me weeks to perfect the consistency of the puree. Chef Smythe tried to copy it, but every attempt she made came out runny. She never understood the chemistry behind the molecular gastronomy of my appetisers. More precise than some equations that come out of the science labs."

I nod my head, "I've always thought appetisers are the most under-appreciated course. I mean, anyone can roast a leg of lamb and serve it with a side of mash. It takes a true genius to meld together unique flavours without making something that immediately fills you up."

"Exactly! Exactly as I've always said. Why didn't you start here a few months ago, Natalie?"

I've got her talking, now to move the conversation in the gala's direction. "So, it's true, you're really leaving St Margaret? I mean, now that Chef Smythe is out of the way, surely you have a good chance of landing the top spot permanently."

Turning, Claudia launches the sponge into the sink where it lands with a splash. "Ha! You'd think so, but even from the grave that old hag is keeping me hidden in the shadows. I'm sure Dr Radcliffe won't even consider me. It doesn't matter though; I can barely stand to be in this room."

Hmm, I wonder whether it is fear or guilt making her want to leave. I try a new angle. "You must have really hated the chef. I've only been here two days and I've yet to hear anything nice about her. Working with her must have been sheer misery."

With a sharp chuckle, Claudia walks over to the desk, her response muffled by the sound of her shuffling papers. "Misery is the right word. That woman thought she was Gordon Ramsay, always yelling at everyone and criticising every flick of a spoon. Nothing we did was good enough for her. But then she'd swan out the door at the end of every dinner and take all the credit and the compliments. Never said one nice word about any of us."

"I met Beatrice at lunch today and she said much of the same. She mentioned that Chef Smythe refused to give you a recommendation. How could she do that and get away with it?"

Tossing a pile of papers onto her desk, Claudia twists, her cheeks red with anger. "She did it because she was a complete beast of a person. She couldn't care less about our hopes and dreams, only her own. She treated our suppliers even worse. Chef Rousseau at Oxford Maison knew the truth, but what could he do? He offered me space in his kitchen several times, but I'd had enough of working underneath someone. He was happy to take me on as help, but didn't have any interest in supporting me where I might end up as competition. That's the way these chef personality cults work."

I don't have to fake the shudder. That sounds awful. "You must have confronted Chef Smythe about it?"

"Plenty of times. Not that it did any good. Nothing would make a difference." She pauses, taking in a deep breath before carrying on. "It was time for me to take matters into my own hands."

Take matters into her own hands? I realise in a flash that this woman could very well be a person who can bury a cleaver in someone's back. The thought of it shakes me. Quietly, I slide around the metal island until I'm standing on the far side of it.

Claudia fails to notice my movements. She picks up a dagger-like metal letter opener, slicing through envelopes. Lost in thought, she looks to be reliving some past event, talking more to herself than to me. "It was my only way out. It was a risk, but I had to take it."

Is she talking about what I think she's talking about? My eyes dart around the room, searching for something I can use for self-defence. I spot a cast iron frying pan resting on a nearby countertop and breathe a sigh of relief when my fingers wrap around its handle. Unfortunately, it's heavier than it looks. The metallic bottom scrapes across the counter, drawing Claudia's attention.

Turning around, Claudia looks at me and bursts out laughing. Not exactly the reaction I expected, but it's better than her coming at me with that letter opener... or a meat cleaver. Claudia wipes her eyes with a dishtowel while I debate whether it's safe to set the skillet back down.

"If I needed any signs I'm making the right move by getting out of here, having the new hire look at me like I'm a murderer is a good one."

I abandon the skillet, flinching as it hits the counter with a clatter. "If murder wasn't your way out, what are you talking about?"

"I'm going on MasterChef!"

I tuck my proverbial tail between my legs and leave, the echo of Claudia's laughter trailing behind me. Hopefully, her notice will run out before she recounts this story to anyone else.

Chapter Eight

H catches up with me as I push my way through the swinging doors to exit the dining hall. "Ow'd you do in there?"

I pick up my pace. "I don't want to talk about it."

Flapping, H matches my speed, undeterred by my efforts to end the conversation. "Did she fess up?"

I can still hear Claudia's laughter in my head. There's no way I'm telling H what happened. "I said, I don't want to talk about it. Move on."

With a few strong flaps of his wings, H circles around to stare me in the face, blocking me from going any further. He reaches out a talon, holding my face in place as he checks my wellbeing. "Yep, it's your blood sugar. Best iffen we go to the Senior Common Room and get a chockie biscuit."

For once, H has a good idea. I could use a whole plate of chockie biscuits after my first few days here. All I ever wanted out of life was to plan absolutely amazing and memorable events. Little did I know that some magical force would pull me right out of London. And why? It wanted to deliver me here in the midst of a murder mystery that will ruin my event if I can't solve it.

Thankfully H knows the way as the door isn't labelled. I twist the handle and open the door to find a spacious sunny room on the other side of it. Its pale blue walls and comfortable seating smooth my battered ego. The coffee and end tables provide a home for an array of magazines and newspapers, the disorder making it clear that they are there to be enjoyed and not just for decoration. I wander inside, pausing to enjoy the art hung on the walls. This is the first room in the main hall that's felt like home instead of an office.

I finally come across a state-of-the-art coffee machine and a plate of chocolate biscuits, tucked away beside an overflowing bookshelf. I bend over, stopping to read the titles on the book spines, but H is having none of it. "I know you 're cream-crackered, but we gotta shake a leg. Grab yourself a bisckey and a cuppa so we can get outta 'ere."

"Out of here? This room is wonderful. What's gotten into you? Our next meeting isn't for another hour. I wouldn't mind finding a good book to read, and there are more than a few here that look interesting."

"Ermm, well, ummm..." H trails off guiltily.

I slide a paperback off the shelf, quickly followed by two chocolate digestive biscuits. I set a St Margaret mug under the coffee machine, pressing buttons until the sound of grinding coffee beans fills the space. H chooses that exact moment to finish his sentence, his words barely audible amongst the spurts of steaming hot coffee spewing into my mug. "You ain't - I mean *we* ain't supposed to be in 'ere. Maybe."

I rewind to the moment we arrived at the door. There was no sign, no note indicating that the space might be closed. Every item in the room, from the comfortable sofas to the well-thumbed magazines to the plate of fresh biscuits, show that the room is ready to welcome all visitors. I sip my coffee, peering over the steam to watch H's efforts to beckon me back towards the door. "Why would someone frown over us being in here?"

"This 'ere is Oxford. Everythin' is a ceremony. Even the common rooms. This 'ere is the *Senior* Common Room." He stresses the word senior, making sure I note its importance. "There's a Middle Common Room an' a Junior one too. I can't never keep up with who can go where. Somethin' about gettin' chosen for membership…"

I take a bite of my biscuit, savouring the taste of chocolate as it explodes across my tongue. It really is the best medicine. Standing here in this space, licking dark chocolate from my fingers, I'm finding it impossible to find the energy to rush out of here. "Does it really make that big of a difference, H? It's just a room."

H scurries across the carpet, stopping at my feet to let loose a jet of flames. I nearly drop my mug when it jumps from lukewarm to scalding. "Ain't you been payin' attention, missie? It ain't 'jus' a room' and ya, it's a 'big difference'. It's a tradition. A ceremony! You outta know better than anybody that these things matter. Now 'urry it up. We can ask 'Arry after you scoffed down a few biskeys and are your normal, cheery self again."

The digestive biscuit turns to ash in my mouth as the seriousness of the situation sets in. There should be a guidebook or an app or something to help a new prefect learn these unspoken rules. We've got enough problems with the magic without me adding to them.

I snag a napkin from the stack, shove a few cookies into it before tucking it away in my pocket. "Come on, let's get out of here before I do any more damage." I cross back to the door, mildly confused when it flies open at the gentlest tug. I jump backwards, but not in time to keep the door from bumping against my forehead.

Wouldn't you know it, Professor Rude is standing in front of me, angry gaze once again in place. He stares down his nose, skipping straight past any apology, instead opting for an accusation. "What are you doing in here?" His tone sharp, each word enunciated perfectly. "This is the Senior Common Room, open to College Fellows and members only." He stretches out the syllables in senior, emphasising its importance.

Rubbing my forehead, I wonder for a moment if I misheard him. Whatever guilt I was feeling over potentially causing more problems for the magic evaporates. This man, despite having never spoken with me, despite having just raised a knot in the middle of my forehead, would rather berate me than check that I'm not concussed. I glance down at H, my hands balled into fists, temper flaring. He wisely backs up a step.

I was on my way out, but I'll be damned if I leave this brute of a man to have the last word. "I don't know who you are or what you do here, but I am confident my cat has better manners than any you've displayed so far. Get over yourself. Get a hobby." I wave around the empty room. "Pick up a book or a paper. Do whatever you want but stop trying to run me out of here. I stumbled across a dead body on my first day here. If I want to come into a room and eat some bloody cookies, you can damn well deal with it. Now if you have nothing nice to say, I'll be on my way."

He raises an eyebrow but steps aside to let both me and H pass. I hear the door bang closed behind us as we make our way down the hall.

"Umm Nat? Do you know who that bloke was?"

"You know what, H? No, I don't. I don't have a clue. I also do not care. That man is rude, plain and simple. I don't care if he is the president of the entire bloody university. Now do you want one of these biscuits or not?"

"Milk chocolate, please."

I spend the next few days in the library, boning up on the history of the college. With thousands of volumes to hand, I am thankful for the help of the Eternals. Between the ghosts of previous librarians and books who show themselves when called, the library seems like the first place within the college grounds that wants to make itself useful.

Despite wracking my brain for a theme for the gala, I'm still stuck at start. Every time I come up with an idea, H assures me that it has been done six times already. I'm down to the absolute dregs.

I sort through my ideas list, searching for anything I haven't already crossed off. "How about 'Come as your favourite prime minister'?"

He is reclining mid-air, tossing wads of paper into the air and using his flames to turn them to ash. "Done it."

I swot a wad away seconds before his flames hit it, forcing him to focus on me. "Seriously, H? Someone put on an event with a prime minister theme?"

He frowns, leaning over to pick up another scribbled page from my pile of discards. "Everybody came as Churchill. It was embarrassin'."

I go back to my list, skimming until I reach the very last line. "Cops and robbers? We could make our murder mystery the centrepiece instead of hiding it under the carpet."

Every Eternal within ten feet stops, furiously shaking their heads at me.

Tossing my pencil onto the table, I glare at my team of magical assistants. "Help me out here! Are you sure there's nothing else available from previous events?" The Eternal librarian shakes her head mournfully and leaves me to the well-thumbed stack of notes before me.

"Oh H, I think the magic made a mistake. Look at me! I've been working on this, the very first step in the planning process, for hours on end. And what have I got to show for it? A paper cut, an inch of ash and an empty trash bin. Fate got it wrong. I'm not meant to be here."

I bury my head into my arms, sniffling to hold back the fat tears that threaten to spill. H swoops down beside me, nuzzling his snout into my shoulder in solidarity.

"Listen to me, Nat. I swear on my old stone at the Bodleian, the magic has never, ever, ever got it wrong. Look at the past week. You left all your friends and family in London and moved up to Oxford. You found a dead body on your first mornin' at work. Then you discovered your cat is a wyvern, an' your grandpa's fairy tales were real. Your family has magic in the blood. You barely batted an eyelash. Who coulda dealt with all that better than you did?"

I wipe my nose on a scrap of paper, snickering when I realise what I've done. H is right, I'm being awfully hard on myself. I mean, my entire handover and training consisted of a single letter tucked into a locked desk.

Blowing my hair out of my face, I push back from the table, smoothing out my wrinkled top. "H, we need to get out of this library. When event planning block hits, there's only one thing that solves it."

"Sure thing, Nat. Wot's that?"

"Ice cream. Ideally salted caramel, but I'm too desperate right now to be picky."

"Yassssss! Iffen you want ice cream, you can't do better than a G&D's special."

H and I head out onto the pavement. The sun is shining. The birds are singing. This is probably one of our last days of late summer before the autumn chill sets in. Perfect weather for a walk. I wander down the block, passing the entrance to my townhouse. There are four cars in the front carpark, I wonder if one of them belongs to my neighbour. I've heard him bumping around up there a few times but have yet to meet him. Another item for my To Do list. But not now. Now is for ice cream.

I pause at the corner, realising I've lost my partner in crime. "H? Aittcchhhhh??? Where did you go?"

He's five meters behind me, sitting at the bus stop in front of Dr Radcliffe's mansion. I turn back, marching until I'm facing him.

He looks at me, a picture of confusion. "Wot?"

I wave my hands at the idyllic scene around us. "What are you doing?"

"I'm waitin' for the number six, should be here any minute."

I glance upwards, checking again to see if there's some black cloud looming on the horizon. For once, the sky is empty except for a few birds. If I squint my eyes, I can make out the city centre off in the distance. It can't be that far to this ice cream shop. "We're not taking the bus. The whole point of this little adventure is to get some fresh air and hopefully inspire some fresh ideas for the gala."

H, still seated on the bus stop bench, looks up in confusion. "I thought the point of this 'ere trip was ice cream. 'Ave you thought about how short my little legs are? Or 'ow tired my wings get flappin' around? I can't go that far."

Right as the guilt settles into my stomach, I remember the scene I spotted from my kitchen window last evening. "You spent 45 minutes running laps around the college gardens last night. Your leg length and wing span didn't seem to bother you then."

"That ain't a fair comparison. There was a mouse."

"Well, now there's an ice cream waiting. Come on." I nod my head encouragingly a few times and move on. He'll catch up if he wants his own cone.

After another couple of blocks, I remember that I have no idea where we're going. "What was the name of the ice cream place? A&Bs? C&Ds?"

H huffs, reducing a small pile of autumn leaves into ash. "G&D's. It's an Oxford classic. There's one not to far from 'ere... Can I 'ave sprinkles on my cone?"

Brushing ash off my trousers, I give H the side-eye. "Do cats like sprinkles?"

Winking, he replies, "No, but wyverns do."

We cross over in front of the Radcliffe Observatory. Oxford is so different from any other university I've seen. Rather than having a discrete campus, their buildings ramble across the city and even out into the countryside. Homes, shops, restaurants and schools intermingle with historic halls and modern departmental high-rises. The thirty-eight colleges which make up the university sit tucked away behind stone walls and iron gates.

I can feel the itch to explore crawling up my back. I probably should have ventured out over the weekend instead of closing myself in the library, but the weather was so dreary I couldn't work up any enthusiasm. This is the problem of living a hundred meters from the office.

H's shout snaps me out of my doldrums. "Oi, Sid! Gatherin' up for the winter yet?"

I follow H's gaze, spotting a bushy-tailed squirrel scurrying up a tree trunk. After it deposits a nut, it turns around and waves an arm in our direction. Until that moment, I didn't know a squirrel could give someone the finger. Hopefully, this is part of the magic that only I can see.

H flaps up, whacking my arm with his wing. "See, I told you there're more of us Eternals. Just think, you coulda been stuck with the nutty lad instead."

I pause my steps, pretending to mull over the option. "Hmm, I bet nutty lad wouldn't eat all of my cheese or sleep on my feet. Is it too late to request a change?"

"Hrmphh."

The college walls turn into shopfronts as we get closer to the centre. H turns down a cute alleyway, the street lined with cafes and restaurants, chairs spilling out beyond the sidewalk. A string of lights crisscrosses above, I'm sure it is achingly romantic when the sun goes down. It's a perfect date spot, and here I am with a pet wyvern.

We duck into a colourful doorway where a life-size cow cut-out beckons us inside. Creamy, milky goodness glistens under the lights of the glass freezer case. The mound of chocolate in the back corner captures my attention. Forget about salted caramel, I need chocolate.

"I'll have a cone please, with a scoop of, uh..." I don't remember my local gelateria advertising this flavour. "Um, super #?*! chocolate." I can't help it, I blush.

"Gimme a cone of the fig and mascarpone, will ya, Nat?"

I'm not surprised that H has found the one cheese item on the menu.

Nabbing an empty table outside, I settle in to enjoy my treat. I hope the Oxford magic will keep people from noticing that I'm sitting with a cat holding an ice cream cone.

As I watch people walk by, I have a bit of a revelation. "Hey H, maybe we're going about all of this the wrong way."

"Whatcha mean, Nat? Searchin' for the murderer or tryin' to find a theme for the gala?"

I take a few more licks of my ice cream, narrowly preventing it from falling on my skirt. "Both, I guess. We've been looking in all the obvious places. I thought for sure we'd find the murderer in the kitchen and an event theme in the college annals. Maybe we need to take a broader look at our problems. We could look more into the people that have come in through the gates at St Margaret, see if there is some hidden passion we've failed to uncover."

H's eyes light up, providing a momentary distraction from the ice cream smears dripping off his snout. "'Idden passion? I know just the missie to ask."

"Really?" I can't believe it.

"Yep, and you know her, too. Catherine Morgan."

Forehead scrunched, I struggle to remember where I heard that name before. "The portrait in the main building hallway?"

"Not the paintin', the woman sittin' inside it. Remember what Dr Radcliffe said? Cathy knows all about 'idden passions, plus she's been 'angin' in that spot for as long as I can remember. If she ain't seen it, it ain't 'appened."

I steal half the shop's napkin stack to sort out a very sticky wyvern and then we turn back the way we came. This time, though, we catch the bus. I've got a new angle of attack and not a moment to lose.

❖

The security guard calls out my name as H and I enter St Margaret main gate.

"Ms Payne, I'm glad I caught you. Harry was in here a little while ago, looking to see if you'd left. Something about car sharing?"

Oh no! In between my hours in the library and ice cream sugar high, I'd completely forgotten about my dinner plans. Harry had invited me and H over for a roast dinner and to meet her husband. After days in the dining hall, I was craving a home-cooked meal.

Flashing him a quick smile, I call out my thanks before dashing up the front steps. "Thanks for letting me know, I'll go track her down now. Cheers!"

I look back in time to catch him doffing his cap. "Anytime, Ms Payne. I'm always here to help."

"Looks like our plans to meet with Catherine will have to wait until tomorrow, H." I shoo him in the front door and clack my way down the long wooden hallway to Harry's office. We make a quick stop in the common office to check in on my assistants.

Jill and Will look up when I stick my head in the door.

"Hiya team, any luck on finding us a caterer for the gala?"

Both shake their heads no. Jill points to a stack of post-its on the corner of her desk. "I've called every chef and caterer in town, but they all claim to have no availability on the night we need them."

Will pipes up before I can formulate my next question. "We'd believe them, except some gave the excuse before they even heard the date. We've never seen anything like it. Normally our inboxes are overflowing with requests to arrange tastings or offering discounts."

"Do either of you have any good news?" I ask.

"I do!" Will pipes up, shuffling through a pile of papers. "Here it is. I've finalised the guest list and 150 people have confirmed their attendance. The marquees are on order, tables and chairs rented, heaters..."

"Basically, everything we can do without knowing what the final theme will be," finishes Jill, both of them looking at me expectantly.

"Not to worry, team. I've got a lead on a new avenue for exploration. I should have the theme nailed down in the next day or two." I cross my fingers behind my back, hoping Catherine Morgan will come through with a genius suggestion.

Both Jill and Will grab their notepads, ready to take my next orders.

"Anything we can do to help?" asks Jill.

"I'm always happy to do background research," offers Will.

Waving my hands, I motion them to put their pens down for the moment. "Thanks, Jill and Will, that's generous of you to offer. However, I suspect you two will have trouble reaching the person I have in mind. Stay focussed on the caterer challenge. You may need to broaden your reach out into the Cotswolds."

I wish them both luck with their work and promise to check back in tomorrow. With any luck, hopefully I'll have the theme challenge sorted.

I pop into my office to shut down my computer for the day. Dr Radcliffe is away at a conference, so Harry suggested we take advantage of the quiet to leave early. Given how many days we're the last ones to leave, it doesn't exactly feel like we're cheating.

"Come along, H. We've got a roast dinner with our names on it."

"I hope the old bag's got Yorkshire puddins and gravy. And a cheese board." H spins in mid-air, chasing a spot of ice cream on his tail I failed to catch at the shop.

Giggling, I reassure him, "Knowing Harry, I doubt you'll starve."

After knocking on my door, Harry leads us out to her car, chatting away on the drive as she tells me about her day. She's still steaming over Professor Green who failed to submit his paperwork on time.

"I wish you had been there to see his face, Nat. The bloke was a week late on submitting his student interview notes despite me chasing him multiple times. He seemed unfazed that he was holding up the entire recruitment process for his department."

"There's always one person who believes that deadlines are mere suggestions and don't apply to them. Always one. But what you can do about it?" I ask. I don't really expect an answer, but Harry is ready with a reply.

"I know exactly what I'll do about him. Those high table seating arrangements don't happen by accident. He'll find himself next to Baron Wadsworth for the next few dinners."

"Who's Baron Wadsworth?"

"He's a local celebrity. His wife attended St Margaret, so he took a shine to it. She passed away ten years ago, but he still asks to come to high table dinners. I guess he does it to avoid another dinner at home alone."

Aww, bless him. "That doesn't sound too bad. Poor man, I'm sure he wants some company."

I'm caught by surprise when both Harry and H snicker.

"He definitely wants company. But he's half-deaf and nearly a century old. As penance for holding up the department, Professor Green will spend the whole night shouting across the table while trying to keep the Baron from pinching the serving staff's behinds."

I can picture the scene in my head. A stodgy middle-aged professor seated by a white-haired elderly man. The dining hall is anything but quiet once it's filled up with students. Between loudly repeating himself and running interference with the serving women, Professor Green will have a night to remember. Or should I say nightmare to remember? I'd feel bad for him, but it seems like just desserts after leaving prospective students waiting an extra week for word on their applications.

"I always get my revenge, Nat. Professor Green was well over the line; this lesson will be one he remembers."

Harry's home ends up being a cottage in a nearby village. Her husband is waiting out front when we pull into the drive. With bristle-brush grey hair, a checked shirt, rugged brown trousers, and leathery sun-kissed skin, he is the very picture of a typical Cotswold farmer.

He meets me halfway down the pathway, bright smile matching his twinkling green eyes. "Welcome, Nat. Pleased to get a chance to meet you. I'm Rob, Harry's other half."

"My worser half," pipes up Harry from behind me.

He leads me into a cosy front room, a bright rug and glowing fireplace bringing warmth into the space. H makes himself at home on the sofa, while I wave away offers of seating. The walls are lined with portraits and paintings, hardly a clear space left.

"We travelled a lot when we were younger and I could get around more easily," explains Rob, his weight held up by a beautifully carved wooden cane. "Harry fell in love with that seaside picture on our first trip. It became a bit of a hobby to collect some kind of art from every place we went."

"You must have travelled loads to have collected these. I love how they're all so different and yet work together."

"Sheer luck, that is. Now if you want to see something that's taken hours of work, come on through to the back."

Rob leads me down a hallway and past the kitchen where Harry is already hard at work prepping potatoes for the oven. He pulls open a sliding glass door that leads into a small conservatory.

I gasp, "This is amazing! I didn't think it was possible to get so much land here in Oxford!" Beyond the glass walls lies a perfectly sculpted garden fading into pastureland as far as my eye can see. The back patio is lined with raised flowerbeds run riot with bright colours. Pear and apple trees dot the lawn, their branches heavy with fruit.

Rob points out a small fence further back, barely visible from our position in the conservatory. "We only own to the edge of the garden there, but all the land beyond is protected for farming and river overrun. That's why we chose this place. We knew we didn't have to worry about losing our view to a new high-rise or housing development."

Sighing with house envy, I realise I've seen some of these flowers before. "Your garden is gorgeous. Reminds me a bit of the college, if I'm honest."

Rob preens, pleased with my comment. "It should, I was the master gardener there for years until I had to retire early. My knee got too bad to stand it, too many hours kneeling down weeding when I was young."

Harry's voice rings out before I can ask any further questions. "Come back into the kitchen, you two. I need someone to open the wine and pour us a glass while I finish up the cooking."

We tuck into dinner, all four of us seated around the table. Even H has been offered a seat, complete with a Yorkshire pudding swimming in brown gravy. He and Lillian must have spent many evenings here.

In between bites, I pause long enough to thank my host. "This tastes delicious, Harry. I feel terrible, I hope I didn't put you to too much trouble."

"Don't you worry a thing about it, Nat. I love having people over," Harry reassures me.

"That's the truth," replies Rob. "She's always adopting some homesick student or lonely professor, sometimes whether they like it or not. Take your neighbour, for example. We've had Edward over for many an evening. He's not everyone's cup of tea, but we've uncovered his weakness - homemade mince pies. Harry makes them every time, no matter what the season."

I've yet to run into my neighbour, probably due to my lost days working in the library. I'd honestly forgotten about him, but now that Rob has brought him up, I confess to my curiosity. "How did you get to know him? I mean, other than work."

Harry laughs out loud, "We didn't get off on the best foot. He turned up at the college, full of himself. He's a prodigy, you see. Graduated from Cambridge early, publishing heaps of papers and hundreds of citations. The department wined and dined him to convince him to come over, so he shows up convinced that the sun rose and set on his head."

"I'm not sure we've managed to convince him it doesn't, Harry," Rob interjects.

"I'm doing my best, Rob. Now, where was I? Oh yes, so in he waltzes expecting everyone to drop everything and cater to his needs. I could see he needed a small attitude adjustment if he didn't want to alienate everyone around him. That would have ruined his career and made Dr Radcliffe look bad."

Food momentarily forgotten, I beg Harry to continue with her story.

Nodding at the bread basket, she carries on as she butters another slice of bread. "When he showed up one day, demanding to speak to Dr Radcliffe with no appointment or care for the others sitting in my office, I told him she wasn't in and to try back day after and I sent him right out the door. The next day I did the same thing again. I kept up this routine for a full week until he happened to be standing there when Dr Radcliffe walked out of her office. He blustered around and I told him in no uncertain terms that if he couldn't respect his colleagues and the college staff, then Dr Radcliffe would continue to be unavailable to him."

Rob jumps in to finish up the story, "He turned up the next week with a bouquet for Harry and has found Dr Radcliffe to be available ever since. My Harry has a core of steel and no patience for people who mistreat others."

Chapter Nine

After dinner, Rob drops H and me back at the college, bellies stuffed and barely in time for me to make it to my first official prefect meeting. A walk seems like the perfect way to clear my head of gala stress and organise my thoughts before seeing the others.

When we spoke over the weekend, Mathilde insisted that the prefect group always met well outside of normal business hours so that no one would question why or how the group had connected. As promised, she'd texted me the address of the wine cafe she and Kate had selected.

As I turn to leave the college carpark, H takes off in the opposite direction, swooping past me on his way towards the garden gate into the college grounds. Shouting, I stop him before he disappears. "H, where are you going? I need you to show me the way to this cafe."

Perching on top of the iron bars, H refuses to budge. "Oi, Nat, you can get there on your own. All you gotta do is walk straight down the road for a mile and then turn right."

Confused, I look around, wondering what other plans he has

in place. "What are you going to do while I'm gone? There won't be anyone to let you into the flat."

H sneezes, lighting a column of ivy on fire. Whatever response he gives is swallowed up by the sounds of furious flapping as he tries to blow enough wind to snuff the flames out.

When he finally settles back again on the railing, I try again. That sneeze is a dead giveaway that he is nervous about something. "You were saying something about your plans? Could you repeat it? I didn't quite catch it."

Clearing his voice, he dusts plant ash from his tail before straightening up and puffing out his chest. "I said that I'm steppin' out with my lassie. Princess Fluffy, not that it's any of your concern."

"Princess Fluffy?" Incredulity drips from my voice.

"Hrmph. That's right. She's a Persian cat. I promised to take her 'untin' for mice in the garden." His eyes dare me to make something more out of it.

Backing away, I wave him on with his adventures. "Too much information. Fine, I'll go on my own, so I don't interrupt any more of your love life."

Thankfully, the route is exactly as H described, my phone alerting me when it is time to make the right turn into the street where the wine cafe is located. It is hard to miss, its brightly lit windows casting a glow onto the surrounding pavement. I climb three steps to enter the front door, pausing at the bar to ask if the others have arrived. The barman points me down a hallway, telling me they're seated in the conservatory.

Mathilde and another woman are tucked away in a small booth sipping red wine when I arrive. Mathilde is once again in t-shirt and jeans, making a sharp contrast to the well-dressed middle-aged woman next to her who must be Kate, the third prefect. With sleek chestnut hair smoothed into a sharp bob, diamonds winking on her ears and hands, and her starched white shirt collar flipped up, Kate looks more like a continental socialite than a university staffer. I bet she fits right in with the international art community.

Somehow I expected Kate to be close in age to me and Mathilde, but she appears to be in her early forties. Now I see why we keep our meetings a secret; we're all so different from one another, on top of working in different departments, that we would struggle to find an explanation for being together.

Mathilde spots me first, pointing me out to Kate. I wave them to keep their seats, saying it isn't worth the effort required to crawl out of the booth. Kate quickly pours me out a glass as Mathilde does introductions, allowing me to settle into the space in the cushioned booth.

After handing me a glass and calling for a welcome cheers, Kate launches right into it. "Sorry it's taken me so long to meet you, I've had my hands full at the Ashmolean and I've been using all my spare time to visit the statues around town."

Sipping my wine, I reassure her I haven't taken offence. "Please don't apologise, I should have found time to track you down myself. We're all together now and we've got a lovely wine, so I don't think we're doing too badly. So how do these meetings normally go? Is there a pledge we recite or minutes?" After the episode in the Senior Common Room, I'm not taking anything for granted.

Mathilde chuckles, "It's nothing so formal as that. From the few I attended, we mostly chatted while we polished off the better part of a bottle of wine. Lillian would entertain us with stories of her run-ins with various professors or staff. She wasn't much of a planner."

I shake my head. "Yes, I heard that about her. As much as I love a good gossip session, I don't think that will be helpful in figuring out what has gone wrong with the magic. We might need to be more methodical, at least for the time being. I brought my notes from our call last week. Now, where are they?"

As I dig around in my seemingly bottomless handbag, Mathilde nudges a disbelieving Kate. "See, I told you she loves lists."

Kate buries her head in her hands while I pull out my trusty notebook and three different coloured pens.

"Now then, where were we? Oh yes, our action plan. H seems pretty convinced that the magic is out of alignment, opening us up to bigger problems, including Chef Smythe's death. Let's start with a report on our assignments. Mathilde, did you want to go first, or shall I start?"

Mathilde chokes on a sip of wine when she finds herself on the hot seat. "Why don't you go, Nat? I bet you've got notes written. I can gather my thoughts while you update us."

I flip open my notebook to see a woefully short list. "Well, I've not made too much progress. I spoke with a few of the Eternals at St Margaret, but no one seems to have seen anything out of the ordinary."

Mathilde pats my hand, "Good of you to make the effort, but I thought that was the case. If anyone had seen anything suspicious, I'm sure they'd have let H know by now."

Looking down, I move onto the next item on my list. "Still on the investigation, from what Harry mentioned, the police have made no headway. I tried to nose around, speaking with Chef Smythe's kitchen staff, but everyone so far has a solid alibi. Other than that, I've been locked away in the library searching for some event inspiration. Sorry, I know it isn't much."

Kate seems more impressed with my efforts, rushing to reassure me. "Do not apologise, Nat. That sounds like a fair amount of work for less than a week's time! How is the search for suspects? And the gala? Do you have a theme yet? I always loved it when Lillian would reveal her vision for the events. Always so, well, magical."

"Ha, yes, magical. It will be magical. Just as soon as I come up with it." As the words come out of my mouth, all the warm fuzzy feelings I gained from mid-afternoon ice cream and Harry's roast dinner disappear. I've got a mountain of urgent tasks, and after almost a week of work I've got nothing to show for them. My wineglass wobbles in my hand, wine sloshing precariously close to the top. Kate reaches over and plucks it out of my hand before I spill.

My gaze jumps between the two women, finding encouraging smiles instead of judgemental stares. Kate and Mathilde are literally the only two people in the world who can fully appreciate my challenge. "Do you ever doubt yourselves? Maybe think the magic made a mistake and you aren't up to the task?"

Kate barks out a sharp laugh in response. "Definitely. Sometimes more than once a day. I had a rough start, ending up in a physical fight with one of the museum staff and having to order him escorted from the building. He thought the hiring committee should have awarded him my job. Just when I found my feet again, I picked up my magical key and discovered that my statues and paintings talk."

Reaching over, Kate gives my arm a gentle squeeze. "We may have inherited a magical legacy, but we're still human. It's natural to feel overwhelmed, or have doubts. We work hard and worry about doing a great job because we're passionate about what we do, and we care about ensuring that this legacy lives on."

I let out the breath I'd been holding as relief rushes through my veins. Wine glass in hand once again, I take a tentative sip, letting the flavours blossom in my mouth. If Kate, a picture of perfection, had an actual altercation in her first week, maybe I'm not doing so badly. At first glance, she seemed cool and aloof, leaving me worried I'd struggle to find common ground with her. Instead, she's turned out to be just as lovely and personable as Mathilde and Harry.

Fishing around in her pockets, Mathilde draws out her phone, typing in her passcode as she speaks. "Deep breaths, Nat. You can't solve a murder or a magical mystery on a timeline. If it were that easy, the police would have sorted it all out on day 1. I've got a great meditation app; I'll text you the name. I think you need to schedule yourself some chill out time."

Kate eyes my notebook and pen, leaning over to Mathilde to whisper, "I don't think she knows how to chill out."

She might be right. I'll book some chill out time into my schedule, I think I've got a free space next Tuesday. "I think I've done enough talking, can I hand over to you now, Mathilde?"

"Right, yes you can. Let me see, I was supposed to be investigating our book archives for information on the issue with our magic. I have made some progress... or maybe preparation for progress is a better way of putting it. I've put out a recall notice for books on loan to the college libraries."

"Maybe this is a daft question, but won't someone notice if you recall all the loaner books?" I ask.

"Ha! I'm not recalling all of them. I have a list of autobiographies by egotistical men throughout history that we call on in situations like this. They're more than happy to let us know their theories on why things are going wrong. My predecessor put one book in each college a few months ago when Lillian was diagnosed."

Kate and I crack up into our wine glasses. When we get ourselves back under control, Kate steps in with her report. "Better you than me, Mathilde. The artefacts and antiques in the museum don't talk - well, mostly. As I mentioned earlier, I've started visiting the statues, but they're all there and in good condition as far as I can tell. I've assigned one of my junior staff members to update our catalogues, but much like the library, I've got objects spread throughout half the rooms of all thirty-eight colleges in Oxford."

I shudder at the thought. Suddenly my lack of a gala theme doesn't seem like such a monstrous problem. "Right, it doesn't seem like we will get to the bottom of the alignment issue as quickly as we'd hoped. Is there anything else we can do in the meantime?"

Mathilde and Kate both mull over my question as we sip the last of our wine. Finally, Kate breaks the silence. "I think we need to focus on boosting the magic that is here. You've got the gala coming up, Nat, that will bring in a large group of people. Mathilde, could you call in a favour at Cambridge and have them send some books your way?"

Mathilde nods, her smile a sure sign of her acceptance of the plan.

"Great, I've got a couple of mates from uni working at the National Portrait Gallery. I'm sure they'd be happy to support me by loaning some artwork for a special exhibition."

I finish writing, tearing out two pages from my notepad and passing them over to my fellow prefects. "Excellent, I've documented our plan here and noted each of your next steps."

Kate waves for the waitress as we gather our things, "This round is on me."

"Oh Kate, you don't have to do that!" I reply as I dig in my handbag for my bank card.

"Actually, I do. Mathilde bet me a round of drinks that you wouldn't let us leave tonight without a written assignment."

"I tried to tell you, Kate." Mathilde snickers.

"Oh wait, that reminds me..." I fish my notepad and pen back out and scribble one last note before we leave.

"Would you like to share your note with the rest of the class?" asks Kate.

"I forgot to assign myself to chill out."

After a good night's rest, H and I wait until the early morning rush ends before we pay a visit to Catherine Morgan. It'll be my first time trying to strike up a conversation with a portrait. I'm crossing my fingers that I won't embarrass myself.

"Oi, Cathy, 'ow's it 'angin'?" H turns a flip in the air, laughing himself silly at his own joke.

Turns out I worried about the wrong person being an embarrassment.

Nudging him out of the way, I apologise to the woman in the painting. "I'm so sorry, Ms Morgan. Four hundred years of existence and apparently he never learned any manners."

"It's quite all right, Natalie. I'm well aware of H's antics by now. Please call me Catherine. I'm happy to speak with you. It was so frustrating to have you stop here in front of me on your first day and to not even be able to wink a hello."

"At that point, I'm not sure seeing a portrait wink at me would have been the best for my sanity. I was so nervous. First day jitters and all that. And then Dr Radcliffe and I found Chef Smythe..." my voice trails off.

"You poor dear, what a day. Every time I've seen you pass by, you've been distracted or frazzled. Am I correct in imagining that this isn't a casual visit?"

"I wish it were, Catherine. I hate to start our relationship by asking for a favour, but I'm in rather desperate need of some help. I promise, as soon as this gala is over and murder solved, I'll come by with a cup of tea and we can get to know one another better."

Catherine bestows a gentle smile. "That sounds lovely, dear. I will hold you to that promise. Now, what can I do for you?"

I run through my mental list, weighing up whether it's best to start with the search for the murderer, help identify suspects or suggestions for a gala theme. They're all equally important, making it impossible for me to pick a place to start. "Um, the murder, potential suspects, the gala... everything? Because that's what I need help with. Sorting out everything. Or a time machine so I can add more hours into my days."

"Poor darling, it's a shame that the magic doesn't allow us to slip back in time. Life would be easier if we could see the murder as it happened. But let's talk about the gala first. You need a theme, something unexpected and yet quintessentially St Margaret. Let me think..." she rubs her chin, deep in thoughts.

The sound of the main hall door opening provides a momentary distraction, a student dashing in from the rain before continuing past us without even a sideways glance. It's almost as though he didn't see us standing there. The main door slams shut in a gust of wind, blowing a wayward leaf down the corridor. H flips over backward once again, this time attempting to catch it.

Before I can chastise him, Catherine clears her throat, recalling my attention. "Back in time... yes, that might do it!"

"Back in time? Like a decade party?" I can't see how a sock hop will be appropriate for a formal college gala.

Leaning out of her portrait frame, Catherine nods towards the seating alcove to our left. "Pull that chair over, dear, and let me tell you a little story. It all begins with a search for an assistant, a fateful trip to Paris and a shared vision which would bind two women and this college together for years to come."

I can hardly believe the fantastical tale that Catherine recounts. The setting is the early 1900s. Two women, lost in the gardens of Versailles, somehow slip through time to glimpse Marie Antoinette waiting to hear the outcome of the sacking of Paris, an event which happened over one hundred years before.

"This is a fascinating story, to say the least, but what does it have to do with St Margaret?"

Forgiving my interruption, Catherine continues, "The two women in our story were both learned scholars here at St Margaret, one the college principal and the other the assistant principal, and they were devoted spiritualists. They were desperate to tell the story, but feared being ridiculed, so they wrote a book and published it under a pseudonym. Their tale shook the core of London, selling over 11,000 copies. Scholars still argue over the truth of what happened on that fateful day when the women disappeared in Versailles."

Leaning back in the chair, I can feel the familiar spark of an idea blossoming in my brain. "I won't do a Versailles theme, that would be too obvious. But yes, I think... I can see a pathway from here to something incredible. Oh, thank you!"

Catherine reaches out of the painting again, this time to pat me on the shoulder.

"You're welcome, dear. If there is one thing I've learned, both during my lifetime and in these long years afterwards, it's that we women must stick together. Some women here could afford to learn that lesson. Take Chef Smythe. That woman would sooner cut a woman down than hold out a hand to lift her up. What she did to poor Harry... oh, perhaps I shouldn't say."

Harry? I'm thunderstruck. I wasn't aware they had any history beyond being colleagues. "What did she do to Harry?"

"I wouldn't dare to bring it up. It's horrid, really. Worst thing a woman can do to another. But I saw Harry come out of the dining hall last week looking absolutely gutted, and I wondered if the whole thing had started up again."

Edging forward onto the edge of my seat, I plead with Catherine to share whatever she knows. "Tell me everything. If it might hurt Harry, I'd rather be the one looking into things than have the police find out. Sounds like the poor woman has been through enough."

Catherine ponders my words, quickly arriving at the same conclusion. Although Harry isn't aware that Catherine Morgan is anything other than a painting, Catherine has had ample opportunity to watch her over the years. "Harry is certainly one of the loveliest women to grace our hallways, always cheerful. Dr Radcliffe wouldn't have half the success she has had without Harry standing behind her to sort out any messes. That's what makes Chef Smythe's actions that much worse. Harry's husband used to be the head gardener here at the college. He retired early because his knees were giving him trouble."

"Rob? Yes, I met him yesterday. I didn't think he'd been around the college in a while. How long ago did this thing with Chef Smythe happen?" I ask.

Casting her eyes to the ceiling, Catherine searches her memories. "I'm not entirely sure. It's so hard for we Eternals to keep track of time, particularly since I spend so much of it hanging here on the wall. One day seems much like the rest. Maybe eight or nine years ago? Chef Smythe was younger then. Although she was loath to admit it, I believe she was jealous of Harry, how much everyone respected and frankly adored her. She felt she should get more of that adoration given her superior skill set. She'd moan about it every time she walked between Dr Radcliffe's office and the dining hall. She decided that if she couldn't convince everyone, she could at least tempt away Harry's husband. Show her in no uncertain terms that Harry was not her equal."

"NO! That's terrible! She tried to steal her husband?" I can't believe it, although it explains the animosity in Chef Smythe's gaze on the day she stormed out of Dr Radcliffe's office.

Shrugging, Catherine carries on, "I don't know how far it went - not too far, I'd imagine, given Harry and Rob are still married. Chef Smythe tempted him with special meals and his favourite desserts. She was always there with a plate of food, a kind word and a smile whenever he worked in the herb garden outside the kitchen. Most of the fellows ignore the gardening staff, Rob would have noticed the special attention she was paying."

Shaking my head and waving my arms, I interrupt Catherine before she can say anything more. "Ugh, stop there. I don't want to know what happened. I'd rather know nothing than imagine Chef Smythe and Rob in any intimate relationship. Anyway, if it happened years ago, what made you think of it now?"

Settling back into her seat, Catherine replies, "Harry was here one evening last week, shortly before your arrival here at St Margaret. It was late, after a high table dinner. She stayed until the end and helped the staff reassemble the room once everyone had left. It was dark here in the hallway, only the emergency lighting on, Harry thought she was alone. She came out, sat down in that very chair and had a long cry. She was mumbling into her handkerchief and all I could make out was her husband's name and phrases like 'I can't believe we're going through this again' and 'how will I get through this.'"

Looking at my chair, I try to picture the scene. "Poor Harry. For her sake, I hope you're wrong. For all of our sakes. If she ends up being a murderer, she'll have fooled us all. I could never imagine her doing it, she's just too good-natured."

H swoops to land on the chair beside me. He'd been so quiet, I'd forgotten he was here with me. Nearly falling out of my chair, I reach over to hold his snout shut before he can let loose with another one of his infamous sneezes. He swallows it back, steam pouring from his ears. "Thanks, Nat. That was a close one. You 're right in the line of fire."

Wiping wyvern snot onto the chair cushion, I arch an eyebrow in his direction. "No worries, but you only sneeze when you're stressed. What's going on?"

H sinks into the chair, his leathery wings scratching against the seat back. "I was rememberin' them stories she told last night at dinner. 'Arry's got a dark side."

My mind whirring, I mentally replay everything I heard. There was the story about getting even with Professor Green and the funny tale of her putting Edward Thomas in his place. Sure, she doesn't hesitate to hold her own, but murder? It seems like a huge stretch.

But then again, what would a strong woman do to make sure she held onto her husband? Could Harry be the culprit? If so, what does that mean for me? My one friend here at the college, um, human friend that is, and I might have to point the police in her direction.

I'm so lost in thought I leave without saying goodbye, wandering the hallway until I exit into the gardens. In a mindless trance, my feet move along the worn path towards my flat. I need a quiet space to think this over and figure out what to do next.

Chapter Ten

I move mechanically around my kitchen, boiling the kettle and dropping a tea bag into my favourite mug, pacing in a circle as I wait the requisite three to five minutes for the tea to steep.

After pouring in a spot of milk and stirring in a spoonful of sugar, I make my way over to the window seat. When I imagined spending hours here, I wasn't planning to pass them away wondering if a woman I genuinely like might be a cold-blooded murderer. I'm relieved that H didn't follow me back. If he were here, I'd be forced to give voice to my thoughts, making my suspicions real.

I replay every minute of time I've spent with Harry. Could she have done it? It seems unfathomable. I have countless examples of things she has done to welcome me and make me feel at home.

"Would a murderer stock your refrigerator?" I ask my empty living room. Unsurprisingly, the sofa cushions fail to answer.

My grandfather's picture sits on the mantle. Was it only a week ago that I showed up, bright eyed and ready to take on everything the college had to throw at me? I had no idea what I was getting myself into. I wish his face would come to life, offering advice on what to do next. Sipping my tea, I stare at the photograph, willing the mouth to move. "Grandfather, are you there? I know about the magic now. We need your help." Silence is my only response.

Back into my bedroom, I toss my work clothes onto the bed before digging my workout wear and trainers out of my cupboard. I need to get out of here, out of the college and away from everything that the college keeps throwing at me.

For the first time, I turn toward my front door. I don't want to jog through the gardens, waving hello at every student I pass. I want out of here, now, without being forced to speak to a soul. Earbuds in, volume cranked up, I tuck my key into the pocket of my leggings.

I fling my front door open, head down as I search through my music for my cardio playlist. Not looking where I'm going, I jog into the narrow entry hall straight into the path of someone, my shoulder banging into a man's chest, nearly causing me to drop my phone. I rip out my earbuds to apologise, looking up to find Professor Rude glaring back at me.

Of course I do. That seems about right for how my day is going.

I can tell he's gearing up for another round of criticism, so I open my mouth, jumping in before he can get a word out.

"Well, well well... Are you policing the housing now? Not content with complaining about me to the Principal in the dining hall or ensuring I don't invade your precious senior common room?" Waving towards my open apartment door, I explain, "I live here, in this very flat, whether you like it or not."

Eyebrows arched, he stares down his nose at me. "I have plenty of better ways to spend my day, Ms Payne, than wander around after you." He pauses, pointing towards the ceiling, "I also live here, right up these stairs."

I stare at him as the words trickle through the muck of my

brain. The shopping tote on his shoulder and the stack of mail in his hand are evidence of the truth of his statement. He lives here. That means he must be... can it be?

I lean against the hallway wall, chuckling at the irony of the situation. Harry's favourite professor, the one she's been promising to introduce me to, is the one person who has repeatedly made me feel unwelcome.

Maybe the universe is trying to send me a sign. But is it saying I should pack it in and head back to London or alert the police I've identified the murderer? Harry is clearly delusional if she thought this belligerent, snotty, know-it-all and I could ever be friends.

"First Harry, now this... can things get any worse?" And with that thought, my chuckles subside.

I look around the entryway, deciding what to do next. It is smaller than I expected, leaving little room for myself and Edward to stand side by side. We can either face each other or turn tail and run out of the door. If the indecision on his face is any sign, he's weighing both options.

Between running into each other around the college and now discovering we're neighbours, it's clear we need to find a way to be civil to one another. The college is too small to allow for anything else. My run can wait for a few minutes.

I pull my apartment door shut and slide over to the stairway, climbing up a few steps before lowering to perch on one. "If we're going to be neighbours, you might as well sit and get to know me. You know, the real me, not the one you've been imagining."

Having blocked his escape route upstairs to his own flat, I've left him little choice but to agree.

Edward lowers himself down, awkwardly folding his arms to avoid bumping me. "I could say the same about you. You were quick to take my head off just now."

"We agree then, a fresh start." I turn in his direction and hold my hand out. "Natalie Payne, pleased to meet you. My friends call me Nat, you can call me Natalie."

"Some fresh start," mutters Edward. "Pleased to meet you, Natalie. I'm Edward Thomas. My friends call me Edward Thomas."

Edward shrugs his shopping tote off his shoulder, letting it rest on the stairs in between us. We stare at one another in silence until Edward finally succumbs, opening his mouth to fill the awkward gap. "I believe you uttered something about Harry earlier. I couldn't make out the words, but if you're having a hard time getting acquainted with her, I might be able to assist you."

I snort. "Assist me? With Harry? That's a right laugh. From what I hear, it's the other way around. I should offer you a hand."

"I have no idea what you mean, Ms Payne. Harry and I get along well enough now. When I first arrived, I admit I didn't find her comportment to be suitably austere for such an important role. I've since learned that she can be austere when she chooses to be... and I really don't want her to be that way with me."

"Back to Ms Payne, already? Are you always so formal with other college staff?"

Edward looks me over, from my bright pink Nike trainers up my floral leggings to my turquoise jumper. "I'm not sure anyone could make you fit into the mould of a formal Oxford staff member."

I think about correcting him and then decide it isn't worth the effort. Although we're both trying to break the ice and give one another a fair chance, it is definitely an uphill battle.

"Getting back to Harry, I've got a few reasons for having her on the brain, but foremost are her efforts to introduce the two of us. She said you're the college liaison with the police department for the murder. Did you learn anything about their investigation?"

I don't think Edward could look more aghast if I'd told him I was the murderer.

"Why would our Head of Ceremonies need to know confidential information regarding a formal police inquiry? I cannot fathom what you'd have to do with the situation or why on earth you and Harry would spend any time discussing the matter in the first place."

I stare in disbelief. "What would I have to do with it? I bloody well found the body. Of course Harry and I are going to talk about it. As to why I need confidential information, well, that's simple. I can't get another chef to agree to cater our gala. No one is willing to set foot in our kitchen until we find out who killed Chef Smythe."

Edward huffs out, "That's ridiculous. There's no indication that her death is part of something larger which would put others here at the college at risk."

Holding my hands up, I say, "Don't blame me, I'm not starting any rumours! People are shocked. Crimes of this nature never happen at a college. But if we don't sort this out soon, Dr Radcliffe may cancel the gala all together." I don't need to fake the concern on my face.

Unfortunately, Edward seems unfazed by this possibility. "Perhaps Dr Radcliffe should cancel the gala."

"What? How can you say that?"

Shrugging, he explains, "Investigations require time, even straightforward ones, and this case is far from simple. There were no unexplained fingerprints, no signs of a break-in. The rest of the evidence is still being analysed in the laboratory." He pronounces every syllable in laboratory.

I ball my fists up, holding them tight against the sides of my legs. I want to wave them in the air, shout until I can make him see how important this is. Inhaling and exhaling, I calm myself. "Edward, do you understand how important this gala is to St Margaret?"

He sneers, "It's heels up for a group of benefactors and

alumni. How important can it be? Surely no one will complain if we push it back a few months."

Horrified, my voice squeaks up a notch. "The gala is much more than a 'heels up' as you call it. It is a ceremony that takes place between the college and the individuals who provide important funding. Dr Radcliffe expects to raise tens of thousands of pounds in critical donations. What do you think will happen if we postpone that amount of money coming in the door?"

Seeing I'm finally starting to catch Edward's attention, I continue on. "The St Margaret gala has taken place every October for the last fifty years. Should we postpone the event, or worse yet, cancel it all together, it will make the papers. Local and potentially national. Do you want to see Chef Smythe's murder splashed on all the broadsheets? St Margaret's reputation for academic excellence replaced by a sensationalist tabloid headline?"

Face now green, Edward stammers out a reply. "I had... well, I hadn't any idea that could happen. Surely you must exaggerate..."

I don't wait for him to finish, my voice rising in volume. "I am not exaggerating. I may not have a doctoral degree from Oxbridge, but I know public relations. I know the press. Most importantly, I've seen how people respond to bad news."

My words echo up the stairwell, Edward at a loss for further arguments. I lower my voice back to a level barely above a whisper. "Do you have any idea why your snap judgement made me so mad?"

Edward's face snaps towards mine, confusion written on his wrinkled brow. "Because I assumed you were incompetent?"

Shaking my head, I explain, "No, not that, although I'll admit it frustrated me. However, what lit my temper on fire was your assumption I am an outsider, someone who can't possibly understand how important ceremony is to Oxford, and who won't respect Oxford's history or unique place in British society. I grew up listening to my grandfather tell me stories about his life as a librarian here. The Oxford colleges were sacred ground for him. He planted the seed in my mind that my greatest accomplishment in life would be to find a career here within the University system."

"Ms Payne, Natalie, I'm sorry, I should have..."

Using the stairwell, I pull myself onto my feet, taking a small leap down the last few stairs to land near the main exit. Resting my hand on the door handle, I turn back, getting in my last words. "I have as much right to be here as anyone else within St Margaret's iron gates. And I'm not letting you, the investigation team, or anyone else stand in the way of the Autumn gala taking place. Not just happening, but it being an incredible success. So, either get on board with St Margaret's priorities, or get out of the way."

If Edward had anything else to say, it got lost in the slamming of our front door.

As my feet pound the pavement, I replay every word of the conversation with Edward. It's clear to me Edward has little time for anyone and anything which doesn't suit his ideal of Oxford. For the life of me, I can't figure out why Harry was so insistent on introducing the two of us. We have nothing in common. I can't see us bonding over episodes of the Great British Bake off.

He's far too lackadaisical about finding Chef Smythe's killer. Left to his own devices, he'd sit back and let the police investigate for weeks, months, probably even years. He'd find some way to publish a paper on their efforts, unaware about the impact on the college.

Is there something more to Edward than meets the eye, or is this some kind of Machiavellian plot to distract us from finding out that it was Harry who did it? My mind pulls back from that thought, not willing to explore it further just yet.

I dip and dodge through the fields of Port Meadow, trying to avoid other runners and the livestock who call the meadow home. It isn't all that different from the rest of my time at Oxford. Since I arrived, I've been rushing full steam from one thing to another, struggling not to stand in a cow patty or be bowled over by someone coming at me.

By the time I reach the banks of the Thames, my mind is clear and my brow is dripping in sweat. An hour ago, I was praying for a ghost to step in and save me. Between the talk with Edward and the fresh air in my lungs, I might have another path in front of me.

Sure, it isn't the path I chose for myself. I signed up to throw amazing parties in historical venues. But I, Natalie Payne, am not a quitter. I didn't quit as a child when I struggled to learn to read. I didn't quit when my teachers said I would never be better than middle of the pack. I found my way of learning, ignoring their instructions and sketching my notes into my memory. By the time the dyslexia diagnosis came, I had already figured out how to use my brain difference to my benefit.

Between my pattern-seeking brain and my insights into people, I am more than capable of getting to the bottom of the mystery of who killed Chef Smythe and what is throwing the magic out of alignment.

Maybe Harry did it. Maybe she didn't. I know better than most that people, places, and things here at Oxford are more than they seem on the surface.

But there's no reason to rush over and accuse her. I've finally got the start of an event theme in my head. Plenty to keep me busy for a day or two. Perhaps I've lit a fire under Edward and he and the police will interrogate Harry before I do it myself.

Working on my idea for the gala theme is now my top priority. I'll go back into the office, assign out a few new tasks, check in on the search for a caterer. If I order some supplies, update my charts and cross items off my To Do list, I'm sure I'll feel better... be more in control.

Once I'm standing comfortably on my feet again, then I'll speak to Harry. I've got the weekend to figure out what to say.

Chapter Eleven

Saturday gets written off with a quick jaunt to London to have lunch with my parents. My mother offers to treat me to a manicure, and before I know it, it is nearly teatime.

I spend all of Sunday and half the night talking over my gala ideas with H, finding him to be a surprisingly good sounding board. I couldn't sleep until I was sure I had a solid plan to take into Dr Radcliffe.

Before I can present my idea and ask Dr Radcliffe for approval, I need to find Bartie, our top Eternal. I've barely seen him since our chat in the hallway that first day, although we have passed each other a few times and waved hello. I scour the main building, whisper-shouting his name with no luck. Would the Head of Eternal Affairs go for a walk in the garden? Only one way to find out.

I slip out one of the side doors into the terraced garden behind the main building. I check all the hidden seating nooks, spotting plenty of squirrels and birds but no Bartie. Carrying on, I enter a deeply shaded pathway, double-checking to make sure Bartie hasn't climbed up a tree to hide himself away from his Eternal paperwork.

Finally, hearing the welcome sound of leaves shuffling, I quicken my pace to catch whoever it is before they can move elsewhere. I track the sound to a line of oversized shrubbery growing against the college fence. Right as I realise that the space is too small to hide Bartie away, H comes strolling out. "H! Where have you been? You disappeared after breakfast. I need your help!"

"Sorry, missie. Princess Fluffy snuck outta the door when her 'umans went to work. A wyvern 'as needs you know."

"Blech! Now I've got that vision in my head. You know you've got leaves stuck to your tail, right?"

With one flaming exhale, H resolves the problem of the leaves before turning an arched eyebrow in my direction. "You're one to talk. I saw you yesterday, you was gettin' all chummy with Edward Thomas in the stairwell."

I cross my arms, indignation colouring my cheeks. "I was not getting 'chummy' with him, far from it. What were you doing spying on me?"

H flaps up to eye level, one long black talon pointed in my face. "You left me behind, remember? Went wanderin' off, leavin' me to wrap things up with Catherine Morgan. I was not spyin'! I was tryin' to get in the flat. I deserved a biscuit as a reward for my 'ard work."

Oops. I left him behind, and then I went off running without a thought. Time for a distraction. "Good news, H. Here's your chance to earn another reward. I need help to find Bartie... There's a plate of Lincolnshire Poacher Cheddar in it for you."

Licking his lips in anticipation, H nods his agreement. "It's Bartie you need? Lemme think... What time is it?"

I look down at my watch. "Half-past nine, give or take a few minutes."

H snaps his fingers. "That's easy, I know right where 'e'll be. Follow me, mate."

We follow the pathway along the fence until it twists back

towards the centre of the college grounds. I eye a signpost as we pass by, trying to guess where we might be headed. With our back to the main building and student dorms on either side, there are few options.

"H, are we going to visit the new conference centre?"

"Nope."

We walk between student housing buildings, turning again to pass by my own flat's back entrance. H flaps a few steps ahead of me, keeping on until the far gates are within sight.

The next signpost I see has two lone indicators attached to its top. "I thought you said that we weren't going to the new conference centre."

"We ain't. I told you. Be patient, you 're scarin' the birds away."

I look around but can't see anything else nearby, a sick feeling growing in the pit of my stomach. If we aren't going to the conference centre, the only other sign said 'Principal's Lodge'.

I speed up, circling around in front of H, forcing him to pay attention. "We're not sneaking into Dr Radcliffe's house, H. If Bartie's there, we can wait until he gets back."

"Settle down, mate. We're not going to Dr Radcliffe's place neither, although she must 'ave some sweet snacks in her kitchen cupboards."

Refusing to budge, I force him to confess. "Then where are we going?"

"Right 'ere." H nods his head towards a wooden gate I had completely failed to notice in my rush to question him. He slips by me, swooping to land on the top of the gate. His tail taps beside a metal placard.

The placard is spotless, but I can't make out the words in the sun's glare. I walk over, holding up my hand to block the light. "Fellows Garden?" I squint at H, suspicious. "Is this going to be like the Senior Common Room all over again?"

"Nah, 'ardly anybody goes in 'ere. You'll be fine." H flies off into the garden without another word.

I lift the latch and pull the gate open with a reassuring creak. Stepping under a leafy arbour, I emerge onto a landscaped lawn, complete with a burbling fountain and wrought iron benches. From here, there's no sign of the gate which encloses this hideaway, leafy green bushes and russet-hued trees line the perimeter.

H is well ahead, coasting on an invisible air current as he leads me towards a glass-encased gazebo. From the outside, I can see window seats stretching along the inside. If that room is as warm as your typical conservatory, I may never leave.

As I get closer, I spot a masculine set of somewhat transparent shoulders sitting against a chair back, deep within the room. H raps on the door, startling Bartie enough that he rises from his seat to come let us in. As the door opens, warmth spills out, pushing back the chilly October air.

Bartie steps aside, waving us in out of the cold. "Ms Nat, H, what a surprise. What brings you two out here to the Fellows Garden?"

I cast a longing eye towards a padded window seat near a radiator but turn my heels towards the seating area in the middle of the room. Bartie and I settle into a pair of garden chairs while H stretches out on a sun lounger. "I was looking for you, actually. I need to ask for your help."

Without a word of complaint over the fact that I've interrupted his private time, Bartie smiles and invites me to continue. "Of course, Ms Nat. I'm always happy to help our Ceremonies team. What can I do for you?"

I glance over at H, but he's looking at the other side of the room. Apparently, it's up to me to pitch Bartie on my plan for the gala. I sit up, looking Bartie right in the eye, leaving no doubt that I'm serious. "Bartie, I'd like your help to bring the magical field to life. For everyone. To see...." Bartie is already shaking his head, but I rush on, "For everyone to see that magical people exist."

Looking at me as though he is questioning my sanity, Bartie furiously shakes his head. "No, absolutely not. I'm sorry, Ms Nat. It isn't done."

"It isn't done, or it can't be done?" I clarify.

Bartie freezes in place, my question catching him unaware. "Both? Either? I have no idea, but it simply must not happen. If everyone knew that Oxford had magic, we'd all find ourselves torn apart and locked up in some laboratory being studied by scientists."

I lean forward, placing a hand on the armrest of Bartie's chair. "What if people didn't know that they were seeing magic?"

Bartie wipes a hand over his face. "I don't understand. You want to show them the magical elements, but don't want to tell them it's magic? How would that work?" He prods H to wake him from his impromptu nap. "H? Were you aware of this? How could you allow her to even ask such a question?"

"'Ear her out, mate." H yawns and rolls back over. "She kept me up 'alf the night jabberin' away. I thought she'd lost her marbles at first, but iffen you give her a few minutes, you'll come around."

Arching back in surprise, Bartie scrunches his brow, staring at H as though he's waiting for him to turn this whole conversation into a joke. When the silence stretches on, Bartie turns back towards me. "Somehow, I doubt that, but very well. Explain away, Ms Nat. The floor is yours."

Once again, I launch into my idea for the gala theme, revealing the secrets which will move it from merely interesting to leaving the gala attendees with a memory that will last a lifetime. Bartie's help will be critical if I want to pull this off.

I start with my conversation with Catherine Morgan and her tale about the former St Margaret scholars who thought they went back in time. I reassure him I don't want to recreate Versailles in our gardens, but instead want to organise an event where the attendees can see the history of St Margaret come to life.

Frowning, Bartie asks, "Why can't you hire actors to play the role of the historical figures?"

"I could, but no matter how good they are, no modern-day actor could ever compare with the authenticity of our Eternals. My idea hinges on the attendees believing wholeheartedly that they are speaking with the real people who walked these very college grounds years ago. They have to be able to ask any question they want and get a truthful answer."

Bartie is still unconvinced. "Surely we could write up some notes, you could brief the actors and actresses..."

I interrupt before he can go any further. "Bartie, the gala is two weeks away. Even if I could find an acting crew tomorrow, they still wouldn't have time to properly prepare. Have you forgotten who attends these events? Actual historians! If even one detail is wrong, it will undermine the entire event."

After a moment of silence, I pull out the last card I have hidden up my sleeve. "Bartie, if you won't do it for me, will you at least think about doing it for the magic of Oxford? You know that the magical field is out of alignment. Our connections are weakening. We need this gala, this ceremony, to be an incredible success." I lift my eyes, locking them with his. "This is our only hope. Our best hope. Don't kill it before you properly consider whether it could be done."

Bartie is the first to break our stare, standing from his chair. As he paces around the room, I can hear him mumbling under his breath, barely loud enough for me to make out the words. "I would never have imagined! I mean, we've never done it before, but there's no reason to think we couldn't. We'll need to talk to some others, perhaps Ms Morgan first given she was the original inspiration?"

Having decided, Bartie lifts his head and nods at the doorway. "Let's go, we don't have a moment to lose."

It isn't until we step into the Fellows Garden that we realise we're missing someone. Poor H nodded off during my discussion with Bartie, exhausted from the hours he spent brainstorming with me the night before. I go back inside, gathering a sleeping H into my arms, before following Bartie as we retrace our steps across the college grounds. When we reach the main building, I beg Bartie to stop so I can deposit H in the cat bed in my office. For a magical creature, he's awfully heavy.

Closing my office door with a soft click, Bartie and I navigate the main building hallways, following the signs for the entrance where Catherine Morgan's portrait hangs. As we grow near, Bartie calls Catherine's name, his ghostly voice booming down the hallway with excitement. Thank goodness no one else can hear him.

Catherine leans forward, stepping clear out of the painting when she sees our excited faces bearing down upon her. Shocked, I glance up at the canvas to see if it is empty, but her smiling face still gazes down upon me, although now much more lifeless and flatter than before.

Catching my eye, Catherine explains, "It requires a small amount of effort, but we can climb out of our paintings when we're suitably inclined. Our image remains behind whilst our spirits wander the hallways. Now, what has the two of you so excitable this morning?"

This time I let Bartie explain my idea, hoping that it will go down better coming from a fellow Eternal. Thankfully Catherine clues in to the necessity of such extreme measures and immediately gets on board with the plans.

"Like Bartie, I believe it could be done. You can run the idea past Dr Radcliffe, but we'll need to try it out in advance on someone unrelated to the magic, preferably someone here you can trust with a secret in case anything goes awry. Does anyone come to mind?" asks Catherine.

There's only one person who fits the bill here at St Margaret. Harry. Looks like my plans to dip and dodge her for a few days will need to be revised. But first, I need to get Dr Radcliffe's approval for my gala theme.

❖

Despite working again until the wee hours, I bounce out of bed in the morning before the sun is even up. After several cups of coffee and reviewing my notes, I'm ready and raring to go. I shower and get dressed in my most sedate black skirt and a black peplum top, not wanting anything about me to distract Dr Radcliffe's attention away from my gala plans.

H sneaks a peek in her office window, confirming that she's in and not in a meeting. I can't risk getting caught up chatting with Harry until I figure out what to say to her. But with her desk sitting between me and Dr Radcliffe's inner office door, I must be clever if I hope to get past her.

When H gives me the all clear sign, I quickstep down the hallway, arriving at the door to Dr Radcliffe's waiting area with a mountain of notes threatening to tumble out of my handbag. I don't dare pause for a breath. "Morning, Harry. Is Dr Radcliffe in?" I shove my notes back into place as I march into the waiting room, eyes focused on the inner office door.

Harry drops a letter onto her desk, my sudden arrival catching her by surprise. "Nat? What are you doing here so early... and how much coffee have you had?"

I can see Dr Radcliffe's door is slightly ajar, a sure sign that she is there and isn't in a meeting or on a call. "Five cups, I think. I lost count. I can see that she's there, don't get up, I'll see myself in."

I blast past Harry, leaving her sitting behind her desk with her mouth hanging open. I am in a hurry to make my big pitch, but I'm also doing my best to avoid having to give my friend the third degree.

The inner office door opens smoothly, a slight creaking noise alerting Dr Radcliffe to my presence. She looks up, a small smile crossing her face when she sees that it's me hovering in her doorway. "Morning, Dr Radcliffe. I hope you don't mind me popping in without an appointment, but I wanted to update you on my plans for the gala."

Setting her paperwork aside, Dr Radcliffe leans forward, waving me to come in. "That's quite all right, Natalie. Have a seat. I'm eager to hear how you're getting on."

After closing the office door, I pick a seat, choosing again to sit with my back to the portrait. Now I'm aware the man pictured is glaring down at me. Probably an old stuffed shirt like Edward who doesn't think I belong here.

Back straight in my seat, I shuffle through my notes, finding the page with the talking points I prepared for the meeting. Given the gala is only three weeks away, I've only got one chance to sell Dr Radcliffe on my plans. I'm not leaving anything to chance.

"Dr Radcliffe, I'd like to tell you a story about two women and their rather unusual trip to Versailles."

She seems perplexed when I tell the story, both intrigue and confusion flitting across her face in equal measure. However, as I explain the connection with St Margaret, segueing over to the gala and my vision for the event, Dr Radcliffe gradually eases back into her seat, an invisible stress falling off her shoulders as a smile grows on her face.

"... so you see, Dr Radcliffe, as soon as our guests walk into the main marquee, it will seem like they have accidentally fallen back in time."

Although her smile reassures me that she doesn't hate my gala idea, I wait to see if she thinks it is good enough to approve. She's lost in thought, her gaze unfocused as she no doubt tries to imagine how the final event might look. When she finally opens her mouth to speak, I catch my breath.

"My word, Natalie. I will admit to having been nervous when I spotted you noodling away in the library. I was concerned that you were at a loss for ideas. I can see now that you were simply researching a plan. A brilliant plan, I might add."

I release the breath I'd been holding. Thank goodness! Leaving nothing to chance, I ask for a final confirmation. "I take it you approve my proposed theme?"

Beaming, Dr Radcliffe replies, "Not only do I approve, I fully endorse it. I've never heard of anyone doing anything like it, and yet it is so quintessentially St Margaret that it seems near impossible it's been overlooked."

As the stress falls from my shoulders, it's all I can do not to collapse against my chair back. "I'm pleased you like it. I really want my first event here at Oxford to be a roaring success."

"If you can execute your vision, it will be."

Now that I've got the approval to proceed, I move on to the next item on my list. It's an unusual request, and I'm not sure whether Dr Radcliffe will agree. "I'd like to keep the theme a secret, not to be revealed until the guests arrive." I cross my fingers underneath my note paper.

Dr Radcliffe sits up in her seat, tilting her head to the side as she mulls over my request. "It is rather unorthodox; we will get questions from attendees curious about the dress code."

I'm prepared for this question. "We printed the dress code on the invitation - simple black tie - after all, it isn't the guests who will be the ones dressing up."

"No, I suppose you're right..." she mulls my request for another moment before nodding her agreement. "I believe Harry can handle any concerns, but have you thought this through, Natalie?" Her sharp gaze searches my face for any hint of uncertainty. "It will put even more pressure on you to make the gala a night to remember."

Holding strong, I raise my head high, confidence brimming on my face. "Don't worry, Dr Radcliffe. I have it all under control. Trust me when I say that every guest who attends will leave feeling that they had a truly magical experience."

We spend a few more minutes chatting about budgets and external support staff and my ongoing search for a replacement caterer. To distract her from any further questions about my lack of success finding a new chef, I tell her I've got a call booked with an acting agency.

"Will you need any help to audition the actors for the gala? I'm sure Harry would be happy to assist." Dr Radcliffe offers as I stand up to leave.

"No." The word slips out of my mouth. "I mean, no thanks, that is. I won't be auditioning people per se."

Her brow furrows. "How will you find actors for the roles we discussed if you don't hold auditions?"

I'm not holding auditions because all the "actors" are already here in the building. But I can't exactly explain that. Thankfully, I'd prepared an answer to this question.

"I know a group from my days in London. Kept in touch as I knew I might need them again. They're brilliant, can step into any role and you'd be convinced that they were the individuals themselves, brought back to life."

I make a quick goodbye and dart out the door before she can ask or suggest anything else.

I don't dare to hesitate as I make my way through the reception area. Thankfully, Harry is on a call when I step out of Dr Radcliffe's office. Harry uses her free hand to mime drinking a cup of coffee. I shake my head and hold up five fingers to remind her how many cups I've already had today. I mime the universal signal for 'I need a loo break' and wave goodbye before practically running out into the hallway.

Hopefully, in the next few hours I'll find the courage to put some serious questions to Harry.

❖

I invite Jill and Will, my trusty assistants, into my office to share the good news that we've got an approved gala theme. Once again, I start with the story of the two women and their fateful trip to Versailles, building up into an explanation of my vision for the Autumn Gala. Both Will and Jill are buzzing with excitement by the end, spending the next two hours discussing decorations, lighting, and menu ideas, glossing over the fact that we still don't have a caterer. Having promised to keep my plans a secret, my assistants rush out of my office, notes in hand, ready to take on their new assignments.

I double-check my own To Do list, initially pleased to see I've only got one big task left for the day. Unfortunately, it's the one I was trying to avoid. 'Talk to Harry' is in big letters, impossible to miss. I force myself up from my chair and out of my office door.

Why is it that when you want to avoid someone, they're around every corner you turn, but when you need to find someone, they're nowhere? I seem to be perpetually one step behind Harry. In every room I visit, there's someone saying, "She was just here. You just missed her." Just, just, just.

When my energy flags and my stomach growls, I put my search on hold and grab lunch in the dining hall. I stop by the gardens to call H, knowing that if I leave him behind, I'll never hear the end of it. Plus, I promised him some cheddar, a staple on the dining hall cheese board.

We walk into the dining hall; me moaning about how much my feet hurt. "I give up, H. I've walked every inch of the college grounds and I still can't find Harry."

"That 'Arry?" H points across the room.

Yes, that Harry. The missing woman is sitting alone at the end of one of the long student tables, sipping a cup of coffee and looking as though she hasn't a care in the world. Maybe she doesn't since she offed the one person who was standing between her and marital happiness. Or maybe she didn't do it, communing away with her clean conscience.

I rush through the serving line, grabbing a plate of the day's special. Harry spots me waiting to pay, waving me towards the empty seat across from her.

Beatrice, the cashier, is once again sitting at the pay counter. I thought Beatrice would be happy to be free of the brunt of Chef Smythe's anger, but she seems subdued. I chat with her as I wait for her to scan my ID card. "Hiya Beatrice, looks busier in here. I guess things are back to normal now."

Beatrice stares at me, eyes unblinking, before shaking herself back into the here and now. "Yeah, normal. Everything is normal, as though Chef Smythe never died." Her expression is glum, discouraging me from any further conversation.

They say you never can tell how grief will hit you. Maybe Beatrice was fonder of Chef Smythe than she realised. Or maybe she's upset over Claudia's departure at the end of last week. That makes more sense. I make a mental note to check in on her later.

As I set my tray and H's plate of cheese on the table, Harry's smile flips to a frown when she gets a close-up view of my dishevelled state. "Nat, dear, have a seat. You look positively haggard. Did you forget to go to sleep last night?"

"Thanks, Harry. I got caught up in party planning again and didn't go to bed until the wee hours."

Harry swipes a chip from my plate and dips it into my tomato ketchup. "What have you been doing all morning? I imagine you have your hands full now that Dr Radcliffe has signed off on the theme." She chews the chip, narrowing her eyes at me. "I expect you to tell me everything, as Dr Radcliffe refused to say even a peep. On you go, out with it. What are you up to, Nat?"

I know she means the gala plans, but all I can think about is her and Chef Smythe. Postponing this conversation will not make it any easier.

I duck my head down into my shoulders and whisper my question. I wasn't planning to hold the inquisition in front of a studio audience. "Did something happen between you and Chef Smythe?"

Harry's expression shifts from excitement to confusion. "Why on earth would you ask me that? I mean, I disliked the old biddy as much as the next person, but that's it. Anything else is ancient history."

Ancient history? That phrase reassures me that the situation might not be as bad as I thought. Nonetheless, I need to get it all out. I cough and stop for a sip of water. "I heard something the other day... something about Chef Smythe, you and Rob... a friend spotted you crying alone in the hallway one evening, a few days before Chef Smythe was killed."

"Oh no, someone saw that did they?" Harry's cheeks pink with embarrassment. "I'm so embarrassed. I don't know what got into me that night, making me break down in the college hallway. I was sure I was all alone."

I give her a soft smile of apology, allowing her to collect her thoughts.

She sits back in her chair. "Must be someone who's been here for a long while if they managed to connect up those dots. That is absolutely ancient history." Her eyebrows arch, waiting for me to tell who spoke with me.

I can't reveal that my source is the portrait in our hallway, so I wave off her question. "Yes, they've been here for ages, years really. I wouldn't want to embarrass them. They said that it was late, after a high table dinner, and you were muttering something about not being able to go through it all again. When Chef Smythe turned up dead, they, well, wondered if the two things might be connected. Maybe she was trying again to start up a tendre with Rob."

Sitting up straight, Harry leans over the table, her voice a harsh whisper. "I bloody would kill the woman if she tried something like that again. Nearly ruined my marriage and my life because of her own unfounded jealousy. Thankfully, Rob was oblivious to her efforts. He thought she was being nice. When she made an actual pass at him, he sent her packing. How he could stomach her in the first place, I'll never know. Guess he was only thinking about how good her food was."

Now I feel terrible. I've drudged up bad memories, practically accused my friend of murder, and I still haven't gotten to the bottom of why she was crying. In for a penny, in for a pound.

"I know I should mind my business," I start off.

"Do you know how to do that?" Harry interrupts.

"Ha. Yes, I do. I hate to ask now that I've aired your dirty laundry, but is everything okay?"

Thankfully Harry takes pity on my tired, stressed face. "Let's go grab a cup of fresh coffee and I'll tell you what happened."

I put my tray away, once again calling H back from Beatrice's arms. Together we follow Harry along the hallway. When she turns into the Senior Common Room, I grab her arm to stop her. "Maybe we should go somewhere else? I don't want to disturb anyone."

"Nonsense, dear. This room's relaxing environment is exactly what we need to brighten our moods back up. Not to mention it houses the best coffee machine in the college. Why wouldn't you want to go inside?"

I release her arm but remain frozen in the doorway. "Am I allowed? I know there are rules about which common rooms people can use, I don't want to intrude where I don't belong."

"My dear, you can go anywhere you want within St Margaret walls. You are the university's Head of Ceremonies. There is nowhere that you would be unwelcome."

Having said her piece, Harry leaves me to follow behind her, with little idea of how much I needed to hear those very words.

I wave her to sit, crossing the room and picking up two teacups and saucers from the serving tray. I push buttons until we each have a steaming latte, add a few biscuits to each plate and walk over to the armchairs Harry has claimed for our use. Thankfully, they are tucked into a little nook, providing a semblance of privacy in the open space.

Once I'm seated, Harry dunks a biscuit into her coffee before picking up our conversation where we left off in the dining hall. "It's all fine now, Nat. I was crying over Rob. Do you remember him mentioning his bad knee the other night?" I nod mechanically. "He had some tests done to see if the extra physio was working, but the early results didn't look good. I was concerned he'd need more surgeries and medicines, requiring me to take an extended leave of absence to care for him. Rob is a terrible patient, nursing him back to good health requires more sympathy and forgiveness than I can muster up. By day two I'm ready to feed him to the foxes that come into our garden."

She takes my hand and gives it a squeeze. "Poor you, Nat. All this stress and pressure associated with planning the gala, and then someone gives you reason to worry about me."

Harry passes me one of her biscuits and I take it gratefully. I need all the sugar-fuelled energy I can get today. "I'm sorry to have dredged up bad memories, but I am glad to hear that everything is okay now. I am feeling a lot better about the gala plans after meeting with Dr Radcliffe this morning. But I didn't have the nerve to tell her we're coming up dry in our search for another chef or caterer. I'm afraid we're out of luck unless someone identifies the murderer."

Harry nods sagely, "I must speak with Edward, get him to prod the Detective Inspector to speed up his interviews. That reminds me, I wonder if they've interviewed the veg man?"

I stop, biscuit halfway to my mouth. "The who?"

Sipping her latte, Harry explains, "The veg vendor. We try to source the bulk of our produce locally and we have a veg delivery service that brings us a daily delivery. That's why Chef Smythe was in the office on your first day. She'd had some run in with the veg vendor and emailed every chef in Oxford to let them know. The veg man was livid and complained to Dr Radcliffe, not that I can blame him."

"Hmmm, sounds like a promising avenue of investigation. It's good you remembered it."

"That it is. Now, speaking of mysteries, what's this gala theme you've got in your mind?"

Chapter Twelve

The prefect group normally meets up twice a month, but given our current predicament, we've increased the frequency. To balance out the stress, Mathilde and Kate put together a meeting schedule designed to take us to seemingly every pub and wine bar in Oxford.

Back in my flat after a long day of work, I stare down at H as I pull on my coat. "I can see you're comfortably ensconced on the sofa, so don't worry about it, I'll go on my own."

H's only response is a yawn.

"Any last-minute directions? Says the address is on Cowley Road?" I expect H to offer some advice, but he leaps off the sofa and does a perfect downward dog in front of me. "Does this mean you are coming? What did I say to convince you? Not that I'm saying no to a personal tour guide."

"Cowley Road? It's on the other side of the centre. You gotta take two buses. Even iffen you keep your loaf outta the clouds, you'll still struggle to find it. I'm comin' along with you to keep you outta trouble."

With H leading the way, I'm free to let my gaze wander as we take our first bus into the city centre. The university buildings and colleges lining the road are flooded with light, subtly inviting scholars to come in from the nighttime cold. We step off at the end of the line, close to the Bodleian Library - or at least that's what H says. Nothing looks familiar to me.

We slip down a narrow lane called Turl Street, walking past still more college entrances. The tiny shopfronts catch my eye as we pass, each one different from the next, yet somehow equally at home in Oxford. A hipster cafe shares a wall with a charity shop. Two windows advertise student discounts on their high-end wine and beer while the next sells souvenirs for both the University of Oxford and Hogwarts, in equal measure.

We emerge onto a high street, wide lanes separating one side from another. Bus stops line the pavement, tiny paper displays listing out the number and destination. I'm glad H is along, saving me from spending minutes trying to find the right one. People pack into the bus like sardines, but H uses two well-placed swipes with his claws to carve us out a space. By the time we get to the bar, I'm ready to pour my own pint. We're the first to arrive, so I send H over to reserve a table while I order drinks.

Standing at the bar, I wave my hand to attract the bartender's attention, scanning the taps to decide what I want. "What did H say he wanted again? Stout? Why does that sound familiar?" I wrack my brain but can't come up with anything. He's older than the legal limit. Who am I to refuse him a drink after he came all this way with me?

Kate and Mathilde soon join me at the bar and we all head towards the table with our drinks in hand.

As usual, I've come prepared with all the note-taking necessities. This time I skipped out on bringing multiples of everything, having recognised that I was the only one likely to write anything down. I flip open my notepad, tuck my pen behind my ear, take a sip of my ale and launch into my update.

"You'll be pleased to know that I've made significant headway in my gala planning and I can assure you both that it will be beyond all imagination."

"That's great news, Nat. What's the theme?" asks Kate.

"Top secret." I mime zipping my lips and throwing away the key.

Kate frowns at my unexpected response. "Top secret? Like Mission Impossible? Definitely an unusual choice, but..."

Shaking my head, I interrupt her before she goes any further with that thought. "Not mission impossible! No, I'm keeping the theme a secret from everyone outside of my Ceremonies team."

Mathilde eyes me over the top of her pint glass, "Fess up. How did you get it approved? I have to prepare a PowerPoint presentation just to get permission to swap out a single book in a display."

"Um, well I had to tell Dr Radcliffe most of it, but I've left out a few key details... like the fact that I'm planning to staff the event with Eternals."

"Eternals?!?!?!" both Kate and Mathilde gasp in perfect harmony.

I wave them to lower their voices. "Calm down, The Eternals at St Margaret have agreed with the plan. I'll put you two on the guest list so you can see for yourself."

Mathilde rubs her hands together with glee. "I've never been invited to a gala. I don't care what the date is or what else I might have planned. I'll be there. You don't even have to bribe me with the Eternals."

I smile at Mathilde; her excitement is contagious. "Excellent!" I put a tick next to one of my tasks, double-checking that I haven't missed any other news. "That seems to be it for me. Other than that, I have little else to say. All my Eternals are accounted for. They're working so hard on the event they haven't had time to look into anything else."

I flip the page over and write a new heading. "Mathilde, you were going to recall a book from each of the thirty-eight colleges, to see if they had any information or ideas on what is going wrong with the magic. I should have asked before, but how does that work exactly? Do the books talk to you? Can you ask them anything you want? I didn't think we had any texts about our magic."

"We don't have any texts about the magic, unfortunately. That would be a big help right now. I recalled an autobiography from each college library. Those are the only books that can speak. They've also got to have a photo of the person somewhere in the book, as that's what talks. Kinda like your portraits," explains Mathilde.

I think back on Catherine Morgan and Dr Thicke, chatting away from within their picture frames. "Oh! That makes sense. I've spent plenty of time in the St Margaret Library researching, but I hadn't consulted any autobiographies."

Mathilde pauses for another sip of her beer. "You can ask any of the rest of the books a question and if they have the information you seek inside of their cover, they'll flip open to the correct page."

Nodding, I reply, "Yes, that was exactly my experience. I was researching the history of the college. Being able to ask the books was much faster than digging through a bunch of indexes. Thanks for answering my question. Now, where were we? Oh yes, your talking autobiographies. Did you learn anything?"

"It isn't good news, I'm afraid," Mathilde reports.

"Are your books missing?" asks Kate.

"I almost wish they were."

Kate and I look at one another. What could be worse for a librarian than missing books?

Mathilde launches into her tale. "Most of my books reported back in, but one of them didn't. The one from Iffley College. At first, like you, I thought maybe the book had gone missing. I phoned up the college librarian, and he assured me it was right there on the shelf."

"What did you do?" I ask.

"I made an excuse and taxied over to the college to check for myself. He was right, it was sitting there on the shelf, in plain view."

Concerned, Kate interjects, "Did it say why it hadn't reported back in?"

"It didn't say anything. In fact, none of the books in the entire library said a word. They didn't move at all." Mathilde explained.

Kate's eyebrows climb to her hairline as she looks at Mathilde in confusion. "None of them? What does that mean?"

"I shoved three of them in my bag and practically ran the distance back to the Bodleian. When I brought them inside, for the first hour they sat there in silence on my desk."

"And then what happened?" I ask, completely enraptured in the story.

"One minute they were quiet and then the next they were gabbing on about deep sleep and missing memories. When I calmed them down again, they said that the last thing they could remember was being on the shelf at Iffley. After that, the next thing was my desk. In between that, nothing. The magic just disappeared."

With a crash, H sets down his empty pint glass, causing us all to jump. He'd been unusually quiet, and we'd forgotten he was there. "Iffley College? Whatcha mean there's no magic at Iffley? The magical field covers all the colleges. Iffley can't be left out. The magic can't disappear."

Mathilde shakes her head, "I can't say that I checked everything, but as far as I can tell the college has no access to the magical field."

"I'm gonna need another stout," H announces before folding his head into his hands.

"Me too," echoes Kate and heads up to the bar to place another order.

I look around the table, waiting for someone to share more

information. H is too busy blubbering into his hands to take note of me, and all of Mathilde's attention is focused on her pint glass. I rap on the table, jolting both H and Mathilde out of their deep thoughts. "Is there anything special about Iffley?" I haven't been here long enough to know where all 30-something colleges are located.

"It's not far from you," explains Kate, returning with another round. "Maybe 3, 4 blocks away from St Margaret."

"So Iffley has no magic at all, and St Margaret is showing signs of a weakening connection. Are there any other colleges around our area? Did you check them?" I look at Mathilde and hope she has some good news.

"There are two more in your part of town - LMH and Norham College both seem fine. I don't understand how Iffley could end up outside of the magical field. I hate to say it, but if we don't strengthen St Margaret's connection, you might lose the magic there. Your autumn gala should provide temporary help... it is a Ceremony. But no amount of parties will save us if we don't get to the bottom of the problem with the magic."

With that grim report, we all turn our attention to our pint glasses.

When I step out of the bar, the cool night air hitting my cheeks, I look at H and remember why the word 'stout' sounded so familiar.

It was in the postscript on Lillian's welcome letter, where she said I'd regret letting him have stout. She wasn't wrong about that. I think about bundling him into a taxi, but the greenish tinge to his scales makes me think some fresh air might be better.

Throwing out a hand, I block H's attempt to take flight. He's unsteady enough on his feet as it is, and I need to keep him close by.

Turning back, smoke leaking out of his nostrils, H makes his dissatisfaction known. "I dunno why you gotta make me walk, Nat. I'm fine, you see."

He'd be more believable if he didn't trip over his own tail. I walk in lockstep behind him, like a mother guiding an unsteady toddler. We barely make it through the crowd of students lining the pavement outside a popular nightclub. I call out sorry to the few who end up with singed ankles, wondering how the magic makes them accept that as normal behaviour from a cat.

Gradually, we make our way over the Magdalen Bridge and back into the centre of Oxford. H mutters along the way, his drunken accent impossible to understand. Every once in a while, he throws out a hand, mumbling incoherently at a statue or building.

I breathe a small sigh of relief when we make it to Broad Street. I recognise it from our trip to the bar; it is near the end of the bus line between St Margaret and the city centre. The road is closed to thru traffic, a large bollard preventing anyone from attempting to use it as a shortcut. The streetlights shine onto the stripe of bright yellow reflectors that circle the top of the post. H seems dazzled by them, careening off the pavement to wrap his arms around the bollard.

"Come on, H, we're nearly at the bus stop. It's only a few minutes ride from here." I spot a bus pulling up at our stop and grab H's arm to ensure he gets on board.

The driver doesn't raise an eyebrow when a cat follows me on board. He does, however, make me buy an adult and a child ticket. Shoving my wallet back into my bag, I move towards an empty row of seating in the back. The bus departs with a lurch, sending H tumbling down the aisleway until he comes to an abrupt stop against one of the metal poles.

Before I can help, I hear his wings flapping. My eyes widen in horror as I find him spinning around the shiny chrome pole in mid-air.

"Lookie 'ere, mate," his drunken voice calls out to me.

My efforts to reach H are once again hampered, this time by the bus grinding to a halt at a red light. His talons slip off the pole, tumbling head over heels through the air.

"Wheeeeeeeeeeee!" he caterwauls, jets of flame spurting from his nostrils. A display of bus route pamphlets disappears into ash and then reappear like magic.

Fortunately, one of his feet catches on the rubber straps, arresting his movement. Now he's dangling from the ceiling by an ankle.

I glance around, checking what the other passengers are making of the scene. An old man catches my eye. He raises a finger in H's direction, asking in a creaky voice, "Get a hold of your cat, you old cow."

My cheeks blaze in embarrassment as I try to stop H from using the rubber handholds as monkey bars. "He escaped out the garden gate, and now he's scared. Nothing to worry about though, I've got it all under control."

Except I don't have it under control, not at all. H's wings are slapping against my shoulders as I pry his talons loose. Our battle continues until I slip off my coat and wrap it around his body.

I gather my wriggling parcel into my arms, pushing my hair out of my face. The old man is glaring at me, distinctly unimpressed by my gallant efforts. He reaches up a gnarled finger, jamming down on the red call button. The bus slides to a stop at the next stop. His glare deepens as his gnarled finger turns in my direction, first pointing at my chest and then at the door.

Right. I've got the message. Drunken wyvern in arm, I step down off the bus as though it had always been my intention. We've made it exactly one stop along the line.

When H stops squirming around, I slow to a more sedate pace when I spot a free park bench ahead on the pavement. Shivering with cold and yet somehow also burning with anger, I loosen the coat flaps, rolling H out of my arms and onto the seat.

Whatever response H has prepared withers under my blistering gaze. He dusts himself off before tumbling to the ground.

"I'm fine. Lessss go," he mumbles. Let's go indeed.

We pass the cute side street that's home to G&D's ice cream parlour, the strings of overhead lights twinkling just as I imagined they would on the afternoon H and I enjoyed ice cream cones.

"Almost home, H. Just a little further... keep going. No, straight. Keep going straight, not turn. We don't live here. H!!!"

It's no use. H drunkenly stumbles off the pavement into a large front garden, shouting loud enough to wake the block. "Sid! Bruv, are you there? 'Elp a mate out!"

"Shhhhh, H. Leave poor Sid alone in his squirrel home, it's the middle of the night." I corral him again, nudging him to turn towards the pavement and our route home.

"I dun feel so good, Nat."

"What?" The word is barely out of my mouth before I click in on the meaning of his gibberish. I leap back, dodging a spray of flames. Rushing to stamp them out, I get too close to an unwell H and catch the edge of the sick that follows. Gross. Looking down at my shoes, it's safe to say I've learned my lesson about H and Stout the hard way.

By the time I unlock the front door to my building, I'm hoping feverishly that I don't run into Edward. I don't have a clue how I'd explain the wyvern vomit on my shoes. When I get into my flat, I exhale a giant sigh of relief.

"Easy does it, H. Lie down here on the nice, cool tile floor."

H slumps down on my bathroom floor while I run my shoes under the tap. I debate giving him a rubdown with a wet towel, but leave him be when I see his eyes are closed. Carrying on with my nightly rituals, I brush my teeth and hair, wash my face and pull on my nightclothes. As I'm about to switch off the lights, I hear H murmur my name.

"Nat? Will you remember me after I'm gone?"

I kneel next to his little body, stroking his scaly head as I reply, "Where are you going, H?"

"I'm gonna disappear. Poof. Gone. When the magic goes, I go." A giant tear leaks from his eye, sliding down his snout to disappear in a sizzle.

I settle myself more comfortably on the bathroom rug, sensing that this discussion will not be a quick one. There's no way I can go to bed with my favourite Eternal in such a state. "Oh H, you're not going to disappear! What made you even think such a thing?"

H is quiet for so long that I almost convince myself that he's passed out again.

"I 'eard you and them other missies natterin' on tonight. Iffley College. No magic left. Books not sayin' a word... Iffley's a few blocks from 'ere. I'll be next to go."

Reaching out, I tap his snout to make sure he's awake and paying attention. "Did you tune out the rest of our conversation? We're working as fast as we can to discover what's wrong with the magic. Other than the murder, everything seems fine here at St Margaret for the moment. The gala is only two weeks away. That will surely help reinforce our connection to the magical field. That's the whole point of it all, remember."

H belches and immediately grimaces. "Oh. The gala, I forgot about it. I stopped listening after a bit, lost in my pint glass. It's rare I get to enjoy a stout or two."

"More like a stout or five. I saw how many empties you left on the table."

"You don't need to kick a wyvern while 'e's down, Nat." He rubs his stomach, sending off alarm bells in my head, before burping up a small flame that almost lights the loo roll on fire.

I stroke his forehead again and try to breathe through my mouth, avoiding the smell coming off him. I really should have washed him when I had the chance.

"Listen up, H. I know I'm new here, and new to all of this magical stuff, but I don't think the magic is disappearing."

With a groan, H rolls over to face me. "What makes you say that, Nat?"

"Think about it, H. Mathilde told me that the magic is everywhere, but only Oxford and Cambridge have the right tools or set-up or whatever it is to see it. How could the magic disappear?"

For the first time in a long while, H perks back up. "By jeez, you may be right on that, Nat."

I mentally pat myself on the back, both for making H feel better and for saving the rest of my bathroom decor from the risk of flames. "Let's think about this logically. If there's no magic at Iffley, that must mean that something is wrong with the set-up, something is pulling the alignment way out of place. Could the magical field be sliding around, rather than disappearing? How could we check that?"

"I can tell you 'ow to check, missie. The magical field goes from Iffley College at the top, down to the Arboretum at the bottom." H crosses his eyes, struggling to recall the rest of the information before giving up. "I can't remember what the other two sides are, but if ten there's somethin' wrong at the top, the bottom is the next place to check."

"See, now we're talking. And planning. I need my notepad." I dart back into my bedroom and return with my trusty bedside pad. You never know when a great idea or urgent task will come to mind.

H is snoring when I kneel back down, I nudge him until he snorts back to consciousness, sitting up in a rush causing a black ring of smelly smoke to rise from his nostrils. "Where'd you go? What'd I miss?"

I gently lower him back to a safe position on the bathroom floor, patting his shoulder to keep him awake. "I went to get a notepad. Tell me about this arboretum."

"Eh? Oh ya, well, I ain't been there in ages, so lemme see. It's a giant park with woods. Full of peacocks. Nasty birds, strutting aroun' tryin' to peck my loaf off."

Raising an eyebrow, I ask, "Really? I've never seen a peacock get that aggressive. They're so beautiful to look at."

"Meh, they're all for show. Anyway, the Arboretum is south of the city. You'd need a car to go there, too far to take a taxi."

A big smile crosses my face. "We're in luck then, as Harry has offered me use of her car tomorrow. I'm planning for us to pay a little visit to our ex-veg vendor."

"Not we. No way I'm goin' to a farm or the arboretum. All this 'ere rain, I'll never get all the mud outta my cat fur."

Cat fur? I run my hand down his scaly back and along his tail, reassuring myself that my eyes aren't deceiving me. "I thought the cat fur wasn't real."

"You know what I mean. 'Ave a good time on your trip. I'll probably still be 'ere, lyin' in the floor, prayin' for my death when you get back."

On that note, I jot a few instructions onto my notepad and turn in for the night. H may have begged off, but I've got a busy day tomorrow.

Chapter Thirteen

W arm rays of sunshine light up the interior of Harry's car.
I get settled inside after finding the correct college
carpark. With spaces dotted around the entire perimeter, it was
no easy feat. I buckle myself in and double check my task list.
"Get car, check. Next up, buy wellies."

After a drunk H planted the seed in my mind, I woke up at
4am and added a new pair of wellington boots to my must have
list. He already ruined one set of shoes last night, and I can't
afford to sacrifice another pair so soon. After setting the address
in the sat nav, I turn up the radio and sing my way out of the
college grounds.

As I wait for my turn to cross the roundabout, I mull over the
background information Harry gave me on the veg vendor. The
Johnstons, a husband and wife team, own a small farm in the
surrounding countryside. According to Harry, they were reliable
vendors, always turning up on schedule with the order at the
ready. Neither she nor Dr Radcliffe was clear on what set off Chef
Smythe in the first place, both having their doubts that the
Johnstons might have been at fault. That was why Dr Radcliffe
had called the chef into her office. She hoped to resolve the

argument before it got any more explosive. Finding Chef Smythe's body had put an end to it instead.

As far as Harry knows, I'm on my way out to see if the Johnstons might return to the college. I didn't mention my plans to check for their alibis while doing so. This time around I'm taking a much subtler approach. I don't need to confront anyone; I can leave that to Edward and the police.

I spy one of the large chain supermarkets on the edge of town, stopping to raid their limited clothing section. Deep in the dark depths of the clearance rack, I spot a pair of Cotswold dog printed wellies in my size. Wellington boots are the one item of clothing where English women are encouraged to go wild, the bolder and brighter the print, the better. I always saw it as a personal challenge to see how crazy I could find them.

I circle through the aisles, restocking my kitchen before turning towards the checkout. One swipe of my bank card later and I'm the proud owner of a lush pair of wellies... so cute that I don't want to get them dirty. Hmm, maybe I should have thought this through. At least this pair of shoes is washable.

Back in the car, I follow the road through endless roundabouts before I see a sign for the farm in question. Bumping down a muddy track road, I say a silent prayer that I don't cross anyone coming from the opposite direction. I'll take London traffic over narrow back roads any day.

Three blind curves and one tractor trailer later, I finally turn into the drive. I park next to a shed, slip on my wellies and climb out. No one comes out to investigate my arrival, and with multiple sheds and barns spread across the property, I don't have a clue where to look.

"Might as well start with the closest one," I murmur to myself. Right as I give the door handle a gentle tug, a woman comes careening around the corner.

"Aha! I finally caught one of you. I've had enough of you kids sneaking in and stealing our tools. Whatever you've taken, you can set right back down again."

I turn around slowly. The woman in question is armed with a shovel and seems ready to use it, her blonde hair slipping free of a loose ponytail, her cheeks bright with anger. She appears to be in her mid-forties, stoutly built with enough muscle to hold up a shovel at length without her arms shaking like mine would. Her rugged trousers and mud-crusted wellies stand in stark contrast to my tight jeans and shiny new wellies. I raise my hands in the air so she can see the only tool I'm carrying is a moleskin notebook.

I pack as much soothing tone into my voice as possible. "I don't know what farm thieves typically look like, but I doubt they wear dog print wellies. I'm Nat, Natalie Payne, that is. From St Margaret College. I didn't mean to snoop around, but I couldn't see anyone."

She doesn't lower the shovel. Tough crowd.

"I'm not sure that St Margaret differs greatly from a group of thieves. Nearly ruined our business. Haven't you lot done enough already?" She raises the shovel up and I fear for my head. I thought Harry was exaggerating when she suggested the veg vendor might be a murderer. Now I'm worried I'm the next victim.

Trying to calm her down, I slowly work my way back towards the car in case I need to make a quick getaway. "I'm new at St Margaret, I heard from Harry about what Chef Smythe did and I wanted to come out and make my apologies on behalf of the college."

"New, you said?"

I nod my head in reassurance. "Brand new, so new that I discovered the chef's body on my first morning at work."

"Ah, you're that Natalie. Sorry about that." She finally lowers the shovel down and leans it against the wall of the nearby barn. "It feels like we've had nothing but grief coming out of there lately, I didn't have the energy to deal with anything else."

Relaxing my shoulders, I hold out my hand to her in a fresh attempt at an introduction. "Please call me Nat. I'm the new Head of Ceremonies for the University, temporarily at St Margaret as their gala is my first event."

She shakes my hand and returns the intro, "Karen Johnston. As you must know, I run a fruit and veg delivery service."

"Pleased to meet you, Mrs Johnston. I know it's unusual for the Head of Ceremonies to come chat you up, but given the circumstances, I'm having to take a hands-on approach to planning the catering for the gala."

She shakes her head in commiseration. "I've heard that they're struggling to find a replacement chef. You've got a right mess on your hands, haven't you dearie?"

"That I do, but I'm guessing you must be feeling relief rather than more stress." I cross my fingers behind my back and hope that she'll talk on the topic.

"That woman was pure evil, always out to ruin someone. We'd had a long run with no issues, so it was just our turn in the draw. Mr Johnston was livid, determined to march over there and let her know how he felt about her fake complaints and broadcast email. I sent him off to the pub with his mates and stayed here to take care of the kids. I didn't hear the news until the middle of the next day. Just as well he never made it there or else I imagine we'd be hearing from the police instead of you."

"How many kids do you have, Mrs Johnston?" Maybe they wouldn't have noticed if their mum slipped out to kill somebody.

"I've got four of them, youngest one only 4 and the oldest at uni. The little one was a surprise for us, nearly had one child out the door and along comes another one who is determined to never leave our bed."

So much for that theory. Time to wrap this visit up before my wellies get any muddier.

"I have little sway over the hiring of the new chef, but I can select which vendors we'll use for the gala. If it's okay, I'd like to put your company back on the list."

Mrs Johnston's face lights up. "We'd love that. St Margaret has a special place in our hearts."

Seeing her smile, I check if I can get anything else useful out of her. "While I'm here, you wouldn't happen to know of any chefs or caterers who might be free on the evening of the gala?"

Although I haven't made progress in finding the murderer, at least I secured fruit and vegetables for the gala. Now if only I could find someone willing to prepare them.

I've exhausted all the obvious suspects within the college. Could the culprit have been an outsider? As far as I know, the police haven't found evidence to show a break-in or failure in the security system. Surely one of the Eternals would have spotted a stranger walking the hallways. No, it must be someone we all know, but who?

My mind cycles through possibility after possibility as I let the sat nav tell me how to get to my next destination. The traffic queues provide plenty of time for me to come up with names and discard them just as quickly. Everyone seems to have had a reason to dislike Chef Smythe, but to kill her? Nothing obvious jumps out.

When I turn onto a smaller road, the speed limit drops to 20, causing me to sigh in relief. I wasn't looking forward to everyone sounding their horns at me while I look for the entrance to the Arboretum which the sat nav shows floating in the middle of a field. When I spot a large sign, a quick right turn under a wooden archway puts me on a paved drive. Before I can celebrate, I slam on the brakes. For a peacock. I can't say that H didn't warn me.

When my heart beats again, I navigate my way through the people and birds milling around the carpark until I nab a free space. I tromp back through the mud to the hut that is doubling as a welcome centre and pay the entrance fee. Map in hand, I'm ready to check the perimeter.

I gaze around, spotting a fence off in the distance. "Great, that doesn't look too far. I should have this wrapped up in no time."

I follow the path until I reach the fence line, which doesn't turn out to be the end of the Arboretum. "How big is this place?" I wonder aloud as I unfold the map. Skimming down, I find the information section. "Formerly 8 acres, the park has grown to encompass 130 acres outside of Oxford... 130 ACRES!"

It's time to call in reinforcements.

After fishing my mobile out of my bag, I scroll through my contacts until I track down the one I need. Our longest serving prefect is my only hope. It rings and rings, but Kate finally answers.

"Hi Nat. How's it going? Does H have a sore head today?"

"Hi Kate. Yes, poor H. Sore head doesn't begin to cover it. And as soon as he recovers, his pocketbook will be hurting. He owes me a pair of shoes."

"Blech! Don't take this the wrong way, but I'm glad Mathilde and I left when we did."

"Haha, yes, you're lucky you missed our walk home. But enough about that disaster. I need some help." I barely get the words out before a peacock screeches, startling me.

"Help? Where are you and why does it sound like someone is screaming behind you? Oh my, are you okay, Nat? Nat?"

I can hear Kate's voice calling out from my phone in my hand, but I'm too busy waving furiously, trying to frighten off an aggressive bird. When it literally turns tail and saunters off, I wipe the sweat from my forehead before lifting the phone to my ear. "Sorry, Kate, didn't mean to frighten you. I'm fine. That's not a woman screaming, it's a peacock."

"Peacock?" Confusion colours Kate's voice. "Seriously Nat, where are you?"

Leaning my back against the fence post, I position myself so I will get plenty of warning of any other approaching fowl. "H and I had a theory there might be something wrong with the magical border around the city. He said I should check out the southern end of town."

"Arboretum?"

"Got it in one. How'd you know?" I ask.

Laughing, Kate explains, "I went down there during my first month at Oxford. There's a kiln in the park, and we were hosting a visiting artist. I had to double-check that none of his creations were coming to life. I remember the peacocks all too well."

"Good to know that it isn't only me and H that the peacocks hate. Anyway, I'm here, I have the most spectacular new pair of wellies on and I'd rather not walk 130 acres in them if I don't have to. You wouldn't know whether the magical perimeter covers the whole park?"

"Hold on, let me check." The rattle of fingers tapping on keys echoes through the line. "I've got a map saved somewhere on my computer. Now what did I call the file?"

"Arboretum Map?" I ask helpfully.

"I wish," Kate laughs. "But we can't leave any information on the magic within easy reach. I had to bury it somewhere no one would think to look and name it something bland and uninteresting. Oh yes, here it is. Visitor statistics 20 May 2007. It's opening up."

How did she remember that file name? It definitely hit the mark she was aiming for.

After a few mouse clicks, Kate comes back with a response. "You're in luck. It looks like the magical perimeter only extends over the main research areas. If you follow the yellow path around, that should give you a good idea of where to check.

Anything well outside the yellow path shouldn't show any signs of magic."

I look over the map and say a silent thanks when I see that the yellow path is only a mile long.

"Thanks, Kate, you're a star. I'd better run, still got a mile to walk here and the peacocks are getting antsy."

I stow my phone back in my bag and make my way towards the trail indicators. The foliage really is incredible here, so much so I regret putting my phone away. I could get a cool new headshot for my Facebook profile.

The trees eventually open up to reveal a wide meadow. I haven't seen anything out of the ordinary, and I'm thinking our great idea might not have been as genius as it seemed last night. That's the problem with fuelling your planning with alcohol.

I've only walked about half the route when I hit the southern edge. "Might as well get that photo as proof of my efforts."

I put my phone into selfie mode and spin around, trying to find the perfect angle for the light. I was hoping to get the trees in, but my face is hidden in a deep shadow. Looks like it will have to be the meadow. Not very autumnal, but the grazing fluffy white sheep should save the photo from complete boredom.

I line up with the light and abandon trying to get my feet into the shot. My arms aren't that long, and I haven't reached the point of carrying a selfie-stick in my bag. Bright natural light, check. Chin up, check. Fluffy sheep in the distance, triple check.

"Think she will pay us for being in the photo, Vern?" asks a gruff male voice.

I take my finger off the button and look around in confusion. Other than the couple I passed in the picnic area, I haven't seen a human being in the last 10 minutes. If there's one here, I'm asking them to take the photo for me. Left, right, nope, no one? No one at all. "Hmm, I must have been imagining things."

I adopt my pose again and reach my thumb over towards the button.

Another male voice pipes up, this one slightly higher pitched. "C'mon Steve, you know they never pay. Chase us all over the bloody meadow trying to get the perfect shot and never say so much as a thank you before they go."

Meadow? Can it be? But the perimeter is behind me.

I abandon my selfie efforts and turn around to face the sheep.

"Excuse me, but your names wouldn't be Vern and Steve, would they?"

The two sheep open their mouth and I'm sure a loud bleat is about to come out.

"Who's asking?" says the sheep on the right in a familiar high-pitched male voice.

The other sheep tilts his head, rapping his horns against the other one. "She's asking, Steve. What are you talking about? You can see her right there, talking in our direction."

Oh god, it is the sheep.

"Hello Vern, Steve. I'm Nat. Nice to make your acquaintance."

The two sheep dip into a bow. Definitely something magical afoot.

Tucking my phone in my pocket, I brave the mud to get closer to the fence separating me from the meadow. "Have you two been talking for very long? Talking to humans, I mean."

Vern is quick with a reply, "It's the darnedest thing. We were gardeners over there at the Arboretum for most of our lives. We died together, a falling tree catching us unawares. Freak accident. We woke up in the Arboretum, it was as though we'd never left, except people couldn't see or hear us."

I dig in my handbag for my pen and notepad. "Ok, so you two are Eternals? That makes more sense. But then, if you were ghosts, how did you end up inside the sheep?"

Steve picks up the story, "One minute we were Eternals, gardening same as always, the next minute we were staring at the Arboretum from the other side of the fence. Only we weren't ghosts anymore. We were sheep."

Uh oh, that's not good news. I massage a hand cramp as I ponder over my next question. "Is it just the two of you who can chat?" I mentally cross my fingers and hope for something positive.

"Oh no, it's right bunch of us. Several other sheep here, plus three or four in the next meadow south. The one beyond it, too, if the gossip is right. As far as I can tell, it's several hundred years' worth of former gardeners from Oxford, finally able to set foot outside our former workplaces. We've started up a sheep network, sharing gossip all the way down into Berkshire."

I feel sick to my stomach and I don't think it's the aftereffects of last night's beer. It's time to make tracks so I can talk to H about this.

"Have either of you spotted anything else odd out here?" As though talking sheep isn't weird enough. But I've come here, I'd better make sure nothing else is amiss.

"That flower bed behind you needs weeding, but I guess that's to be expected with all us gardeners stuck in sheep bodies. Other than that, no."

"Thanks for your help. It was nice to meet you both. Enjoy the rest of your day."

Vern and Steve are still arguing with one another as I pivot towards the carpark. If any peacock comes between me and that car, it will definitely regret it. I was right about one thing. The magic isn't disappearing. It's leaking.

Chapter Fourteen

For the first time since I've arrived in Oxford, I pull a car into the drive in front of my flat. Harry reassured me I could leave her car anywhere on college grounds, and given the mountain of groceries in my boot, I aimed for as close to my front door as possible.

I drop my muddy wellies on the front steps and hope that no one tries to walk off with them. I know they were only a few quid, but what's the likelihood I'll find another pair of them on the clearance rack? Not happening. On second thought, I stash them in the bushes.

I kick open the front door, juggling shopping bags in my hands. "H, I'm home. Are you still alive?"

H is draped across the window seat, looking like a giant lizard as he absorbs sun rays with a damp cloth over his forehead. Other than flinching at my abrupt entrance, he shows no other signs of life. "Stop your shoutin', Nat. My loaf is slicin' itself into pieces as we speak."

Guess he isn't recovered from the hangover yet. This news ought to help. As I set my shopping bags onto the kitchen counter, I call out in a singsong voice. "Oh Aitchhhhhh, the magic isn't disappearinggggg."

H struggles back into a sitting position before pumping his wings to fly-lurch his way into the kitchen. He skids to a stop, barely avoiding landing in the sink. I watch in awe as he pops a couple of paracetamol into his mouth, chugging water straight from the tap. He looks up at me with hope in his bloodshot eyes and asks, "It's not? 'Ow d'you know?"

I pause my unpacking to look over at him. "You told me to check the border, so I did."

H gives up his effort to remain vertical, sliding down to lie across the kitchen counter. "What border?"

"The magical border. You know, the edge of how far the magic should be accessible? We had a whole conversation about this last night." Leaning carefully over H, I put my canned goods away in a cupboard. He doesn't show any signs of remembering our conversation, so I try again. "Do you remember any of what you said? You advised me to go to the Arboretum."

Shivering, H gets a pained look on his face. "I 'ate that place and all them screechy bird brains. Sound like somebody's dyin'. Sendin' you to check it out wasn't a 'alf bad idea. Drunk H is a pretty bright fellow." He tries to pat himself on the back of a wing but rolls over instead.

Nudging him back onto the safety of the counter, I grumble, "I nearly had a showdown with one of those peacocks while trying to get into the car. Pretended like it couldn't understand a word I was saying, but it moved quickly when I started weighing the idea of a peacock feather shawl."

"Iffen drunk H didn't warn you bout them birds, he shoulda. But back to the magic. What'd you find down there?"

"I found Vern and Steve." Sipping from my water glass, I wait to see if H knows the pair.

"Vern and Steve?" H scratches his chin in confusion. "I don't think I know a Vern or a Steve. Are they wispies? Old researchers or gardeners?"

"They used to be. Now they're sheep."

"Sheep? Baa baa sheep? 'Ow'd they end up as animals iffen they was already Eternals?"

"That's the million-pound question. One minute they were Eternal gardeners, weeding for all of eternity. The next minute they were chomping down on grass in a meadow."

I don't know whether it is the hangover or my story, but H seems to get more confused with every word I say. "Sheep? At the arboretum? But there ain't any sheep at the Arboretum. The peacocks won't share the space with another animal. Are you sure you were at the Arboretum? Did you see a sign?"

"I saw the signs, I bought an entrance ticket, I fought off the peacocks. I was definitely 100% in the right place. But that's my point, H. Vern and Steve weren't at the Arboretum. They were in a nearby meadow on the other side of the border. They weren't the only sheep in the field who could chat. They bragged about a sheep gossip network that stretches all the way to Berkshire."

H opens and closes his mouth a few times as he struggles to make sense of my words.

"But that's impossible! The magical field only works in Oxford and Cambridge. Everyone knows that. That's 'ow they set it up, and that's 'ow it's been for the last three 'undred and somethin' years."

"Not anymore, it's not. Now we've got sheep setting up a social network." Pushing off from the counter, I head towards the living room, calling out behind me, "While I bring the rest of the shopping in, can you see if you can get Kate and Mathilde on a call?"

I toss H my phone before going out the door.

I double-check the shrubbery as I bring my third and final load into the house. My wellies are still there. Hopefully they'll stay hidden until I finish up this call. I make myself a note as soon as I get into the flat, so I don't forget to retrieve them later.

H activates the speakerphone when I walk into the kitchen. "Alright, missies. All 'ere on the call. Over to Nat for an update."

"Good news, ladies. I've uncovered a clue to our magical problems."

"At the Arboretum?" asks Kate.

"What were you doing at the Arboretum?" interrupts Mathilde.

Maybe I'd better back up a step. I bring Mathilde up to speed on my late-night musings and subsequent trip to our southern border.

"I'm loathe to say it, but H had a great point, drunk or sober."

"Your welcome, Tildy. Anytime, Tildy. Nay need to thank me, Tildy." H's sarcastic tone overwhelms the phone line.

I give him a pat on the head, stopping myself when he winces. "All right, H. We all owe you some cheddar. Now, back to my findings. Kate, I found the yellow trail and followed it down to its southernmost point. It juts up against the edge of a lovely meadow that's home to a flock of sheep. Very talkative sheep, I might add. They hadn't been out to graze for too many weeks, but they were pleased as plum to explore the far side of the Arboretum walls."

Kate laughs at the thought of it. "I can't imagine what kinds of conversations sheep have with one another. But the better question is, why were you able to talk to them?"

"Their story wasn't dissimilar to H's. One day they were a pair of Eternals, the next they were staring out at the world through sheep's eyes. I chatted with them long enough to find out that the magic is leaking straight down past the county line. There are now Eternal sheep sunning themselves in Berkshire."

H and I sit in silence as we wait for Kate and Mathilde to respond. When a minute ticks by with no answer, I double check that the line hasn't dropped.

"Hello? Mathilde? Kate? Are you still there?"

"I'm still here, I'm trying to wrap my head around your last statement," clarifies Mathilde. "I'm positive that the magical field should not be reaching that far south, but I have no idea why it would be, or what we can do to fix it."

"On the bright side," Kate chimes in, "At least now we know that the magic isn't disappearing."

"No, but it is moving." I interject. "Iffley College sits at the northern-most point of the magical boundary, right?"

"Ya, that's the top," confirms H.

"Ok, after Iffley, the next college moving south is St Margaret. While we still have access to the magic here, it isn't working as it should. On the other end of the boundary, the Arboretum, the magic is reaching well beyond what we'd expect."

H looks thoughtful, but Kate speaks up first. "I see where you're going with this, Nat, and I think we can narrow our search into two areas, both having to do with the boundary. Either someone has stolen or damaged the artefacts at Iffley and St Margaret or someone has stretched the boundary on the other side of town. If they haven't extended the magical boundaries properly, they could cause damage at the top end without even realising it."

"What do we do next, Kate?" I ask.

"Let's start with the simplest possibility first. It's my turn to pay a visit to Iffley. As the Museum Curator, I'm best placed to identify if an artefact is damaged or missing."

With a new plan in place, we wrap up the call, promising to regroup soon.

After we hang up, I find my trusty post-it note underneath the last shopping bag. "H, I'm going back out front to rinse off my new wellies. Can you make sure the front door doesn't lock behind me?"

He nods his head and goes back to enjoying the plate of Lincolnshire poacher I set out for him.

I find a hose hanging on the side of the building and unwind it until it reaches the front garden. Turning my back to the road, I aim the spout so that any run-off will go into watering the front flower beds. No point wasting the water. My mind wanders off, replaying the events of the last twenty-four hours.

The sound of a male throat clearing cuts through my daze, causing me to swing around in surprise. Completely forgetting about the hose in my hand, I take a second to realise I'm drenching Edward's shoes in a spray of cold water.

"Oh, my goodness! Sorry, I didn't hear you coming. You startled me." I drop the hose, causing it to arc off the ground, covering both myself and Edward in another jet of water. Edward takes pity on me, walking around to turn off the water before I can do any further damage.

Wiping water from his trousers, Edward arches an eyebrow in my direction. "Must our every encounter result in a scene, Miss Payne?"

Water drips from my hair and my shirt, raining onto the surrounding ground. "If anything, Edward Thomas, I'd say that I came out worse in this battle. I am sorry I sprayed you with the hose. I didn't notice you driving into the carpark."

Edward has the good grace to blush. "I didn't drive, I was returning from a walk in Port Meadow. I should have realised you couldn't hear my footsteps over the water hose."

Edward and I stare at one another, the moment stretching into uncomfortable lengths as we each wait for the other to make the next move.

Finally, he clears his throat, succumbing to the awkward silence. "I've spent the day at the police station comparing notes with the investigative team. They've had the initial evidence analysis reports back, and the mud found on the doormat did not come from the college grounds."

Staring down at the mud around my feet, I wonder how they could tell. "Did the report suggest where it might have come from?"

"Unfortunately, they could not narrow it beyond the Cotswolds. The only reason they knew it wasn't from our grounds is because several years back, Harry's husband Rob had new topsoil brought in. He turfed most of the garden areas, including around the dining hall kitchen. Our garden soil is an unusual find here in Oxfordshire, and the mud on the doormat didn't match. Whoever turned up that morning and brushed their feet off before coming inside, came from outside our college walls."

I mull over this information, surprised that Edward was willing to share anything with me without a direct order from Dr Radcliffe. Out of the corner of my eye, I spot my new wellies, still crusted with mud from my morning adventures. "I don't think we can exclude everyone from the college a priori." I pick up my boots, waving them in the air. "Someone from within could have spent the day before out in the Cotswolds like I did. This clay is nearly impossible to get off without a scrub brush."

"A priori? You surprise me with your vocabulary, Miss Payne. Pray tell, what were you doing in the Cotswolds in..." Edwards steps in to get a closer look at my boots. "In dog printed wellington boots?"

"If you must know, I spent the morning meeting our ex-veg vendor. I had a lovely chat, in fact."

"Lovely? The veg vendor?" Edwards stares at me in confusion. "Our veg vendor?"

I look around to make sure I haven't stumbled into a different dimension. "Yes, the family which used to provide all the local fruit and veg for the dining hall. I met Mrs Johnston this morning. Bit of a rough intro. But once she realised I wasn't there to cause her more angst, she softened right up. She didn't seem too sorry about Chef Smythe's passing, but I can't say I blame her. She said she was home the whole night before caring for her children."

Edward's face hardens into stone, his gaze searing into me. "Home the whole night? Were you out questioning her? Checking her alibi? You mustn't meddle in police matters; you could cause more hassle than you know."

Rolling my eyes, I scoff at the notion. "I wasn't questioning her. We need a chef. I need vendors for the gala dinner. If she mentioned what she was doing the evening in question, that's hardly my fault."

Edward weighs up my response, unconvinced by my story but finding no further evidence to support his claim of meddling. "You didn't meet Mr Johnston, by any chance? Perhaps gather his alibi?"

I shake my head no. "Why do you ask?"

"I've had more than my fair share of encounters with Johnston. Blustery fellow, a right tosser, always shouting about at the local, creating arguments out of thin air. I have no notion why he comes into Oxford for his evening pint, perhaps he stops there on his way back home. He wouldn't be much missed if he took his patronage elsewhere."

"Really?" I raise my eyebrows and explain, "But Mrs Johnston was so lovely. You could see that she was genuinely broken up over the whole matter, from the fight with the chef to the abrupt end. She even remarked at how special St Margaret is to her family. She's certainly keen to come back in as a supplier."

"Be that as it may, the muddy doormat suggests someone came from beyond our walls. If it isn't them, then it must be someone else coming in from the Cotswolds. Perhaps a gardening service or the milk delivery boy? A proper investigation by trained professionals will no doubt get to the bottom of the matter in the next few days."

A few days? I can't wait that long, not with the gala time clock ticking louder and louder. Now that I've discovered a clue to the magic mystery, it's time to turn my full attention over to the search for the murderer.

Chapter Fifteen

I had promised Harry I'd return her car keys first thing in the morning. She'd gotten her husband Rob to pick her up after work and bring her in this morning, as we weren't sure how long my errands would take. I head straight to her office, betting I can convince her to sneak away for a quick coffee before we each get to work.

H trails along behind me, putting on a good show of recovery after his stout-fest and a day of rest. I'd think his coming along was a sign of true companionship, but I know he's only here this early hoping to get a sausage roll from the dining hall.

Knocking on the open doorway, I call out a greeting. "Morning, Harry. Are you up for a cheeky latte before we hit the grind?"

Harry is bent over her desk, shuffling furiously through a stack of papers, pencil gripped tightly between her teeth. It's the first time I've come in to find anything less than spotless perfection.

"Whfhaft?" Her muffled words remind her to remove the pencil before trying to say anything else. "Sorry about that, Nat. What were you saying? Something about sneaking?"

"Not sneaking, Harry. I asked if you wanted a cheeky latte... a quick trip to the senior commons room?"

Harry surveys her paper-covered desk, file folders peeking from beneath the chaos. She tries to push the mountain into some kind of order before blowing her hair out of her face, shoving back her chair and standing up. "I've been staring at these documents for the last hour, and I'm no clearer on what they mean than when I started. So yes, I think a cheeky latte is absolutely in order. Let's go."

I chatter away as we walk to the senior common room, telling Harry about my visit with Mrs Johnston at the farm. Once inside, I fill the silence while we wait for the espresso machine to prepare our lattes, describing my new wellies in great detail. It isn't until we're back in the hallway, coffee mugs in hand, that I realise that Harry has barely said a word. That is not like her, not at all.

"Can you spare a minute to stop by my office? I left your car keys in there." Harry nods a yes, failing to note that my handbag is hanging from my shoulder.

After unlocking the door and waving all three of us inside, I pull out the chairs at my meeting table and gesture for Harry to make herself comfortable. H jumps up onto my desk, his glare promising retribution if I don't wrap up my chat and get him over to the dining hall for a sausage roll.

I mouth, "Five minutes," to H, then settle into my guest chair at the table with Harry. As she wraps her hands around her mug and lifts it for a sip, I notice her fingers.

"Oh my, Harry! Your nails! What have you done to yourself? If you were this nervous about loaning the car out, you should have said something. I could have gotten a hire car instead."

"I wasn't nervous about the car, you ninny," Harry reassures me, but her grip tightens around the mug, a deep line creasing her forehead. She stares into her coffee mug for a second before raising her head and looking me dead in the eye. "I'm worried about the college. I think we've been cursed."

I nearly shoot latte out of my nose at her response, and even H stops breathing. I grab around for a napkin to wipe the coffee-induced tears from my eyes.

"Cursed?" I squeak out. "Weird choice of words, Harry. What makes you say that?"

Nothing in Harry's gaze suggests that this is a laughing matter. "You cannot tell anyone I shared this with you."

Shaking my head, I rush to assure her, "Of course not. Chatham House rules - what happens in this room, stays in this room."

Harry nods in approval. "Exactly. Although the murder investigation has rightly captured everyone's attention, it isn't the only crime going on."

"Wait, what?" I look up in confusion. "What other crime? Here at St Margaret?"

Pointing toward her office, Harry explains, "Dr Radcliffe had me pull together a report of recent complaints. That's what all of those papers and files were on my desk. As far as I can tell, petty crime is up 22% in the last few weeks. Students have complained of jimmied locks and stolen rucksacks. One candleholder is missing from the high table."

I glance at H, but he is as concerned as I am. "That isn't good, but a far cry from another major crime investigation. Maybe we've got a stolen keycard on the loose?"

"I wish it were that simple, Nat. But the incidents are spread all over the college and we immediately deactivate any lost keycards. It's almost like we've hit a run of bad luck. I can't find any other way to explain it."

I laugh nervously as I fumble around for a response. She isn't far off, but obviously I can't tell her that. "I'm sure the petty crime will sort itself out. A bad apple somewhere in the bunch; the security team will soon catch them. Look on the bright side, Harry. At least you haven't lost any other staff members. Or students, as far as I know."

Harry sets her mug down with a sharp clatter. "That's the other thing."

"What other thing?" I steel myself as I wait for the other shoe to drop.

Harry doesn't respond straight away, instead picking up her spoon and stirring her coffee absentmindedly. I'm ready to prod her when she speaks up. "The search for a replacement chef has stalled out."

"No good candidates?" I ask.

"No candidates at all, more like it. I can't explain it, we've never had trouble recruiting before. We're a highly reputable employer with a stellar reputation."

I nod my head in agreement. I hate to admit it, but I wish my contract was with the college instead of the university. Unlike Harry and Dr Radcliffe, my time at St Margaret is temporary. Soon after the gala, I'll be off to another college to help with a new event.

While I'm lost in thought, Harry carries on, "And yet we've had no one express an interest in taking leadership over our dining and catering facilities. I phoned several chefs who had previously reached out to see if we had an opening and every single one of them said no with no further explanation."

Harry waves her hands in front of my face, making sure I see every ragged nail. "Look at me, Nat. I'm a right mess. I spend all night tossing and turning wondering what we could have done to have deserved this, then I chew my fingernails off during the daylight hours, worried that the word will leak out to the wider public."

I sneak another glance at H, my eyebrows raised in a silent question. We can't let Harry go on worrying that this might somehow be her fault. Eyes wide, H gives a subtle shake, his eyes cautioning me from saying too much. My mind races looking for something, anything to reassure her an end to the problems is within sight. Finally, I land on a temporary solution.

"I ran into Edward yesterday evening. He seemed fairly confident that the police would have the matter wrapped up within the next week or two. I'm sure that as soon as they announce they've captured a suspect, life here at St Margaret will quickly return to normal."

Harry looks at me over the top of her coffee mug. "We don't have two weeks, Nat. If the police don't solve the crime within the next couple of days, we'll have no choice but to cancel the gala."

Harry's words keep running through my head long after she leaves. Cancel the gala? We can't afford to have that happen. The gala is critical to keeping the magic strong here at St Margaret. If it gets any weaker, a few petty crimes will be the least of Harry's worries.

The sound of H's talons shredding my paperwork reminds me of my earlier promise. "Do you want to go to the dining hall now?"

"For the first time in four 'undred years, I ain't 'ungry. I'm too worried about 'Arry to eat."

"I know exactly how you feel. Did you see the state of her fingernails? When she stood to leave, a ray of sunlight illuminated the bags under her eyes. I can't even think about the gala. Cancelling it? That would be devastating." I slump in my chair, depressed and overwhelmed.

Harry is right, Edward and the police inspectors aren't moving fast enough. If we're not careful, Chef Smythe's murder will end up in the cold case files. And then there's the rise in petty crimes. I can see both Harry and Dr Radcliffe will feel somehow at fault. If only there was some way to let them know that the problem is much bigger than the two of them, bigger than St Margaret.

My mouth moves, vocalising the thoughts spinning in my

brain. "Maybe it would help if they knew the gala was part of the solution rather than another casualty of the crime. But how could we... No, I guess we..." I trail off when I hit a dead end. H was very clear in our first conversation. I can't tell anyone about the magic.

But surely this must qualify as exceptional circumstances, right? Every rule has an exception if you're willing to look hard enough to find it. Nearly everything that has happened since I arrived in Oxford has fallen into the "this has never happened before" category.

I straighten in my chair, a feeling of hope giving me a newfound energy. "H, we need to tell Dr Radcliffe that Oxford has magic."

H opens his mouth, but a giant sneeze slips out, lighting half my gala notes on fire. Without thinking, I grab my coffee mug and splash the now cold brew on the flames. Between the coffee and H's frantic stomping, we put the fire out, but my notes are a complete loss. Good thing the magic will replace them.

Glaring, I snipe at H, "We need to find a better stress relief for you than sneezing jets of flames everywhere."

"Soz, Nat. Does it make it better iffen I say it was an accident?" Using his wing as a broom, H dusts a pile of ashes into the rubbish bin.

"Not really, but I'll let it go since we've got bigger problems on our hands. Where was I? Oh yeah, Dr Radcliffe. Can we tell her about the magic of Oxford?"

H gives a hesitant snuffle, causing me to leap out of my chair and wrap a hand around his snout. This time he swallows the sneeze instead of setting the room on fire. Only when he nods that it's safe do I let go.

"There's rules, Nat. We can't tell nobody. You know that, I told you myself."

Throwing my hands in the air, I spin around and begin pacing. "Forget the rules! We're in crisis mode here, H! We've got three brand new prefects and no human mentor. The magical field is out of alignment and we haven't got a clue why or how to fix it. And on top of that, we've got a murder to solve and a crime wave to stop. We're in over our heads here, and I don't see any other solution. We need help, H, right now, right here."

I can see H preparing to fire off another immediate no to my request. I throw up a hand, forcing him to stop. "Think about my request the same way you all considered my gala plans. What would it take to get a yes? No isn't an option."

H rocks back on his tail, his wings flared out to keep his body in balance. He stares up at the ceiling, then down at the floor, muttering to himself. I don't dare move, too afraid of disrupting his considerations. Finally, he mutters something unintelligible, nods his head and looks over at me.

"You're right, Nat. This ain't normal and we do need 'elp. 'Uman 'elp. But not Dr Radcliffe."

I try to contain my relief. "Ok, if not Dr Radcliffe, then who? And why not her? She's the college principal. You can't get any more senior than that here at St Margaret."

"College principals come and go, Nat. Iffen we're gonna tell somebody, it 'as to be a person as committed to Oxford as we are. Somebody who's been 'ere for years, knows everyone and everything. Someone whose whole life is Oxford." In unison, H and I both look around the room, searching until our eyes land on Harry's forgotten coffee mug, still sitting on my meeting table.

H flaps his wing, soaring from the desk to the table. He does a backflip before landing across from me. With a sharp talon, he raps against the side of the mug. "The old bag Lillian trusted 'Arry more'n anybody else 'ere. I reckon she's our best choice."

I grab my handbag, ready to rush out the door in search of Harry. H blasts a jet of smoke in my path, arresting my movements. "You can't run out and tell'er now, Nat. Think of the other Eternals! No, I need to talk to all of 'em first, get'em all on board with the plan. Then we can tell 'er."

I see his logic. "That's our plan, then. You track down all the Eternals and get their agreement. In the meantime, I will visit Dr Radcliffe. Edward Thomas and the police aren't moving fast enough. I think it's time for me to take a more active role in solving the murder."

I march down to Dr Radcliffe's office and straight through her outer door. Harry's desk is empty and the inner door to Dr Radcliffe's office is partially open. Most people would wait for Harry to return. Not me, not today. I stride forward, pushing open the inner office door.

Dr Radcliffe sits at her desk, her full attention focused on her computer monitor. She looks dishevelled. I wouldn't go so far as to say unkempt, but her blouse is mis-buttoned and her hair could use a quick brushing. She is so far removed from the flawless, confident woman who greeted me on my first day, I almost wouldn't recognise her.

I step towards her desk, waiting for her to pause her typing. However, when she spins in her chair, her gaze doesn't lift from the cluttered desk beside her. Mountains of files cover the surface, with abandoned coffee mugs dotted in between. She thumbs through the stack, carelessly tossing aside a paper-filled binder. With a quick lunge, I grab one of the coffee mugs before it goes tumbling off the desk, alerting Dr Radcliffe to my presence.

"Hello Natalie, I didn't hear you come in." She looks down at the mug in my hand. "Did Harry send you in with a fresh cup of coffee, by any chance?"

"Erm, not exactly." I point towards the mugs on her desk. "It looks like you've had a few cups already."

Dr Radcliffe seems oblivious to her disarray. I respect her too much to let her leave the office in her current state, so I give a gentle cough and then point towards the front of my blouse showing my neat row of buttons. Dr Radcliffe looks down, flushing in complete mortification.

"I don't know what's come over me, Natalie. Actually, that isn't true. I know exactly what my issue is. It's crime. And unfilled vacancies for critical roles. What I don't know is why this is happening. I've tried every solution I can think of, nothing is working."

After setting the mug in a safe position on the nearby coffee table, I slide into one of Dr Radcliffe's visitor chairs. "I'm sure it is a temporary blip. These things happen every day and everywhere."

"Not here, Natalie. We've never had so many incidents in such a short window of time. The only saving grace at the moment is that the situation appears to be worse at Iffley College. They've had three employees walk out without a word of explanation, and someone has stolen the founder's portrait from the dining hall. What would they even do with such a thing? I don't have a clue."

She quickly re-buttons her blouse and uses her reflection in her computer monitor to tidy her hair. The office is still in shambles, but at least she looks more like her normal powerhouse self. "I spoke with the Chief Inspector this morning, asking for an update on their investigation. He hemmed and hawed, but it was clear they don't have the first clue who killed Chef Smythe."

I lean in close, "What did you say to him? Are they still looking into the matter or have they given up?"

Dr Radcliffe flushes, pink rising from her neck to her cheeks. "Our exchange became heated. I made it clear that slowing the investigation was out of the question, promising I'd phone our MP if needed. Unfortunately, he replied in kind, threatening to hold interrogations for all of our students and staff if I didn't back off and let him do his job."

"Interrogating everyone here? That would be utter chaos." I don't have to fake the shiver that runs down my back.

"The absolute worst, Natalie. If they open up the suspect pool to over a thousand individuals, they might as well take out a front-page advert announcing that they don't have any idea who committed the crime. We'll lose more staff, students will stop applying, donations will slow. It will take us years to recover from such a situation."

I came in here hoping to convince Dr Radcliffe of the urgency of the situation, but it doesn't look like it will take much effort. Time to see if she will support my plan to seek out the culprit.

"Dr Radcliffe, maybe there is something I can do to help."

She arches her eyebrow, an invitation for me to continue.

"I bumped into Edward Thomas yesterday, outside our building. He mentioned the laboratory had identified traces of mud from the Cotswolds on the kitchen doormat."

Dr Radcliffe crosses her arms, "Yes, the Chief Inspector mentioned it on our call. But I don't see how you can help with that."

I shift up straighter in my seat, "I was out in the Cotswolds yesterday, where I met our veg vendor. Mrs Johnston? I went to see if they might know another chef we could contact about catering the gala dinner."

Pausing for a breath, I can see a spark of curiosity in Dr Radcliffe's eyes. "I was rinsing the mud off my wellies when I ran into Edward. He seemed fairly convinced that Mrs Johnston's husband would be a good candidate as a suspect in the murder. I pushed him to contact the police, but he didn't seem to be in any rush to do so."

Dr Radcliffe huffs, "No one is in a rush. I doubt Edward spoke with the Inspector. He didn't mention the Johnstons at all. I can't believe I didn't think of him myself. It's a testament to how crazy things have been here that I forgot about Mr Johnston and his complaints about Chef Smythe completely."

Good, I've got her intrigued. Time to move to the next step. "I know it's unusual, but I managed to bond with Mrs Johnston yesterday. I could go out there, maybe speak with her husband this time..."

"No, Natalie, absolutely not. If Mr Johnston is a suspect, it's too dangerous for you to go out there on your own. I'll phone Edward, he can go. He's probably more qualified than the police, anyway."

Send Edward? That won't do. He's much too lackadaisical about the matter, not to mention his people skills are lacking. I need to act fast; Dr Radcliffe is reaching for the phone. "What if I went along with him?"

"What? Why would you go out there again?" She's not convinced, but at least she's stopped dialling.

"The Johnston's have had rough treatment from St Margaret of late, the only way I got Mrs Johnston to come around was by telling her I'm a new hire. Edward isn't exactly a people-person, if you know what I mean. On his own, he's more likely to get run off the land than invited in for a cuppa."

Dr Radcliffe's eyes dart left and right as she weighs up my request. I make one last push to get her to say yes.

"If Harry can spare her car for another few hours, we can head out now to see what information we can find. I've still got the keys." I dig them out of my handbag, waving them in the air.

"I'm sure she can spare her car, and yes, time is of the essence here. This is rather unorthodox..." Dr Radcliffe wavers.

"We don't have to confront Mr Johnston. We can ask two or three questions, find out where he was on the morning in question. All we need is information we can pass over to the police to verify. Unless you can think of anyone else from the Cotswolds who was angry with Chef Smythe?"

Shaking her head, Dr Radcliffe decides. "No, there was no one else recently. But you must go with Edward and not on your own, do you understand? No confrontations, only a polite chat. I'm counting on you to keep you both safe."

I wrap my hands together in front of my chest, "I promise, Dr

Radcliffe. It will be a quick trip there and back. We'll report in as soon as we return."

Dr Radcliffe's lips are set in a determined line as she hits the button to reawaken the phone before dialling Edward once again. "Hmm, he doesn't answer, but that doesn't mean that he isn't there in his office. You'll have to walk down and get him, I'm afraid. Knock fervently if needed. I insist you wait for him, Natalie. You are not to rush out of here to confront a potentially violent suspect on your own. If Edward gives you any grief, tell him to ring me straightaway."

Chapter Sixteen

I check the Senior Common Room and the dining hall first. I had hoped to find him in a public space, which might decrease the likelihood of him arguing with me about the trip to the Cotswolds. Instead, I only find H with his head buried into the middle of a sausage bap. It looks and smells tempting, but I'm in a hurry. We exchange waves and thumbs up, each of us focused on our assignments.

I consult the directory near the entrance to the main hall, finger trailing down the list of names until I reach 'Thomas, Edward - CC24'. Edward would have one of the prized offices in the brand-new conference centre, reserved for distinguished fellows and rising stars. Looks like Harry wasn't kidding when she said they had to woo him into accepting the position at St Margaret. Prime office space must have been part of the deal.

I tromp through the gardens, past the student housing and my flat. Spying the gate to the Fellows Garden, I carry on towards the modern conference building nearby. Once inside, I follow the signs up the stairs until I reach his office number. There's a young woman sitting crisscross on the floor, her back leaning against his door and her head buried in a textbook.

"He's not in. Popped out for a coffee. You'll have to wait," she says without looking up from her textbook.

I glance over, surprised she noticed my arrival. "That's weird. I didn't see him in the dining hall, common room or at the coffee machine on the ground floor. How long has he been gone?"

Again, she replies without acknowledging my existence. "Dunno, been here about..." she looks at her phone, "about an hour or so, I guess? There was a sign on the door when I got here, and he didn't answer when I tried knocking."

"An hour? For a coffee? Something's fishy. Slide over."

She slips over out of the doorway, allowing me unfettered access to the closed door. What was it Dr Radcliffe said? Oh yes, to knock fervently. If he wants fervent, he'll get it. I fold my fingers into a fist, pull back, and then unleash a knock that would have surpassed the Incredible Hulk.

I don't hear a response, but at least the student has finally deigned to look up at me. "Wow," she says and looks impressed.

Raising my voice, I call out a warning. "Edward Thomas, it's Natalie Payne. I know you're in there. I'll stand here and knock all day if I need to."

To prove my point, I unleash another round of furious bangs. I'm rewarded with the sound of a chair scratching across the floor and the click clack of footsteps across the tile. Edward wrenches the door open, his displeasure with my antics painted all across his face. His eyebrows are angry dashes on his forehead. I take a mental picture so I can describe the scene to H later.

I counter his expression with a beaming smile. "Oh hello, Edward Thomas. Fancy finding you here when you're supposed to be out for a coffee."

Edward swipes the sign off his door and crumples it up in his hand.

"Did you need something, Ms Payne? As you can see, I'm very busy and there are other individuals waiting for a moment of my time."

The student looks around to see who else is waiting and seems genuinely surprised when she realises he meant her.

"It's a private matter, Edward. May I step into your office?" No need for me to discuss a murder in front of his student, even if she is studying criminology.

"If you must," he steps back and waves me towards one of the empty visitor chairs.

I close the door behind me but stay on my feet. The sooner I can get this over with and we can put this trip behind us, the better. "I met with Dr Radcliffe this morning, at her request, and she has insisted that you accompany me along to the veg vendor."

"Really?" He doesn't seem convinced, his voice dripping with doubt.

"Yes, it was her specific instruction. She had words with the Chief Inspector this morning and she's concerned that he isn't focusing enough attention on finding Chef Smythe's killer. When I mentioned our chat about the Johnstons yesterday, she agreed it was worth a quick trip to speak with them."

Leaning back in his chair, Edward admits, "I agree that Mr Johnston merits a visit, but why on earth would Dr Radcliffe suggest you and I go. This is a police matter, hardly an afternoon jaunt."

I'm glad I chose to stand. Sliding over, I position myself between Edward and the door. He's not getting out of here without me. "The police aren't moving quickly. Dr Radcliffe is in agreement that the murderer must be identified as soon as possible. I'm the only person associated with the college who has had a friendly conversation with either of the Johnstons. Dr Radcliffe insists that we accomplish this task together and provide a formal report after the event."

Edward's eyebrows raise in question. "What exactly is this task she expects us to accomplish? I'm hardly going to question a suspect with our party planner along beside me. And certainly not in his farm's carpark."

"She doesn't expect us to put him under a spotlight or pull his fingernails out until he confesses. She asked that we have a short chat with him, get details on his whereabouts so the police can do their job and look into the veracity of his statements. That's it. She'd send you on your own, but, well, don't take this wrong, but you're intimidating. We both thought you'd have more luck with me along."

I can see him wavering. Pointing towards his desk phone, I say, "She tried to call you, check your missed calls. You can ring her back if you don't believe me." The flashing red 'missed call' light echos the truth in my statement. With no other choice but to comply, Edward rises from his chair, grabbing his coat on his way out.

I step out first, clearing the path. He locks his office door and turns back down the hallway without saying another word.

"Um, Edward, aren't you forgetting someone?" I motion over my shoulder to indicate the student still seated on the floor.

"She's well aware that office hours are not until later this afternoon. She was trying her luck, hoping I'd take pity on her. I'm sure she'll be there when I return."

Harsh but true. And exactly why Dr Radcliffe isn't sending Edward on his own. I don't think he even realises how his statements are received by others.

We retrace my steps towards the main building, stopping at my office to pick up my coat and sticking our head in Harry's doorway to let her know where we're headed. As we approach the main doors, the smells of the dining hall drift under my nose.

"Sorry, Edward, we need to make a quick side trip."

"Another one? I thought this matter was urgent, Ms Payne."

"It is, but so is the grumbling in my stomach. A quick bacon bap from the dining hall ought to do it."

The serving windows are closed as we walk in, but I am not to be deterred. I'm sure there are leftovers. I stick my head into the kitchen area to find a madhouse rather than a kitchen crew.

I grab a prep chef and quickly beg for the last bacon bap. Before he goes off to find one, I ask what is going on.

He waves me to follow him into the kitchen, chatting over his shoulder. "It's the new fruit and veg vendor. They're completely unreliable, turning up late, short on produce or not showing up at all."

Oh good, for once a problem I can solve. "I've got some good news. I spoke with Mrs Johnston yesterday. She's happy to reopen our account if we'd like."

The prep chef considers my offer as he spreads brown sauce on my bap before wrapping it in wax paper. "It's a good thought. However, the last time Mr Johnston was here, he shouted the rafters down and said that he'd make Chef Smythe pay for what she'd done. Reliable or not, that behaviour is hard to overlook when she turned up dead a few days later. It's unfortunate, as they are the best in the area."

I raise my eyebrows at Edward as the prep chef passes me a wax-wrapped package before we make our escape. Mr Johnston sounds better and better as our primary suspect.

As we pull out of the college carpark, I can't help but think back on my trip yesterday. That's when it hits me. "Oh no, I forgot my wellies back at home."

"Thank you, dear Lord, for these small favours." Edward bows his head in mock prayer.

Avoiding further conversation, I turn the radio on. This is probably the first time anyone has exposed Edward to pop radio. Perhaps a few tunes will move his mood from sarcastic to sincere.

He reaches over and changes the station. Operatic tones overtake the space in ways that pop singers could only dream. Any other day, I'd enjoy hearing something more soothing and melodic. Not today. I use the button on the steering wheel to discretely change it back.

He changes it again.

I roll down his window. As he rolls it back up, I change the station to pop radio again. I have far more buttons at my disposal and he'd do well to remember that.

He turns the volume down, opens his mouth as if to start a conversation, then closes it and turns the volume back up. Finally, he's caught on.

We complete the ride in silence, although there are a few rough moments when a tractor practically sideswipes me on the single-track road. And when that cow comes out of nowhere. I pull into the now familiar drive, nearly running down a burly man who is trying to sweep it clear.

I throw the car into park before leaping out to reassure myself that he is okay.

"Sir, I'm so sorry, are you all right? I didn't see you until the last second." The man is even larger than he appeared from the car, his thighs and biceps straining his clothing. His bushy beard and eyebrows offset cheeks and eyes practically glowing with anger. This must be Mr Johnston. We're already on the wrong foot.

"Ms Payne, wait," Edward calls from behind me as he struggles to untangle the seatbelt and climb out of the car. All he does is call Mr Johnston's attention to himself.

Mr Johnston raises his fist, finger pointing towards the passenger door of our car. "You! You're that professor from St Margaret. Edmund, something?"

"It's Edward, actually..." Edward interrupts, finally standing up.

Brandishing his broom, Mr Johnston's voice booms across the car park. "I don't care what your name is. I've seen you lording around the college grounds, too good to acknowledge the help. You people are all the same. Stuffed shirts, noses stuck into the air. You couldn't care less what happens to little people like my family. You all sat back and let that bloody woman chef ruin us, our lives, and our business. Now you come here to my home and try to run me over. Get out of here!"

Oh great, this is exactly the scene I promised Dr Radcliffe we'd avoid. I look at Edward, hoping he's about to launch into a very apologetic speech which will bring Mr Johnston's temper down from the stratosphere. As I catch sight of his face, I'm reminded why I'm along for the ride. Anger colours his cheeks and I can see his finger rising into the air, prepared to let Mr Johnston have it right back again.

My mind goes blank, my eyes leaping frantically around the farm, desperate for an idea. I weigh and discard options in an instant. Tractor - too far away. Hay bale - too heavy. A lone rooster crows in the distance. Insane, but it is the first thing I see that might work as both a distraction and a tension reliever.

With no further hesitation, I leap in between the two men, pointing towards the chicken. "Did that bird just lay an egg? Unbelievable, I've never seen one do that outside a henhouse!"

Mr Johnston pauses, confusion crossing his brow as he follows the direction of my finger. "An egg? That's a rooster."

Before I can say anything else, Mrs Johnston rounds the corner of the barn, coming to a halt at the scene in front of her.

Edward looming. Me, finger pointed at a chicken. And her husband, with broom raised to clobber us both.

"Derek, what on earth? What are you doing to Ms Payne? And who is that behind her?"

Mr Johnston lowers his arm and looks at his wife in disbelief. "You know this woman?"

Mrs Johnston nods. "She's the one I told you about. She came by yesterday, introduced herself and offered us a pathway back into supplying the college."

Lowering the broom, Mr Johnston wipes a hand across the

back of his neck. "I'm sorry about that, all the blustering on at you."

Mrs Johnston comes over and wraps an arm around her husband's waist. He doesn't seem so scary now that I can see she has a firm hold on him. "You'll have to forgive my husband, Ms Payne. He's quick to fly off the handle, but he's a gentle old soul at heart."

With his temper gone, I can see a bright twinkle in his eyes and a ruddy cheer in his cheeks. If you put a red hat and suit on him and dyed his beard white, he'd be a dead ringer for St Nick.

Smiling apologetically, Mr Johnston passes the broom over to his wife before reaching out a hand. "My family is my weak spot. Ms Payne, was it? I'm Derek, Derek Johnston."

I accept his offer to shake, grimacing as his hand threatens to crush my own. Edward stays firmly behind me.

Mr Johnston wraps his arm around his wife, smiling at her. "We've worked so hard to build up this life, so we can be able to afford to give our children every opportunity in the world. I get my back up at the mere thought of someone trying to take it all away from us. I'd do anything for her and for those kids of mine."

Relieved that we've got past the initial tension, I reassure him, "I can understand that, Mr Johnston. No harm done. I'm sure it didn't help that I startled you with my arrival."

Edward harrumphs, causing me to motion behind my back for him to keep quiet.

"Our kids worship the ground he walks on," says Mrs Johnston. "The eldest less so now that she is at uni. She's too grown up to admit she still loves her old da. She's a chip right off the old block, you need the patience of a saint to put up with her."

Mr Johnston chuckles, "Come now, dear, she's not so bad. She's got a slower burning temper than I do. If I time it right, I can usually calm her down before she reaches the point of exploding." He looks at Edward and I, "But enough about us, what brings you two back out here again?"

Oops. Instead of fighting over the radio, Edward and I should have been planning our strategy in advance. Too late now, no option but to muster on as best as we can.

"As you know, I had a lovely chat with your wife yesterday about local chefs and the possibility of you returning to St Margaret as a supplier. I was updating Dr Radcliffe this morning, and she wanted to make sure you were both comfortable with the planned return, given how unhappy you were when you last spoke with her." I point at Edward, continuing, "Edward walked through and overheard the end of our conversation. He offered to ride over with me."

Edward steps up to my side, looking at me for confirmation that he should speak. I nod in encouragement.

"I felt, out of respect for the college's long relationship with your family, that it would be best for all if I came out here and spoke with you directly. We'd like for you to return as a supplier, but I believe the inspectors have some questions about your last visit to the college. I thought it best to come myself rather than leaving it to the police. As you've pointed out, you've suffered enough already."

Mr Johnston eyes Edward, mistrust once again appearing in his gaze. "Why would they take your word for it?"

"I apologise, I failed to introduce myself properly. I'm Dr Edward Thomas, a senior fellow at St Margaret and Professor of Criminology and Behavioural Analysis at Oxford. I have a longstanding relationship with the lead investigator, there's no doubt that he'd accept my word as sufficient."

Mrs Johnston gently nudges her husband forward. "I imagine they want to know where you were the other night. Tell them, hun. We've got nothing to hide."

Mr Johnston scuffs his feet, "My wife was here the whole night. She sent me off to the pub to blow off some steam. Our eldest had come home for the evening and she and I were butting heads at every turn."

I ask the next question, keeping Edward's role to a minimum. "What time did you return home, Mr Johnston?"

Looking over at his wife, Mr Johnston estimates, "Must have been close to midnight. I don't normally stay out so late, but I wanted to make sure they'd all be in bed. Thought that was the best way to avoid any further arguments. The pub manager should be able to confirm my departure time. Martin at the Red Lion, up at the roundabout. I was at home until I went to work the next morning."

Excellent, Edward and I have accomplished our task. Now we can pass it over to the inspectors to check his statement. If he's telling the truth, there's no reason to keep them away from the college. If he's not, as long as they are supplying our fruit and veg, we'll know where to find them.

Decision made, I flash a smile at Mr and Mrs Johnston. "We've got that sorted. While we're here, might I make one small suggestion?"

"Certainly you can," replies Mrs Johnston.

"They're having a right time of it trying to find a reliable replacement for your services. If you go over there with a ready delivery, I suspect they'll welcome you back with open arms."

"That's great, Ms Payne. We'll do just that." Mrs Johnston looks over at her husband for confirmation. At his nod, she says, "If there's nothing else you need, we had better get to work preparing that order."

As soon as we're seated in the car, Edward starts in. "Are ornithology lessons not part of the Event Planning degree programme, Ms Payne?"

I knew I'd regret pulling that chicken stunt, but it was better than the alternative. I couldn't imagine having to explain to Dr Radcliffe why Edward had a blackened eye and scraped knuckles. "I had to save you from a round of fisticuffs. Anyway, could you at least let me get out of the carpark before you make fun of me?"

Holding up his hands, Edward says, "Apologies, I would not want to stress you out. You might imagine I lay an egg next."

Grrr. I count to ten as I turn the car around and point it towards the exit. By the time I reach the exit onto the road, I am calm. I will not be baited by the man sitting next to me.

I slam on the gas and fishtail onto the gravelled road, barely missing a passing Mini. Edward grabs a hold of the bar above his window and hangs on for dear life. I look over at him, and an actual snort comes out of my nose. Now I really do feel better.

I slow the car to a more sedate pace as we continue our journey through the Oxfordshire countryside. It really is beautiful out here; the cooling temps have done little to erase the patchwork quilt design of interwoven fields and meadows. I lower my window down to allow a cool breeze to caress my face and turn the radio up when my favourite song comes on. This is the life.

I blank out the existence of the left side of the vehicle. I hum merrily along as I navigate my way from one single track road to another. Everything is blissful and calm.

<KTHUNK>

Edward turns down the radio, glaring in my direction. "I believe we have a flat tyre. Might you want to endeavour to find a safe place to pull to the side?"

Does he always have to sound so condescending? I swerve across both lanes and come to a screeching halt halfway into a ditch. "Is this what you had in mind, Dr Edward Thomas?"

Looking somewhat stunned by my manoeuvres, he fends off further argument. "I think it's best for both of us if I keep my thoughts to myself. Shall I check the glove box to see if Harry has a roadside recovery policy?"

I look at him in disbelief. It's a simple flat tyre, and I spotted a spare in the boot when I was loading my shopping yesterday. "No need to phone in help, I'm perfectly capable of changing a tyre."

I unlock my seatbelt, open my door, and nearly tumble down into the ditch. I wedge my foot into the sideboard at the last minute and avoid another embarrassing moment. "I wouldn't want you to get your cardigan dirty. I'll take care of everything."

Edward's glare sharpens as he waves me on my way. "I bow to your superior skill set, Ms Payne. Carry on, shout if you need anything."

I march around to the boot, digging into its depths until I find everything I need. No surprise that Harry is fully prepared for any hazard. There are the caution signs, a yellow Hi Viz vest, jumper cables and a tyre change set. I wedge the jack near the back flat tyre and hope that the car doesn't tumble further into the ditch when I lift it up. Abandoning any hopes of remaining clean, I ignore the mud and dust clinging to my shoes, tights and skirt. As I work, I wipe sweat from my brow before remembering how dirty my hands are.

"Everything ok back there?" Edward shouts over his shoulder, having taken up position leaning against the hood of the car. His head is buried in his phone.

"Fine," I grunt as I struggle to get the last nut off the tyre. It still refuses to budge.

Typing away on his phone, Edward makes another offer to help. "It sounds as though you are struggling somewhat. Are you sure you couldn't use a hand? Wait a moment, while I put my phone and cardigan in the car."

As I stand up to put my whole body into a last-ditch effort to get this nut unstuck, I hear two things. The first is the sound of a rapidly approaching vehicle coming up behind me. The second is the squeak of a car door opening. Edward's door, to be specific.

"Watch out, Edward!" I shout, but my warning gets lost in the roaring wind as a mid-sized lorry passes inches from the edge of the door, narrowly missing Edward. The wind whips away my sweat, throws the door wide open and sucks all the papers I'd carefully piled onto the dashboard straight out of the car. I watch in horror as papers sweep past Edward, the currents carrying them left and right, up and down, spreading them over several meters of road and off into the neighbouring field.

My mouth opens and a demon's voice comes out, "OH MY GOD, MY WORK. GET MY WORK."

Edward's jaw hangs unhinged, his eyes wide in horror as he realises how much worse his attempt at help has made the situation.

The demon voice spurs him into action, "PICK IT UP. PICK IT ALL UP. NOWWWWWW!"

To his credit, now that his brain has reengaged, he sprints across the street and directly into the freshly ploughed field. He ignores the mud squelching around his ankles, dipping and diving to catch my papers before the wind moves them into another location. I barely notice as I'm frantically doing the same along the roadway. Who knows when another car will pass by? I need all these papers safely back in the car as soon as possible.

I scoop up the last loose sheet seconds before another car passes. I turn around to see Edward standing on the other side of the road, a mass of slightly muddy papers clutched to his chest. We take one look at each other and burst into uncontrolled laughter.

"I thought your request to pick up your wellington boots was overkill, Ms Payne, but now I see I should have stopped for both the boots and a complete biohazard suit."

I cross the street, coming closer until I can pick a stray leaf from his hair. I dislodge the leaf and run my fingers through the dark, wavy locks to restore some order.

I pull my hand back, standing awkwardly once I realise what I'm doing. I bite my lip and look up into his eyes, ready to take on whatever sarcastic remark he's brewing up. Instead of sarcasm, I find a softness which I've never seen. A hint of humanity he normally keeps hidden behind a wall of intellectual stoicism.

"You have a bit of mud," he reaches closer and wipes his thumb across my cheek. "Oh dear, I seem to have made it worse."

I run my eyes over my mud-stained dress, ruined shoes, ripped tights and ragged hem. I must have caught it in my heel during one of my attempts to dislodge the tyre. "A little mud on my cheek is the least of my worries right now."

Edward has the good sense to look sheepish. "I am terribly sorry. It sounded as though you would cause yourself to have a hernia. I was so focused on putting my jumper in the car I missed the warning sounds of the approaching vehicle." He looks around at the now empty road and once again bare field. "It seems we have collected them all, I'll dust and tidy them during the rest of the drive home."

I nod my head in thanks before breaking up this heart-to-heart moment. Pointing at the flat tyre, I admit failure. "You're out here now, might as well give me a hand with this last nut."

It spins free on his first attempt, but he wisely chooses not to highlight this. We complete our tasks in silence, passing tools and parts back and forth until everything is once again orderly, and we can be on our way.

Back inside the car, once again fitted with four inflated tyres, Edward repeats his earlier offer. "If you'll pass me the rest of your papers, I'll see if I can sort them out and put them into the correct order."

I hand him the papers I saved from certain roadway death, settling back into my seat and restarting the car for a hopefully much calmer trip back home. I keep the radio off and the windows rolled up, unwilling to break the temporary ceasefire between the two of us.

When the city limits sign passes by, I realise that Edward has spent the last twenty minutes skimming and sorting my paperwork. "There weren't that many pages, Edward. Is my handwriting that difficult to read or can you not figure out my system?"

Edward quickly shoves the stack back together and drops it back onto the dashboard.

Looking somewhat shellshocked, he asks, "Do you always put this level of detail into your event plans?"

I snort, "That? Oh, that's nothing compared to the bunch back in my office."

Edward's eyebrows shoot up. "There are more?" Shaking his head, he continues, "I'll admit that the bubble lettering threw me at the beginning, but I had not conceived that you would need to utilise fully illustrated charts, spreadsheet trackers, and lists. So many endless lists full of every item one can imagine under the sun."

Pausing at a red light, I look over until Edward meets my eyes. "And you thought I was nothing more than a pretty face. All those conferences and dinners you attend don't organise themselves. It takes hours of planning and coordination; plans and back-up plans and back-ups for the back-up. And that's before we even get to the complexity of adding actual people into the mix."

"I may have underestimated your skills, Ms Payne."

Truer words have never been spoken.

Chapter Seventeen

I stand under the shower until the water runs lukewarm, but I can barely bring myself to turn off the water. My mind is stuck on repeat. All I can see is me and Edward. The two of us standing there on the side of the road. Mud clinging to our hemlines, dust on our faces.

And there we are, staring into one another's eyes like two loons.

I haven't been on a date in months. The dry spell is the only reason I've got stodgy, stuffy Edward Thomas stuck in my head!

As soon as we got back from the Cotswolds, he dashed upstairs to his flat, barely calling out a goodbye. Men never seem to moon over moments the way we women do. In fact, he probably put the entire scene out of his head before even climbing back into the car.

On that note, I turn off the water and step out, wrapping myself in a bath sheet and opening the window so the steam can escape. Pushing Edward out of my thoughts, I focus instead on the Johnstons. I really thought one of them must be the murderer, but I suspect their alibis will hold up to police scrutiny.

If it wasn't either of them, I'm out of ideas of where to go next. What other deliveries come into the college kitchen? Milk? Bread? Wine? I'm pulling at straws, but I'm not ready to dismiss the idea that it is someone from the Cotswolds. There's something niggling in the back of my brain, but with the problems with the magic, gala planning and now Edward occupying my thoughts, I can't figure out what it is.

I use a hand towel to wipe steam off from my mirror. Maybe it's the security guard, and that's why there's no evidence of a break-in. Do any of them commute in from the Cotswolds? I make a mental note to ask Harry when I return her keys and give an update on our trip. Neither Harry nor Dr Radcliffe will be pleased to hear we've eliminated the last reasonable suspect. Hopefully, the news that we'll have regular fruit and veg deliveries again will cheer them up.

I stare at my reflection, wishing she could step out of the mirror and take over some of my responsibilities. I've still got a ton to do for the gala on top of identifying further suspects. "Come on, magic. Can't you clone me already?"

My reflection blinks but otherwise remains silent. She doesn't seem to have any more ideas than I do. She also isn't jumping at the chance to help. "If being angry with my reflection is a sign, I think it's saying I need to go on a holiday."

A nearby church clock tower chimes the hour, reminding me to get a move on it. Digging through my closet, I hunt for an outfit which will fill me with optimism instead of the dread and worry sitting in the pit of my stomach. A pale pink fabric catches my eye. I wrench out a skirt, decorated to look like a perfect cupcake, a pale pink bottom transitioning into a sea of pastel confetti. If I pair it with a simple white shirt and cardigan, I should be able to get away with it.

Once dressed, I put the finishing touches on my hair and make-up, giving a final spin before the mirror before I go. This time my reflection smiles, enthusiasm brightening her eyes.

If I speed walk, I can make it to Harry's office and then the dining hall before it closes. After lunch, I need to grab H to see how his conversations with the other Eternals have gone. Hopefully, he's convinced them of the necessity of bringing someone else into the magical fold. They all know Harry better than I do, having worked alongside her for all these years. Even if she doesn't know the Eternals exist, they'll have had ample opportunity to see her, in both good times and bad. If the Eternals don't trust her, that will be telling.

Once I've got all of that done, I'm looking forward to a few hours working with my assistants. Will promised to have demo tapes of bands to share with us, and Jill should have an update on centrepieces. I can only imagine what Edward would have to say about listening to music being part of the planning process.

After such a long day, I'm relieved to slide into my seat when I meet Mathilde and Kate for dinner. We're tucked away in a back booth at a posh new cocktail restaurant on the roof deck of the Westgate. The place is nearly empty because of a combination of a mid-week evening and the typically terrible British weather. Everyone else in Oxford must have stayed in and ordered a curry.

We spend ages pouring over the menu. All the cocktails have trendy, incomprehensible names, so we have to read all the ingredients to find one we each like. By the time we get to the food options, we throw our hands in the air and opt for a dinner of mixed appetisers.

When my drink arrives, it is wafting a pink smoke into the air that perfectly matches my skirt. I don't know whether to take that as a good sign or be nervous to put it into my body.

Across from me, Mathilde has an array of multicoloured test tubes and an ice-filled glass in front of her. "I think I overpaid; I wasn't expecting to mix my drink."

"We all overpaid," I reassure her. "These places put a massive mark-up on the alcohol. Trust me, I know. I've booked enough events in lounges just like this one."

Sniffing the contents of her test tubes, Mathilde prompts Kate to give us an update. We hadn't planned to meet up this evening, but Kate sent a message earlier demanding we clear our schedules. "Ok, Kate, we're dying to know what happened."

Nodding in encouragement, I take a sip of my drink, reassured to find the smoke is more dry ice and less fiery hot. I must have been thinking about H when I ordered it. After our last drinks evening, I didn't dare invite him along.

Setting her glass onto the table, Kate focuses her attention on us. "I have so much to tell, but let me start at the beginning, ok? When we last met up, I promised to visit Lady Mary Hall and Iffley College this week. Not that we doubted you, Mathilde, but I can reconfirm that Iffley is completely without access to the magical field. They're having their own problems with crime, now that the magical protections are no longer working. A portrait has gone missing, if you can believe it."

"Dr Radcliffe mentioned it this morning. Is it worth much?" I ask.

"A hundred thousand pounds or so."

My drink turns over in my stomach. That is a lot of money.

Rubbing at the line between her eyes, Kate murmurs, "I'm trying not to stress about it. There are three more portraits in the area. When we reactivate the magic, I'm certain one of them will have information to share on the culprit. It is a relatively new acquisition, so I doubt it can be part of the magical infrastructure. In fact, I'm fairly certain that theft isn't the root of our problem." Kate gives us both a very serious look, "That said, in the meantime, we must keep an extra close eye on the premises. Mathilde, can you send an extra library assistant over to Iffley to help monitor the valuables?"

"I'll see what I can do. Staffing levels are always short, but perhaps I can free up someone."

She pauses as the waiter turns up, an array of small plates in hand. We take turns passing around the nibbles until we each have a full plate.

Kate scoffs a quick bite before jumping back into her story. "Now for the crazy update. I had to go into London last night for an event at the National Gallery. I went to catch up with a potential donor about bequeathing his collection to the Ash. That man has two feet in the grave but is still turning up at events. We're all madly competing for his favour. But that's not important."

Mathilde and I hang on the edge of our chairs as we wait for Kate to chew another bite of her food.

"After I finished speaking with the donor, I wandered off on my own, looking for a quiet corner so I could sit and make some notes about the chat. I ended up in a quiet gallery, perched on a bench in front of a giant statue of Victoria and Albert. There I was, pen scribbling furiously, when I feel a tap on my shoulder."

"Who was it?" I ask when Kate pauses for another nibble.

"Why, it was Queen Victoria, can you imagine!"

To say that Mathilde and I look similarly dumbfounded would be a massive understatement.

Kate rushes ahead, "I swivelled in my seat, staring at her much as you two look right now. I was shocked and flabbergasted."

Leaning in, Mathilde whispers, "Did she... did she say anything?" Looking at Mathilde, I can't tell whether she wants the answer to be a yes or a no.

Shifting in her seat, Kate nods. "She asked me if I knew why they'd 'woken up' about a month ago. How she knew I could see and hear her, I don't have a clue, so don't ask."

We let Kate finish her plate of food while we try to make sense of everything she's said so far.

After wiping her mouth and pushing her plate away, Kate continues, "Thank goodness I've had three months of experience speaking with statues here in Oxford. I buried my shock and conducted a mini-investigation. As best as I could see, there is a narrow line of magic running straight through the National Gallery. Victoria and Albert were positioned perfectly to benefit from it. That woke them up."

Having grown up in London, I've got an excellent mental map of the city. The National Gallery is on a near-perfect diagonal from Oxford, one that would cross over a certain set of meadows filled with talking sheep. "Do you think whoever is causing the boundary problem is connected with the National Gallery?"

Kate's face looks grim. "I wish it were that simple, but I followed the line to the edge of the building. There was nothing there which would explain it. My best guess is that it keeps on going to some other location within the city."

"London?" Mathilde looks pained at the thought. "First sheep, now Queen Victoria! There is no way this is an accident. Now I see why you said theft of objects isn't our problem. The only way magic could reach so far south is if someone has tapped into our magical boundary and is attempting to stretch it clear down to London." Mathilde's eyes widen as the reality of our challenge sets in. "That place is huge. It could be anyone, anywhere! How on earth are we going to solve this?"

When all of our plates and glasses are empty, I break the silence. "I am in way over my head already, and I've only been here for a week and a half. I need to make St Margaret my number one priority."

Kate pats my arm, "You are right. We now know for sure that St Margaret is at risk of ending up in the same situation as Iffley. The best thing you can do right now is focus on solving the murder and pulling off the most perfect gala ever."

"No pressure," I mutter.

Mathilde waves for the bill. "Kate's right, Nat. I suspect that your presence in the college is keeping the magic strong despite the bigger problem. Your bloodline is helping to reinforce the magic that is there. And, as you know, ceremonies are important.

The more you can do to engage the Eternals, and the further you can go to encourage people to enjoy themselves, to make the gala evening itself as memorable as possible, the better off we are."

Reaching over, Kate gives my hand a gentle squeeze. "One step at a time, Nat. The gala will be here before you know it. We can all get together afterwards, dividing up whatever work needs to be done to get to the bottom of the problem with the magic after that. Mathilde and I can put our heads together in the meantime, seeing if we can't make a start on a plan for more investigation."

"I was hoping for a day or two in the sun after all this," I moan.

Mathilde beams, "Cheer up, Nat. You'll never be able to complain that your life is boring."

Rolling my eyes, I reply, "I'm not sure that's a good thing, Mathilde, but thanks for the thought, anyway."

Chapter Eighteen

The smoky pink drink worked its magic on me last night. I came home, fell into a dreamless sleep, and I am fairly certain I didn't move between 10pm and 7am. When my alarm goes off, I roll out of bed, taking a quick shower before promising to get H a sausage bap in the dining hall if he'll stop hanging off the refrigerator handle.

As soon as I turn the key in the lock, closing up my flat, H bolts off, hollering that he'll charm a bap out of Beatrice and will meet me in my office shortly. Happy to have that errand sorted, I wave goodbye and watch him run off.

Even though it hasn't even been two weeks, it is strange to walk my daily path through the college grounds alone. I hadn't realised how quickly I'd accepted H as a permanent sidekick. Now I understand why my grandfather's stories so often included the mischievous Humphrey. Except for my few trips outside of the college grounds, H has been by my side day and night.

A few steps from the main building entrance, I remember that I forgot to ask him whether he got the rest of the Eternals on board with our plan to tell Harry about the magic. My impromptu trip into the Cotswolds with Edward, followed by gala planning and then Kate's urgent text all combined to wipe my morning discussions completely out of my mind.

I'll ask H first thing when he gets back from the dining hall. That decision made, I carry on into the building, heels clicking on the wooden floor as I travel the route to my office. My spirits are buoyant this morning, lifted by a goodnight's rest and the cherry red colour of my peplum jumper. I am ready to take on whatever life throws at me.

I open my office door to find total chaos. Catherine Morgan - free from her portrait in the main entrance - is arguing with a trio of ghostly young women. My papers are in disarray, and is that Bartie hiding under my desk? Oh god, it is.

I lied. Easing the door closed again, I step back, determining that a cup of coffee is necessary before I wade into whatever is going on in there.

Before I make tracks to the Senior Common Room, the door to a nearby office opens and my assistants Jill and Will come tumbling out.

"Nat, you're here. That's great." Jill launches straight into an update, barely pausing for a breath. "I booked the band you wanted."

"Finally, some good news. What else do you have for me?" I ask.

Will jumps in, "The decorations have arrived. I stored them in the events cupboard and locked the door tight. They should be safe there until they set up the marquee in the garden."

I hunt through my handbag until I find my notepad. I cross two things off my list and wait for the next update. "Can I cross anything else off? Maybe a caterer?" I cross my fingers.

Jill and Will's shoulders fall in unison. Not good.

"If it's any help, the Mediterranean fish truck is free that night and can do all you can eat fish and chip dinners?" Will offers. I have to force my face to remain neutral.

"Is that the best option we have, team? After all your calls and web searches?"

"It's the only option we have," Will confirms. "Unless you can pull a rabbit out of your hat, I fear the dinner will be greasier than normal."

"A rabbit out of a hat, did you say? Hmmmm." The beginnings of an idea take root in my mind. "Tell you what, you can leave the chef challenge with me."

Jill and Will sigh in relief, once again in unison. I'm thinking they've been spending too much time together. I wrap up our impromptu hallway chat and send them off for coffee and a pastry. I make a quick dash to the common room, grabbing a fresh latte and downing it as quickly as possible. Tongue scalded but now properly caffeinated, I push up my sleeves, march back to my office and shove open the door.

I set my bag and notepad down on the table, dust off my hands, stick two fingers in my mouth and let loose with a piercing whistle.

"Excellent, now that you've all wrapped up your conversations, maybe one of you can tell me what is going on in here? And Bartie, could you come out from underneath the desk or do I need to send out a rescue party?"

All five of them, Catherine, Bartie and the three young women display a flushed neckline despite being semitransparent.

One of the young women speaks up first. "I'm very sorry, Ms Payne, but me friends and I cannot seem to make ourselves solid enough for others to see us. Ms Morgan insists we aren't trying hard enough, and Bartie, well he ducked for cover about an hour ago."

"There's only one way to settle this. We must have a trial run." I hold up a hand when the three women waver out of focus. They are nervous, for sure. "But before we do that, I have another question. Did H speak with any of you yesterday?"

This time Bartie steps forward, "Yes, Ms Natalie, he did. He came to me first, since I'm the Head of Eternal Affairs."

I freeze, waiting to hear the outcome of their discussion, but Bartie says nothing else. "So? What happened? Did he explain why we need to tell Harry?"

Nodding slowly, Bartie looks to his fellow Eternals, looking them each in the eye to ensure they are all still in agreement with whatever decision he has made. "These are strange times, Ms Natalie. Strange and difficult, none of us here have ever experienced an issue with the magic. It was not an easy decision for any of us. The risk is so great, but...." His voice trails off.

"What?!?!?! Just spit it out, Bartie!" My frustration seeps into my voice. So much for starting my day feeling rested and relaxed.

Catherine Morgan glares at Bartie before stepping forward to finish his thought, "Yes, my dear. The answer is yes, you may tell Harry. We will help you. That's partially why we were in here practicing this morning. Saying the words alone may not convince Harry you are telling the truth. We can show her that the magic isn't all in your imagination."

Hand on chest, I close my eyes in relief. "Oh, thank you, thank you all so much. I know we won't regret this decision. We need all the help we can get if we hope to solve the mystery of what is wrong with the magical border."

Looking around the room, everyone's expressions are matching my own, hopeful grins all in a row.

"If it is okay, I'll see if Harry is in her office. I can offer to introduce her to a few of our actors. I'm sure she'll find time to step down the hall." I wave at the group. "Do whatever it is you need to do to, um, solidify yourselves while I'm out. I'll be back in a flash."

It doesn't take much convincing to get Harry to step away

from her desk. I barely had the word actor out of my mouth before she jumped to her feet.

As we walk to my office, she smooths down the front of her dress. "Do I look all right, Nat? Is my hair a mess? Maybe I should pop into the loo first. I've never met real actors and actresses before."

I stop myself from flinching, feeling guilty I'm not being completely honest with her. But if she's nervous now, how would she feel if she knew she was off to meet a bunch of ghosts? I offer soothing words, sticking as close to the truth as possible. "You're fine, Harry. These people aren't superstars. They are regular people, like you and me. In fact, you'll think they've been working here at the college for years and years."

I open the door of my office, double-checking where everyone is standing so I can do the introductions. I might as well not have bothered as Harry bustles past me, straight towards Bartie. When I see her extending a hand, I realise I'd better act fast or she'll stumble on the truth before we can tell her properly.

"Harry, wait. You can't shake hands."

Harry pulls up short, glancing back at me. "Why ever not?"

"I'll explain in a moment. Why don't you take a seat in the chair over there first."

She quickly pulls her hand back and drops it down to her side. Looking around in confusion, Harry looks over at me. "One man and one woman, is that enough, dear? I thought you had more people coming."

So did I. Looks like the trio of young ghosts were right.

Harry leans forward, closely eyeing Catherine Morgan. "Blimey, you're the spitting image of Ms Morgan. I'd know that face anywhere after all these years passing her portrait in the hallway. How did you pull that off?"

"That's what we need to talk to you about, Harry," I say as I slide into the seat across from her. I'd thought hard this morning about the best way to broach the conversation with Harry and had decided to start with my beginnings at Oxford. "Did I ever tell you that my grandfather worked at Oxford?"

Harry shakes her head, mystified by this turn in the conversation.

"He was a librarian at one of the other colleges. He worked here for forty-two years before he retired. My dad grew up in Oxford and was desperate to get out, trying his luck in the bright lights of London. By the time I was born, my grandfather had moved out of Oxford and closer to us in London."

"That's a lovely story, dear, but why are you telling it to me now?" Harry asks.

"Well, when I was little, my grandfather used to tell me stories about an alternate version of Oxford. One which was full of magical creatures, ghosts, talking portraits, books and statues. He was the main character, always accompanied by his best magical mate. A little wyvern called Humphrey. Or... as we know him... H."

"H?" Harry's eyes narrow in confusion. "Like the cat?"

"Not a cat, Harry. A wyvern, albeit a small wyvern. A miniature dragon-like creature who looked like an innocent cat to everyone else. But to those of us who have the magic of Oxford running through our veins, we can see him for what he really is."

Rising from my chair, I cross over to stand beside Ms Morgan. "This isn't an actress. This is Catherine Morgan. My grandfather's stories were real. Magic is real, at least here within the confines of the university. Scholars, staff and donors may pass away, but they never pass on. Some part of their essence stays here in Oxford. Our knowledge lives on eternally ever after."

To prove my point, I slide a hand through the middle of Ms Morgan's body. Then I hold my breath, waiting for the moment of truth.

Harry blinks a few times before tilting her head as she thinks through my statements, weighing up the potential for truth.

Finally, she comes to some decision. Standing up, she strides across the room, circling around me and Catherine.

"How do I know this isn't a video projection?" Harry asks.

Catherine Morgan answers before I can open my mouth. "You could ask me a question if you'd like."

Despite the offer, Harry still seems suspect. "Tell me something that happened here in the college, something only I would know about." She folds her arms, awaiting a response.

Catherine thinks for a moment, giving a small chuckle before replying. "I remember one evening, around 20 years ago, when a younger Harriet thought she was alone in the main building and slid down the bannister of the main staircase. Twice."

Harry's face glows pink. No further confirmation is needed to know the story rings true. She spins, returning to her seat at the table, the empty cat bed catching her eye. "A wyvern, you say? That would explain why Lillian always had so much ash floating around her office."

That breath I was holding in bursts out in a laugh. "That's it! You're going to accept everything I've told you, just like that?"

Harry's eyes glitter with laughter, "Luv, I've been working here at St Margaret for years now. Many a time I've been sure I could hear the sounds of heavy skirts swishing along the floorboards or seen a shadow slipping down the hall ahead of me. And H! Do you know, until this moment, I never questioned why a cat could live for thirty-plus years and still be so spry!"

I cross back, sliding into my chair once again. "Harry, you are a miracle. A godsend. I knew... we all knew that you were the only person we could trust with this information."

Patting my hand in reassurance, Harry says, "Well, now that we've got that mystery out of the way, could you all properly introduce yourselves? And I'm guessing there is a reason you shared this incredible information with me. Out with it, the lot of you. What do you need?"

❖

When H walks into my office, smacking the taste of sausage from his lips, Harry freezes. "He still looks like a cat, Nat. Is there a way for me to see what you see?"

Biting my lip, my eyes dart to H, hoping he has an answer to her question.

"You told 'er about the magic, missie? Glad I missed that talk. Now she wants to see the real H, eh?"

"Is there a way to do it, H?" I ask.

"Yeah, iffen you want 'er to see what you see, we all need to 'old 'ands."

"Hold hands? That's it?" I narrow my eyes. "That seems too simple, like it could happen on accident."

H snorts, a cloud of sausage-scented smoke wafting up. "'Ave you ever seen a 'uman 'oldin' 'ands with a cat?"

I guess when you put it that way... I explain everything to Harry, who immediately jumps at the chance. She and I clasp hands over the table, sticking our free hands out for H to grasp. As soon as H's hand folds into mine, I feel a zing of energy spark up my arm, racing across my body and along to my other arm and hand.

"Ah, there you are. And a handsome devil, aren't you?" Harry lets go of H's hand to pat his forehead. We all break out into laughs when H flaps up, doing somersaults in the air.

"All right, H. That's enough showing off. We've still got work to do today."

H replies by blowing out two puffs of smoke, forming a perfectly shaped "O" and "K" in mid-air.

We spend all afternoon and evening bringing Harry up to speed while the Eternals try and fail to figure out why some ghosts can make themselves seen while others can't. Their age and ghostly tenure don't seem to make a difference.

The solution presents itself as a complete surprise.

Harry, H and I are sprawled over the sofas in the Senior Common Room. It's late enough that no one else is likely to come in and we long ago devoured all the chocolate biscuits stocked by the coffee machine. Bartie and Catherine Morgan are wearing ghostly tracks in the plush floral carpet. The three young women are sharing a settee, backs straight, but heads and shoulders drooping.

I stretch my arms over my head and make a move to stand. "I don't know about all of you, but my brain is mush. I can't think of anything we haven't tried." I fight back the tears that are welling up in my eyes. "Looks like I need a Plan B unless anyone has a last bright idea?"

No one responds.

"We'd better clean up the mess we've left. Would you all mind helping me dust up the biscuit crumbs?"

One woman stands up. "I'll help, Nat. Feels like the least I can do since I don't seem to be good at anything else."

I give her a weak smile, aiming for reassurance. "Don't be so hard on yourself. This was my crazy idea. It's never been done before, we should have known it wouldn't be so easy."

She shrugs her shoulders, moving over to the end table. She tidies up a stack of magazines and then picks up an old candelabra, moving it aside so she can dust off the surrounding crumbs. The moment her hand touches the brass base, her form flickers into solidity. When she sets it down again, she goes back to semi-transparent. Is it that simple?

I call out, "Wait, do that again!"

Confused, the young woman looks at the table. "Oh, sorry, did I not get all the crumbs? It's hard for me to tell how many I'm scooping up."

"Forget the crumbs and pick up that candelabra." She picks it up and sure enough, the same thing happens again. I quickly grab an antique clock and a framed miniature from around the room and thrust them into the other women's hands. Harry sits up straight, eyeing the women who have finally come into view.

"This whole time spent trying to channel more magic, and all we needed was props!" I high-five H, dancing in a circle around the room. "We can weave props into our plan, maybe you can hold a book, another person the candlestick. I'm sure we can find an old serving tray in one of these cupboards."

Harry wraps an arm around my shoulders, pulling me away from the mantlepiece before I can handle any more of the college's precious items. "Leave it with us, Natalie. We know this college and all of its hidden secrets better than anyone. We'll find the perfect items to match all of their roles."

"Yah, let's go, Nat," H whines near the door. "I'm starvin', we finished up the last chockie biscuit 'ours ago. I'm wastin' away to nothin' 'ere."

"Okay, okay. I hardly think you're in danger of fainting from hunger." Moving towards the door, I call back to Bartie, "Bartie, would you have a moment for a last word before I go?"

Head bobbing, he follows me out of the common room door. "Of course, Ms Natalie. What can I do for you?"

I haven't forgotten my magical rabbit conversation from earlier in the day.

"You know everyone who resides within the college grounds, correct? The ghostly inhabitants, I mean."

Bartie pulls a narrow black notebook out of an inner coat pocket. "Absolutely. I have a registry here of occupants and I update it regularly to ensure it is accurate."

I plow ahead, feeling hopeful. "This will sound weird given the circumstances, but I don't suppose that the former Chef Smythe has turned up? I know she hasn't been gone long, but she was here for years and didn't seem to have another place to call home."

"Aye, she is here. I didn't want to mention it as I thought it might make you uncomfortable. She remembers nothing from the day of her passing, if that's what you were thinking," Bartie explains.

"Oh no, nothing of that sort." I wave my hands to dispel the idea. "I had a more, um, traditional role for her. If she'd be interested... and willing. It's a long shot, but do you think she could cater the event? We're in desperate need for a chef who won't be scared off by the murder. If she's here now, she might be the only one within 100 miles who fits the bill."

Bartie scratches his chin as he mulls over the idea. "She's a proud one, already making demands of me and my team. But maybe if we put it to her as a challenge, a last chance to cement her legacy here at the college. She might do it."

I can't help but smile as the last piece of my gala plans hopefully falls into place.

Back in my flat, H asks in between bites of a cheese toastie. "Aren't you going to fix yerself some dinner?"

"Weirdly, I'm not hungry," I shrug. "I'm so excited to see the gala plans come together, I don't think I can make myself sit still long enough to eat. It's like I've found a second wind or something."

Eyes wide, H nods. "I know exactly what you mean, Nat. When I get like that, I usually run a few laps aroun' the gardens and terrorise all the mice."

Shuddering at college mice, I size up the rest of his suggestion. "That's not a bad idea. Maybe I should go for a run, work some adrenaline out of my system so I can rest tonight."

I slip into my running clothes and snicker at the thought of Edward's reaction if he could see them. My leggings have giant pineapples on them. He'd have an apoplexy trying to come up with a snarky remark.

H comes into the living room as I do a few stretches to limber myself up. "I'm gonna stay 'ere iffen it's okay. I gotta meetin' with Princess Fluffy later and I don't wanna miss it."

"How are you going to get out if I'm not here to open the door?" I'm genuinely curious to hear.

Glaring, H explains, "Iffen I'm inside, I can use the doorknob on the door to the garden. I got 'ands, you know. It's only a problem if I'm outside cuz you need the key to get back in."

Weirdly, that makes sense. I call out a final set of instructions as I head out the front door. "Make sure the back door closes behind you, please. I don't want to return and find all my electronics missing."

H gives me a salute as I pull the front door closed behind me.

My feet pound the pavement as I cross the street and aim for Port Meadow. A cool breeze caresses my body while I count out the blocks. The dark clouds on the horizon threaten to bring rain, but I don't worry as I'm not planning to stay out for very long. Dark clouds are the standard here in England, barely cause for concern.

There's hardly a soul at Port Meadow; only a few dedicated exercise enthusiasts are making the rounds on the packed dirt paths. I sink into the zone, revelling in a chance to be alone, with no deadlines and no responsibilities, and no one asking me what we need to do next. The cows and horses are simple beasts, no magic in them to give them a voice. I speed past them, kicking dirt clods up behind me.

I make the loop, turning back to run between the ducks and geese that line the river Thames. A man standing on a houseboat raises his glass in my direction, and I smile in return. By the time I make it back to the park entrance nearest the college, I am drenched in sweat. That's why I take a few minutes to realise that it is rain I keep wiping off my forehead. I look down at my watch and am amazed to see that an hour has gone by. The clouds that had seemed so far away before are now directly overhead.

I pick my pace back up, but it's a futile effort. The drizzle turns into a downpour when I'm still several blocks from home. As I get closer, the light from my front window beckons me home with promises of a warm shower and a glass of wine. I leap onto the doorstep amid a mental debate over chardonnay vs merlot. Reaching towards my pocket, I remember that these leggings don't have pockets. Despite the conversation with H over locked doors and necessary keys, I somehow ran out without one.

I lean on the buzzer labelled with Edward's name. My front door doesn't automatically lock. If he can let me in the main door, I can get back into my flat with no further harm done.

I shiver as the cold soaks through my lightweight clothing. That cool breeze is now an icy blast. I buzz again and again, but no response.

"Ok, Nat, what do we do now?" I ask myself. "Think. Who else has a key to this place?"

The security guard at the porter's lodge! He delivered my suitcases on the first day and Harry made a comment about how convenient it is to have someone around with a master key.

I force my tired feet back into a slow canter. I jog to the end of the block and turn the corner, following the college fence as it leads me towards the main gate. The guard is standing under the lodge eaves, staying dry while he finishes up a cigarette.

"Ms Payne, look at you! Quickly, get inside. What are you doing out on a night like this?"

Wiping more rain from my eyes as I follow him in, I explain, "I went for a run and lost track of time and the clouds. And I forgot my key. Could you loan me a spare so I can get into my flat?"

"Of course, of course," he walks behind the counter and opens and closes drawers. "Here it is, you can keep it until tomorrow morning. No need to get out again tonight."

"Thanks so much. You must see a lot of students in need on nights like this one."

He chuckles, "That I do. You remind me of Beatrice from the

dining hall. Did the same thing as you, except it was super early in the morning. Sun wasn't even up yet."

"Beatrice?" I ask. "The cashier? She never mentioned being a serious early morning runner."

"I thought it strange myself," shared the security guard. "Working here in the lodge, you quickly learn people's habits. That was the first time I'd ever seen her out so early in the morning and caught in the rain, no less. I meant to ask her about it the next time I saw her, but then you and Dr Radcliffe found Chef Smythe and the police turned up and I plum forgot."

"Wait," I interrupt, "Was this the morning of the murder?" Something about that jogs my memory. "Beatrice said she'd been sick that night and had gone home."

"Aye, she goes home regularly, what with her family so close. They seem tight-knit, I always see them chatting when her parents come by to deliver the fruit and veg order. They didn't come by that day as Chef Smythe had fired them."

My brain neurons are firing all across my head. "What is Beatrice's last name?"

"Johnston."

"And you're sure this was that morning? The day we discovered the murder? You didn't mix up the days?"

Grimacing, the guard shakes his head. "I could hardly forget such a horrid occasion. That whole day is permanently emblazoned in my memory."

I'm running out of the lodge before he finishes his sentence. The murderer has been sitting in the dining hall, right in front of us all this time.

Chapter Nineteen

Part of me wants to rush straight to Beatrice's room and get the confrontation over, but the rational part of my brain insists I do this properly. I need Edward. He's our official liaison to the police force, and he has more experience in this area than I do. After all, he is a professor of criminology.

He's also been investigating the murder since the beginning. Our trip to the Cotswolds was evidence enough that we were both on the right path, suspicions in line with one another. I owe it to him to make sure he is beside me if I'm right and Beatrice is the killer.

I know Edward isn't at home; he didn't answer when I rang his bell a few minutes ago. Given the late hour and the dreadful weather, there's only one place he can be: his office.

I'm sure I set a new land speed record with my dash across the college gardens. The rains have cleared all the pathways of people, leaving plenty of space to speed up. Rain pours down on my head, invisible in the shadows. Only when I run under the yellow glow of the pathway lights, can I see the raindrops sheeting down.

I finally reach the conference centre that marks the far side of the college grounds. On the first-floor, one window shines like a beacon. I do a quick estimate, feeling more confident that the lit office is likely Edward's.

"Hold the door, it's an emergency!" I shout at a student exiting the building, the young man's mouth dropping open at the sight of my soaking hair and clothing. He stands as far as possible from the door, holding it wide for me to jog inside. I drip my way up the stairs and along the hallway towards Edward's office, my shoes alternating between a squeak and a squelch. My spirits lift in relief when I spy his nameplate, a light leaking from under his door.

I don't knock. I fling the door open, spraying water droplets across the room, dotting the mountain of papers covering every surface and the man himself.

"What on earth?" Edward thunders before he realises who is interrupting his tutorial session. His student slumps in her chair, bunkering down against his inevitable tirade. Just my luck, it's the same girl who was there the day before.

"Where does Miss Johnston live?" My voice comes out louder and more frantic than I intended.

Edward frowns, a worry line appearing in the middle of his forehead. "What's wrong, Ms Payne? Why are you dripping all over my office? Has something happened?"

Shivering in my wet clothing, I march over to his coat rack and pull his coat off the hook. "I don't have time to explain, but I need you to come. Where does Beatrice live? It's urgent."

His expression grows more concerned as he realises I am deadly serious. Rising from his chair, he apologises to his student. "I realise this is unorthodox, but I need to cut our tutorial session short." He strides around his desk, reaching out an arm for his coat. "Where are we going?"

"We have to find Beatrice!" I blurt, but his face shows no signs of recognition. "Beatrice Johnston. She works in the dining hall. You see her every single day."

"Johnston?" Edward's eyes dart left and right. "Johnston veg? Beatrice in the dining hall is related to the veg vendor?"

A full body shiver races down my spine. We're taking too long. "Yes, she's their daughter. We've got to get to her, now. Do you know where we can find her?"

Edward's student finds her voice. "I, um," she coughs to clear her throat, "Um, well, it's just that I, well..."

"Out with it." Edward's gruff words spur her into completing her thought.

Hunching in on herself, she hoarsely whispers, "She lives two doors down from me. In student housing, building B."

One problem solved. I plead with Edward's student, "Can you take us there? It will be faster than us trying to find her on our own."

Raising a hand, Edward blocks his student from rising. "Is that safe, Ms Payne?"

"She can wait in her room or call the security guard once we're inside." Holding out a hand, I invite her to lead us out of the office. "Is that okay? Can you show us the way?"

She nods, shoving her binder into her rucksack and rising to her feet. Edward and I step aside, bumping into one another in our efforts to get out of her way.

Edward quirks up an eyebrow in surprise, brushing at the wet print mark I made when my thigh bumped against his trousers.

"Don't take this the wrong way, but it would appear that your giant pineapples are rather juicy. Did you go running in pyjamas?"

Outside, Edward and his student match my pace, all of us speed walking in the rain. I feel like I should know his student's name given this is the second time I've inconvenienced her this week.

The rain has slacked off to a drizzle, the pathway lights magnified in the pools of water. Edward offers to share his

umbrella, but I decline. I'm already soaked through to my bones.
A few more drops will not make a difference.

At last, Edward's student pulls out in front, turning left to
follow a short pathway to a lit door. I pick up my speed, urging
Edward to hurry. "That must be block B. Come on, Edward, we're
nearly there."

I make a leap, landing under an awning, finally out of the rain.
Edward's student slides her card in the reader and holds the door
open. We follow her down the hallway until she stops in front of a
closed door.

I raise my fist but freeze before I knock. Edward nudges his
student towards her own door and then steps up beside me. Our
eyes meet in silent conversation. With a deep breath, I pull my
fist back and bang until the student occupant opens it from
inside.

Beatrice Johnston stares out at us, her blonde hair tied up in a
messy ponytail. Her blue eyes seem brighter in contrast with the
dark shadows underneath them. I thought she had been upset
over the sous-chef's departure. Now I know it is likely guilt
keeping her awake at night.

I don't wait for a welcome before pouncing into the room. I'm
soaked straight through to the bone and all out of patience. "Have
a seat, Beatrice."

She takes one look at the crazy gleam in my eyes and does as
I say.

I move into the room, leaving space for Edward to stand in
the doorway. "We need to talk to you about the night before Chef
Smythe was killed. You said you went home sick, stayed away all
night and didn't make it back in time for your shift in the
morning. Is that right?"

Beatrice blinks her baby blues, all wide-eyed innocence. "Yes,
I could feel a cold coming on. I had the shivers, and my throat
was scratchy. I went home to let my mother take care of me. Why
are you asking me this?"

Edward meets my eyes, waiting for permission before
speaking. I give a subtle nod. We're partners, for tonight at least.
"By home, you mean out in the Cotswolds? At your parents' farm,
the Johnston fruit and veg supply company?"

"Yes, that's them. It's not that far away. I took a taxi in the
morning. My mum's always busy taking my siblings to school, so
she rarely drives me back."

I cast a meaningful glance in Edward's direction, pleased to
see a hint of curiosity spark in his eyes. He steps back into the
doorway, leaving the floor free for me to continue.

I clear my throat, calling Beatrice's attention away from
Edward. "If you went home and stayed the night, why did the
security guard recall you returning from a run, soaking wet, well
before the sun came up? You couldn't have been that ill if you
were out running the streets of Oxford in the rain."

Beatrice freezes in her chair, her eyes leaping between the
door and window, searching for an escape. But between me and
Edward, we block every way out. "I don't know what you're
talking about. Why are you questioning me? I'm very busy, I've
got hours of revising left to do. Can you come back tomorrow?"

Any doubts I had fall away. She's guilty. If we walk out of here
now, she'll run away as fast as she can. I can see that Edward has
reached the same conclusion, his phone in his hand, ready to
make a call to his contact at the police.

My voice firm, I reply, "I think revising for an exam is the least
of your worries, Beatrice. I know what you did." Pointing to
myself and then to Edward, I continue, "We know. We both
know."

Her eyes narrow, heat rising along her throat, her fury now
evident. "I can't believe you figured it out - and it would be you.
The outsider. Only another outsider would notice me."

My mouth drops open. I'm gob smacked. "What do you mean,
only another outsider would notice you? Everyone knows you."

"I grew up here, lived my whole childhood dropping muddy

fruits and vegetables off at the colleges' back entrances."
Beatrice's breath heaves in her chest. "I was invisible! Lower than
the lowliest staff member. I was no one!"

Edward interrupts her, "You are a student at St Margaret
College; that's as far from no one as you can get."

Beatrice glares at Edward, her hands gripping the bottom of
her seat, her voice bright with anger. "What would you know,
Professor Thomas? You've been a superstar for your whole life.
Not me. I spent my childhood digging in the dirt. Literally."

Her demeanour brings the memory of our conversation with
her father to mind. That slow-burning temper he spoke about is
ready to explode.

Eyes wide, Beatrice grinds ahead with her story. "I finished my
A-levels and had a chance to escape. I had offers from colleges all
over the country. But no," she chuckles grimly, "my parents
insisted I go here. The college offered a bursary. They knew my
parents couldn't really afford the tuition. I've got four brothers
and sisters; a farm won't provide enough for all of us to go off to
uni!"

The last puzzle piece falls into place. I can see it all now, from
start to finish. "So that's how you ended up studying here and
working in the dining hall."

"Oh yes, Dr Radcliffe thought she was doing me a favour by
placing me there, rationalising that I already knew everyone. That
only made it worse. Here I was, more known to the staff than to
my fellow students. I was part of both groups and neither."

Edward is silent, leaving it to me to get the whole story out
while she will talk. "And then the chef chastised you in front of
everyone? That's what you told me when we had lunch."

Beatrice's cheeks radiate anger, her gaze wild. "She threatened
to report my error at the High Table dinner to the Principal. I
could have lost everything if she had. And the very next day she
fires my parents, claiming that they were providing her with
substandard vegetables. She emailed half the college chefs to let

them know they should look elsewhere, that our quality of produce had dropped."

It's time to get her to admit the truth. "I'd ask if your decision to kill her was spur of the moment, but it sounds as though you put a lot of planning into it."

A nod slips out before Beatrice can stop herself. "I needed my parents to give me an alibi. I went home for dinner and left very early in the morning before they woke up. They assumed that I'd gone back to the college to get ready before I had to be in the dining hall."

"They thought nothing of your early departure because they assumed you were working the breakfast shift." I shudder, thinking of how her parents will react to the news of their daughter's guilt.

Beatrice ignores my interruption, lost in her own world. She murmurs, "I couldn't let the system have a record of my return, so I knocked on the back entrance and the chef let me in. She was rude as always, making snide remarks about how good it was to see at least one member of my family taking her kitchen requirements seriously. It was the final straw."

Edward's voice cuts through. "So you picked up the cleaver and stabbed her."

Beatrice flinches under the harsh accusation. "I must have hit her exactly right, because she immediately slumped over. I washed my hands in the kitchen sink before running back to my room to change into exercise clothing. I used the side gate where the streetlight doesn't work to go out and then ran around Port Meadow until I couldn't see the kitchen and her body any longer. As you said, it was raining. The weather wiped away any final traces of my guilt."

"Not all of them," Edward mutters.

"After my run, I came back in the front gate and used my badge at the main entrance. I needed the security logs to match up with my departure the night before."

As if finally realising all that she's admitted, Beatrice falls onto her bed and sobs.

I cross over, halfway reaching out to comfort her before I stop myself. Who knows if her tears are real? She's had us fooled, even her poor parents.

Edward steps into the hallway, deep in conversation with someone on his mobile. Probably the police inspector. I hover in the doorway, my shivers sending more wet drops showering to the ground.

Edward ends his call with a promise to wait on the scene for the police to arrive. He twists around, his eyes wide as he takes in my shaking form. "The police are on their way over. You can stay if you want..." he pauses as I shake with another tremor, "or you can leave the rest of this with me. Maybe go back to your flat and get into some dry clothes? The police will no doubt want to speak with you, but I can arrange for you to meet them tomorrow."

I smile gratefully, desperate to put all of this behind me. "Thank you for everything. For coming along without questioning why I needed you. Will you ring my bell later, let me know it's finally done?"

"Of course," he reassures me. "Anything you'd like, Ms Payne."

I start down the hall towards the exit, twisting back before I get out of sight. "Oh, Edward?" I call back, waiting for him to meet my eyes, "You can call me Nat."

Chapter Twenty

The date of the gala has arrived, the butterflies in my stomach as much of a signal as the date on the calendar. The final two weeks flew by with the final gala To Do items having kept me busy. I've organised plenty of high-profile events in my career, but this is the first one featuring ghosts. It will either be an incredible success or a total disaster.

In less than an hour, our guests will enter St Margaret's front gate, crossing through the main building before ending up in the manicured gardens. None of the rooms inside are large enough to accommodate a seated dinner and dancing, so we took the event outdoors. A canopy covers the garden pathway, a red carpet guiding guests to the marquee. I left a wide entrance in front at Dr Radcliffe's request so she can stand outside and welcome guests as they arrive.

Once the guests come into the marquee, their first stop will be a smaller tented antechamber and coat check area. I want all distractions sorted before anyone sets foot in the main tent. Jill will stand there while guests are arriving, gathering tickets and checking the guest list. After they have liberated themselves of their coats and bags, one of the greeters at the entrance will pull back the curtain and let them into the main marquee.

As soon as I saw the marquee go up, I decided that's where I'd be, standing watch to make sure everything goes to plan.

I stride across the dance floor, doing my last-minute checks to ensure that everything is perfect before the first guest arrives. I've chosen a solid black gown for the evening. Kate helped smooth my hair into a simple twist and apply my make-up. My insides are liquid, but on the surface, I appear calm, cool and collected.

Jill, on the other hand, is wearing her excitement on her face. Her hair wrap is Oxford blue, coordinating with her white blouse and blue taffeta skirt. She flags me from across the marquee with a frantic wave. "I'm giddy with excitement, Nat. How can you be so calm?"

No point confessing my own nerves. I straighten my shoulders and smooth my dress. "I'll be excited later, after all the food is served and people are well into their cups. Until then, I'm all business." I look around the room, amazed at the transformation.

Two days ago, this was a bare circus tent. Now we've got rich wine-coloured drapes creating small alcoves all round the room. Each alcove is styled with decorations of a different era from the early 20th century, complete with wood panelling and faux fireplaces. They provide the perfect backdrop for our Eternals to play their roles to perfection, inviting guests into their parlours for a glass of champers and a chat. The dance floor lies in the middle of the room, with circular dining tables dotted around it. Guests should start their night chatting with the Eternals on the outskirts of the room and gradually work their way inward.

To my expert eye, every detail is perfect, except for one lone dining chair out of place. I nudge Jill, "Who was supposed to be tidying the chairs back up?"

"That's Will's job, but he's gone to change into his suit. I'll do it right now since I'm standing here." Jill rushes off before I can reply.

Satisfied that everything is as it should be, I look for my next check-in. "Bartie, there you are."

Bartie is standing over in the corner, half-hidden behind a large potted plant. When I arrived tonight, I discovered the Eternals can change clothes, but are limited to choosing styles they owned when they were alive. The cut of Bartie's tux is straight out of the 1940s. He's shuffling side to side while wringing his hands. He stops long enough to motion me over.

Leaning in, I whisper, "What's wrong, Bartie? Tell me so I can deal with it."

Bartie is my rock. If he's freaking out, then it must be bad.

"I forgot my lines." His ghostly face is paler than normal, his voice barely loud enough to hear.

"What lines?" I whisper back.

He shuffles his feet, "I mean, I forgot who I'm supposed to be. What I'm supposed to say if anyone approaches me. Oh, I'm ever so nervous, Ms Natalie. I've never had an acting role before."

I'm shocked. "Not even in the school Christmas play when you were a kid?"

He shakes his head, "No, I was a child during the Great War, we didn't feel much like celebrating in those days." He finishes his thoughts with a whimper.

This calls for a full-on intervention.

I stand firm, head held high, forcing him to raise his gaze from the ground. "Your job, Bartholomew, is to walk our guests through the history of St Margaret. You must introduce the Eternals, tell the guests about their background and then step back and let the Eternals take the lead." I soften my voice, patting his now solid shoulder. "It's very simple, hardly different from a regular day at the office for a Head of Eternal Affairs."

I can hear his knees knocking underneath his long coat, unfazed by my attempt at a pep talk. If nice and reassuring don't work, I guess I can pull out my demon voice one more time.

"STOP BEING A NINNY. SUCK IT UP, GET OUT
THERE AND SMILE AT PEOPLE."

Bartie leans sideways as my words crash over him, then stands
up ramrod straight and salutes me.

I don't hide my grin. "That's more like it. Now that you're not
skulking behind the greenery, could you help me look around and
see if there is anything else we need to do before we throw the
doors open?"

Together we survey the marquee. The heaters have done their
job; the space is warm and toasty without feeling muggy. I pull a
digital thermometer out of my handbag, doing a final check of the
temperature and humidity. "Perfect!" I declare before jamming it
back into my bag.

I can hear the band beginning to warm up, the familiar swing
tones from the early part of the 1900s filling the quiet space. The
waitstaff bustles around the room, placing final pieces of cutlery
on the tables and polishing up glasses. One by one, they step back
from their work and assume their opening positions along the
walls.

Reminding me of a young Mr Carson from Downton Abbey,
Bartie straightens his coattails and gives me a confident gaze. "Ms
Natalie, I believe the room is now ready to receive our guests."

Bartie waves to Will, back from his quick change. Will nods,
stepping to the side and sliding through the curtains to the coat
check so he can open the main doors. The gala has officially
begun.

I mill around for the first hour, watching as the guests arrive
and take a drink and hors d'oeuvre from the passing waiters. They
all wear the same look as they enter the room, wide-eyed delight
and curiosity mingling with a teensy bit of confusion. Perfect.

I step outside the catering entrance to the marquee to grab a
breath of air before I give the sign to serve dinner. The sounds of
conversation and laughter blend with the soft tones of the band,
the buzzing sounds a sure sign that the event is a success so far.

Even catching H trying to sneak into the event earlier in the evening didn't worry me. One Eternal had bundled him out before anyone else noticed

Catherine Morgan rounds a corner, walking in my direction until she catches my eye. Without saying a word, she holds a finger over her mouth and motions for me to follow her. Confused and slightly concerned, I tiptoe around the marquee through the grass until we nearly reach the front entrance.

I peek around the corner to see the man himself. Edward Thomas, Professor of Criminology, senior fellow and master of disappearance. I've barely seen him since we caught the murderer and finished our interviews with the police inspector. Once that mystery was solved, there was no further need for us to spend time together. Or at least that's what I've been telling myself when we've passed one another in the hallway with barely a nod and a hello.

I had doubted that he would turn up, thinking he'd find a conference or some other excuse. But here he is, dressed to the nines in a tailored black suit and black bowtie. He has tamed his unwieldy curls with a heavy hand of gel. He looks so debonair, I hardly recognise him.

Edward calls out to Dr Radcliffe, catching her before she enters the gala. She's been standing outside in a receiving line, welcoming guests since it started.

Exchanging handshakes, Edward quips, "Quite a turnout tonight, Dr Radcliffe."

"I'll say," she replies with a smile. "We're lucky it is even taking place. It is such an important fundraising event, as you know, I feared circumstances would require us to cancel."

"Err, yes, lucky that all of that sorted itself out." He coughs into his hand.

Sorted itself out??? Is that how he describes my soaking wet dash around the college? Fortunately, Catherine is still there, and able to stop me from marching over.

Oblivious to my presence, Dr Radcliffe turns towards the doors. "I believe it is time for a drink. We've all been under a lot of pressure, none more so than Natalie Payne. She took a risk with the theme and the chef. She kept nearly all of it a secret. In fact, I don't even know who the chef is."

Edward flinches, "I imagine she worked very hard on the event. For her sake, I hope it doesn't look like Disneyland."

Dr Radcliffe steps back to allow him to pass ahead of her, and in doing so she catches sight of me peeking around the marquee edge.

She waves Edward on, "Go on in, Edward. I'll let you be the judge of that yourself."

Edward takes a deep breath and steps into the coat check area. Catherine Morgan winks at me, spinning away as Dr Radcliffe waves me over to join her.

My cheeks burn under her gaze, feeling like a schoolgirl caught eavesdropping on her superiors.

She gives my arm a gentle squeeze. "Chin up, Natalie. I haven't been inside yet, but from out here, it sounds like the evening is a great success."

I return her smile with one of my own, raising my hand to show my crossed fingers. "All well so far, I'm literally crossing my fingers it stays that way."

Dr Radcliffe laughs, "You don't need luck. I owe you, in fact the whole college owes you an incredible amount of thanks, Natalie. In less than a month you've not only organised a gorgeous gala, you also unmasked a murderer hiding in our midst. And you've done it all with a smile on your face."

I stand speechless, my throat tight with emotion.

Dr Radcliffe saves me from needing to reply. "I won't ask you to relax now, as I know that would be impossible. But once dinner is done, and the dancing starts, I expect to see you out there enjoying yourself. But enough chatting, let's get inside. If you hurry along, you can probably catch Edward's first reaction. He'll be through coat check at any moment."

❖

The marquee walls look solid, but thanks to having spent the last two days working around the clock to transform them from blank canvas and into a time capsule of St Margaret in its earliest days, I know exactly where every hidden opening lies.

I pull two pieces of canvas apart and slide in unnoticed. I'm in a darkened corner directly to the right of the main entrance. I shift over a few steps so I'll have an unblocked view of Edward's face when he walks in.

The entry curtains peel back, allowing Edward inside. He takes two steps into the room, head turned sideways as he chats with a colleague.

"Turn around, dammit." I mutter under my breath. Any minute now a staff member will see me standing here and force my attention elsewhere.

At last, the colleague laughs and says goodbye, calling out for his wife in front of him.

Edward is always so stoic, I wonder if I'll even notice a difference in his expression. With my luck, he'll tighten up his jaw, blink and stride on, ignoring the magnificence I've spent hours creating. I take a deep breath in and hold it. I wait.

I watch his eyes first. They widen in surprise. He turns his head left and right, skimming the room to take it all in. The corners of his mouth tweak up, incontrovertible proof of his first impression of my work. Although he is mumbling under his breath, the words are clear enough for me to read his lips.

"My god, she's done it."

That's my cue.

I sidle up beside him, careful not to give away my presence until I'm ready.

"Will it do, Edward, or is it too Disney for you?"

Together we take in all the rich details that make up the theme. With Harry's help, we found enough antiques and artefacts tucked away in dusty cupboards and drawers to enable every one of the college's ghosts and portraits to have one to hand. Some carry books, others have candle snuffers tucked away in pockets. Bartie has a worn college journal in hand. Catherine Morgan and Dr Rosemary Thicke are holding court at a small table, their reflections shimmering in the diamond-like facets of the crystal wine glasses they're holding in their hands, keeping them visible to the guests.

I flag down a passing waiter and take two glasses of champagne from his tray, pressing one into Edward's hand before sipping my own. I'm about to slip away when Edward finally speaks again.

"I've never seen anything like this, Ms Payne... Nat. Truly. And I've been to many of these events over the years. It is extravagant, both familiar and unfamiliar at once. It is so utterly and completely..." his voice trails off.

"Ridiculous?" I fill in the gap.

"Perfect," he corrects. "It is authentic and quintessentially St Margaret. I do not understand how you've done this in such a short time. If I hadn't seen your notes myself, I'd swear you used magic."

I try not to laugh out loud as he walks off into the room.

Chapter Twenty-One

Mathilde tracks me down after dinner, grabbing my arm and dragging me onto the dance floor. I pretend to fight her off, but it's a half-hearted attempt. I've been tapping my toe to the music and waiting for an excuse to stop working and let my hair down. The band is a huge hit, skipping effortlessly from swing music to jazz, over to Aretha Franklin and then the Beatles. The guest list is mostly college donors and alumni. This is their era, they know every song lyric by heart.

I lean across to Mathilde, yelling over the music, "Is this how you do the Charleston?" My legs flip out to each side, my feet twisting and nearly sending me tumbling. Mathilde's only response is to burst into laughter. I suspect she's a few drinks ahead of me.

A group of young Eternals dash out to join me. "Ms Nat, stop!" they call out. "You will hurt yourself. Let us show you." Lining up side by side, they lift their skirts so I can follow along with their feet. They make it look effortless, which given they're ghosts, it probably is.

In between numbers, I realise we're missing a member of our trio. "Mathilde, where's Kate? She should be out here with us."

Mathilde stifles a giggle, raising her finger to point towards one alcove. Kate is sitting on a sofa, her feet tucked underneath her, wineglass in hand, chatting away with Bartie. Despite the music and the crowd, they appear to be in a world all of their own. I fan myself, spurring Mathilde to laugh again.

Slowly but surely, as the night carries on, the crowd slims down. I spy Harry slow dancing with her husband Rob, both polished up in their evening best. She gives me a wink when she passes by, reminding me once again why we trusted her with the secret of the magic. She's been my rock for the past two weeks, never breathing a word to anyone about the truth of my gala plan.

Edward slides in and out of my view, always standing on the side, chatting away. I catch him watching me dance with the Eternals, his cheeks colouring slightly before he gives in and raises a toast in my direction. I gather up my courage to invite him to dance, but get distracted midway by a rustling sound coming from behind one of the dessert buffets.

"Oh my word, H!! What are you doing in here?" I hiss when I spy a familiar-looking spiky black tail sticking out from underneath the table. I flip up the tablecloth to find H hunched over the remains of a cheese platter.

"Oi, missie. Why din't you tell me there was gonna be cheese 'ere? A whole wedge of Lincolnshire Poacher, just sittin' there abandoned."

I look around the room, hoping to find someone who can help me smuggle him back out of the marquee. Everyone is caught up in their own fun, the Eternals mixing effortlessly with our human guests.

Maybe one more won't hurt.

I know I'll probably regret it, but I lean under the table, dragging H out by his tail. "All right, you can stay. But try to keep a low profile, okay? They may not know you're a wyvern, but even a cat will look out of place at a formal gala."

H bats his eyes and promises that no one will know that he's there.

I spin around, searching the room for Edward's tall form, but he is nowhere to be seen. I must have missed his departure. Once again, I let Mathilde pull me onto the dance floor. I'm hyper-focused on getting this 1920s footwork right, so I notice nothing is awry until I hear Mathilde gasp.

My head snaps up, eyes scanning the room to find out what happened. Nothing seems out of place, but then I hear the woman next to me say, "Is that a cat hanging from the chandelier?"

I raise my gaze in time to catch H swing from the chandelier like a trapeze bar before somersaulting through the air and swan-diving to land in the middle of the dance floor. He snaps his talons at the bandleader, and the band jumps into action.

"Are they playing Beastie Boys?" Mathilde and I squeal in unison.

A spotlight appears from out of nowhere, casting H in a pool of sunshine and leaving the rest of us in shadow. Fist in the air, wings flapping in time to the music, he abandons all pretence of being a cat.

Head held high, H sings in unison with the lead singer, "We gotta fight... for my right... to parrrrrrrrrrtayyyyyyy."

Mathilde and I shout Kate's name in vain, desperate to make sure she doesn't miss the scene before us. Between the air guitar and spinning himself around everyone's ankles, H is in rare form. But no matter how loud we yell, we're too far away for Kate to hear us over the Beastie Boy lyrics, and neither of us want to turn our heads away for even a moment.

"Are you sure the magic will make the gala guests accept H's performance as boringly normal?" I ask Mathilde, biting my lip to hold back the laughter.

Mathilde waves an arm around the room. What better proof

could we find than the group of oblivious people still dancing away around the dance floor?

H unleashes a fiery shout, turning a nearby woman's glittering gown to ashes. She barely has time to feel a blast of cool air on her bum before the magic replaces the dress. Tablecloths disappear and reappear, coat tails get singed, and ashy dust floats in the air. Before long, Mathilde and I fall down into nearby chairs, holding our stomachs from all the laughter.

When the song ends, a group of Eternals rushes onto the floor, lifting H onto their shoulders and carrying him out of the room before he can get up to anything else.

Hours later, all the guests and staff finally leave for the night. Kate, Mathilde and I are sprawled across the sofas in an alcove, our heels and sparkly shawls abandoned on the floor.

"How come you never mentioned how handsome Bartie is?" Kate asks, sending Mathilde into a fit of giggles.

"He's my colleague. My *Eternal* colleague. The first time we met, my hand slipped right through his. I honestly never looked at him that way."

"Really?" asks Mathilde. "They all seemed fairly solid to me tonight. The gala did exactly as we hoped."

Kate chimes in, "I could see the magic getting stronger as the night went on."

"Did you notice that before or after Bartie kissed your hand goodnight?" Mathilde asks a blushing Kate.

I snicker, "We really need to sign you up for a dating app, Kate, if you're lusting after a man who's been dead for the last half century."

Kate pops up and points the finger at me. "Look who's talking! I saw you getting cosy with St Margaret's star professor, one Dr Edward Thomas, when he arrived. I do not understand why you two pretend to dislike one another. I could sense the attraction from across the room."

Now it's my turn to blush. "That's absurd. I was getting his initial impression of the event. Nothing romantic about that at all."

Somehow, neither Kate nor Mathilde looks convinced.

"Fine," I confess, "we spent some time together while trying to identify Chef Smythe's murderer, but I've barely seen him since then."

Mathilde perks up at the mention of the murder investigation. "You never told us how you figured out it was the woman from the dining hall. How did you do it?"

Leaning back, I explain, "Edward and I were close to solving it with our trip out to the Cotswolds. We each had an inkling that the Johnston family had to be involved, but neither of us realised we had a family member living right here at St Margaret. If I hadn't gone out running and accidentally locked myself out, we might still be trying to solve the case. I never thought I'd be grateful to get caught in a downpour, but my soggy state reminded the security guard of young Beatrice's fateful run on the morning of the murder. When he told me her parents were the veg vendors, I knew she had to be the killer."

Kate grimaces. "I'm glad you got to the bottom of it in time to save the gala from being cancelled, but I imagine her family must be devastated."

I shudder at the memory. "I spotted her mother in the main building a few days later. She looked like she'd aged a decade overnight. But Dr Radcliffe has been doing her best to help the Johnstons, and it looks like Beatrice will end up in a mental hospital instead of prison."

"That's good," says Mathilde. "She's so young, hopefully they can help her salvage some of her life." She leans over to scoop a dessert from the platter on the coffee table. "These scones are to

die for, Nat. Where did you find a caterer? If I didn't know better,
I'd swear Chef Smythe herself made these."

"Um," I cough, "Funny you should say that... because... well, I
needed a chef who wouldn't fear they'd be the next one
murdered...."

Poor Mathilde chokes on her scone, and Kate pats her back to
get her breathing again.

When Mathilde settles down, Kate exclaims, "You got St
Margaret's dead chef to cater the gala?"

Waving my hands, I explain, "Bartie helped me. You can thank
him! It was Chef Smythe or the Mediterranean fish and chips
truck. I didn't have any alternative."

Eyes wide, Kate shakes her head. "Only you would have the
bollocks to pull it off, Nat."

I can't tell whether Kate means that as a good thing or a bad
thing.

"No more talking about murder and death, you're ruining my
last chance to enjoy these scones. Let's talk about something else.
Do you have to move out of the flat now that the gala is over?"
asks Mathilde.

"No, fortunately there's no rush. They won't need it until the
summer term when they have a new faculty member joining." I
can't imagine having to search for a place on top of everything
else going on.

Nodding, Mathilde continues on, "Finding a flat in Oxford is a
nightmare. What's next on your list, Nat?"

Rubbing my feet, I list out my To Do items, "I have to wrap
up the gala, finalise payments for all the vendors, send thank-you
notes to high profile guests, that sort of thing. Once I get that out
of the way, I offered to help Harry with the children's Christmas
party."

"I love a good holiday bash," sighs Mathilde wistfully.

"I used to love them, but after running Mickey and Minnie's

Holiday Party for seven solid weeks one year, I don't find them quite as much fun as before. But at least that will be straightforward and simple. That's it until the university closes for the holidays."

Kate drains the last of her tea, setting her mug on the end table and sitting up straight. "I wouldn't get your heart set on relaxing too much over the holidays. Now that the gala is behind us, we need to turn all of our attention to figuring out who, or what, is damaging our magical field."

Mathilde's face drains of colour. "You're right, Kate. The safety and security of Oxford is resting on our shoulders. We need to get the magical field working properly before something else gets stolen... or worse yet, before someone else dies."

"I've been thinking about that," I say. "We know the problem is in London, but we don't know why or how. I don't think we will understand how someone or something could shift the magical perimeter unless we learn how it was set up in the first place."

Mathilde pauses, deep in thought. "That's a good point, Nat. I suggest we start at one of the oldest colleges first. Their archives will naturally go back the furthest in time. It will save us haring off on a wild goose chase. I do not want to take H to London if we can avoid it."

After seeing H's performance on the dance floor, I'm in full agreement. I still need to bone up on my Oxford history, but I suspect my next big event assignment might help us along the way. Leaning forward, I ask, "Isn't Barnard one of the older colleges?"

Mathilde, as always, has the answer ready. "Some would say the oldest, so yes." Her eyes go out of focus, a sure sign her mind is wandering. "That's exactly the place we need to start. I wonder what kind of excuse we could manufacture to convince them to let us have full access to everything they have in their archives?"

"How about planning Barnard College's annual black-tie dinner next term?" I offer. "I'll have an all-access pass to every room within the college while I'm organising the event. I'll arrange for a tour of the grounds before the holidays so I can learn my way around. We can put together our research plans between now and Christmas. We'll be ready to get to work as soon as the college reopens in January."

Mathilde and Kate nod furiously, both in full agreement with my plan.

After a moment of silence, Kate pipes up, "Seeing the Eternals tonight, I think you've strengthened the magic at St Margaret enough to make it safe once again, at least temporarily. I never met him, but I bet if your grandfather were here, he would be proud of you, Nat."

"Aww, thanks, Kate. I couldn't have done it without the two of you, H, Harry and Edward." I sniffle back a tear.

Kate gives my shoulder a quick squeeze, "So that settles it. Our next stop is Barnard College. We can work together to find out everything there is to know about how the magic works. And hopefully, we can restore the magic at Iffley College and find out who's responsible for the thefts of the missing portrait and artefacts."

Raising a finger, I add, "And don't forget about St Margaret's antique candelabra that's missing from the High Table."

Burglary at Barnard

OXFORD KEY MYSTERIES - BOOK TWO

A secret chamber. A dead body. And one ghost who won't tell the truth!

When Nat agrees to meet a friend in the archives of historic Barnard College after hours, she doesn't expect to find a hidden chamber or stumble across another dead body.

The Master's assistant has been murdered, and although Nat figures out who is responsible, finding the evidence is a challenge. Especially when the one ghost who witnessed the crime refuses to say what happened.

The closer Nat comes to finding the proof she needs, tempers flare and threats fly. The situation becomes a race against time, and just when she thinks she's won, Nat realises the murderer is willing to do whatever it takes to escape justice, including getting Nat out of the way.

Permanently.

Nat's miscalculation will cost someone their life, but whose?

Mince Pies and the Missing Santa

AN OXFORD KEY MYSTERY SHORT STORY

Nat thinks helping Harry with the annual Children's Christmas party at St Margaret will be easy as mince pie. But when Santa fails to show, Nat has to call in favours from everyone she knows to save the event from certain disaster. Mathilde is happy to dress-up as an elf and H is wearing antlers. But Kate is more interested in getting Bartie to stand under the mistletoe than helping out.

If Nat can save the day, she needs to find a new Santa... but can she convince a certain tall, dark-haired Criminology Professor to lend a hand?

This short story is available exclusively to my newsletter subscribers. Sign up on my website at lynnmorrisonwriter.com to find out what happens.

The Eternal Investigator
AN OXFORD KEY MYSTERIES NOVELLA

May 1941 - Money is missing from the coffers of St Margaret College.

Bartholomew Kingston is on the cusp of figuring out who is siphoning funds from St Margaret College when his friend Clark reminds him of their evening plans. He sets his work aside and travels to London for a night out on the town.

When he returns to work he makes a startling discovery: he's dead. Even worse, Bartie is horrified to learn he is being blamed for the theft.

As Oxford's newest Eternal, Bartie has some new tricks up his sleeve. With the help of the other Eternals, can Bartie find the real culprit? Or will his name be tarnished forever?

The Eternal Investigator will be available on Amazon on 1 March 2021. Pre-order your copy now.

Acknowledgments

Writing a paranormal cosy mystery requires two things: a vivid imagination and an audience willing to follow along with you.

I've got imagination in spades, but I owe an incredible thanks to my earliest audience members: my children. When I looked at them one morning and said, "What if our cat could turn into a wyvern?" they didn't bat an eyelash. They nodded their heads and asked what would happen next. That was all the encouragement I needed to put my fingers to the keyboard.

I have to thank my husband as well. He may have grumbled at the start, but he quickly got on board with my dream of being a full-time writer, helping us juggle the family finances to make it happen. When I needed to get out of the house, he opened the door to his office at one of Oxford's illustrious colleges, providing me with endless inspiration.

Next on my acknowledgements is my brilliant editor, mentor and advisor: Inga Kruse. I literally could not have written and edited this book without her help. Despite a nine-hour time difference, she was always there when I needed her. Even when I forced her brain into action before the first cup of coffee hit her veins, she didn't complain. She edited every single chapter of this book, sometimes multiple times, never withholding her honest opinion. She coached me through writer's block and made me believe I could go beyond good and into great. I will love and thank her forever, even though she made me cut out the chicken dance scene.

Anne Radcliffe, grammar goddess, took on the final copyedits, asking critical questions like, "Is H supposed to have a cockney or a Scottish accent?" When I confessed I had no idea, she didn't throw a book at my head. Inga and I could focus on the big picture edits knowing that Anne would make sure we didn't lose track of grammar guidelines along the way.

My parents and my sister - as always a round of thanks to you. They say that your family will always love what you write. I'm blessed to be able to say that isn't the case. My sister didn't hold back on her thoughts of the first draft, giving me insights which helped me transform Nat from a quirky character into an actual human being. My dad immersed himself in the genre, texting ideas and hassling me to send over another batch of chapters to review. My mom read the first draft of my book and proclaimed it a masterpiece. I decided to take her encouragement and ignore the fact that she was on pain meds following a total knee replacement. Sometimes you need someone to pat you on the back to balance out the critiques.

Next, a huge thanks to all of my friends in the writing community. Our secret Facebook groups give me such insights, energy and life.

Last, but far from least, a shout out of thanks to the members of my Not A Book Club group on Facebook. When I needed early readers, you all stepped up to the plate. You stick around, chatting about books and life in equal measure. You accepted me as a writer before I did. Thank you!

About the Author

Lynn Morrison lives in Oxford, England with her husband, two daughters and two cats. Originally from the US, she has also lived in Italy, France and the Netherlands. It's no surprise then that she loves to travel, with a never-ending wish list of destinations to visit. She is as passionate about reading as she is writing, and can almost always be found with a book in hand. You can find out more about her on her website LynnMorrisonWriter.com.

You can chat with her directly in her Facebook group - Lynn Morrison's Not a Book Club - where she talks about books, life and anything else that crosses her mind.

f facebook.com/nomadmomdiary

y twitter.com/nomadmomdiary

o instagram.com/nomadmomdiary

BB bookbub.com/authors/lynn-morrison

g goodreads.com/nomadmomdiary

Also by Lynn Morrison

Printed in Great Britain
by Amazon